Echo

By MJ Douglas

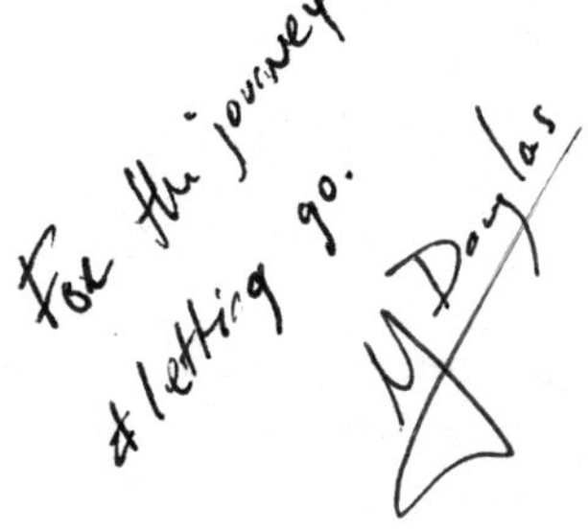

Dragon Tomes Publishing

Additional Works by MJ Douglas

Water Rites (short story)

Augmented

Echo

Published by Dragon Tomes Publishing LLC

Topeka, KS

Dragon Tomes Publishing

www.dragontomespublishing.com

Names: Douglas, MJ, author

Title: Echo / MJ Douglas

Description: First edition / Kansas: Dragon Tomes Publishing, 2024

Subject: Science Fiction

Cover Design: Sienna Arts

Book ISBN: 978-1-963198-01-0

Dedication

To Mary, I am so glad you kept your dreams close. The struggle is real, but it was worth it.

PART 1

Chapter 1

"We have a failure on One."

Pik took a deep breath. She was on load four, still unlikely she'd be alone.

"Failure on Two."

They moved in teams of five. Echoes. Techno-archeologists.

"Failure on Three."

Shit. Deep breaths. As much as she didn't want to fail the load, she equally didn't want to delve alone.

One moment of warning: "Four is green. Go for Four."

The sonic dissonance associated with loading into an isolated pre-Metaverse virtual world isn't easily described to the uninitiated. The truth was that many aspiring Echoes failed out of training, the discomfort too high.

Pik was used to it.

Part of her reveled in the scream of senses as the transfer burned her through oblivion to some unknown region of virtual space. Some people hated the digital equivalent of a near-instant transporter. Pik loved it. The sensory overstimulation signaled the beginning, and she embraced that adventure.

It was always over before she was ready, vision snapping into focus as stretched-out, multicolored lines defined a static environment.

"Four is loaded."

Pik waited for a response. She waited for Five to load.

They had dropped her onto the deck of a spaceship. Her only companion was an engine's low, artificial hum as she waited patiently. Sometimes it took a few moments for the trace to follow her signature and tunnel a communication line to her.

This was the second moment a new Echo feared. Being alone, stuck in an artificial build. Trapped in an environment by oneself without team members or Command to assist.

It happened when teams didn't thoroughly research the environmental stability of the reality when they ported. Sometimes a newt would freak out and reactively block the mental connection back to Command. You had to want to be an Echo. It was challenging and risky.

Calmness was key. Pik was one of the best. She could port into anything and had been the single load several trips. The only person who loaded more consistently than her was Five. That's why they gave him the end-of-the-line load position. Trick was magic.

Light flashed beside her. Colors stretched through the ceiling and floor of the corridor and snapped into place as Trick's face superimposed on a military marine build. He grinned at her.

"Miss me?"

"You wish."

Trick grunted, noticing her ridiculous build. An Echo's ability to dive was directly proportional to the malleability of their self-image. In the Metaverse, Pik was mainly a young Asian woman with strong bangs, blue-streaked hair, and dark eyes. Here she was, a six-foot tall, overly bosomed blonde with muscles and a couple of tacky tattoos.

"That's some build." Trick's voice was gravelly like his character's persona. He came off in real life as a long-haired, dust-addicted flower child. Those who worked with him knew better.

"Yours too. What do you think? Typical alien survival game?"

"The green goo on the walls is definitely a hint."

"Horn wins the bet again."

"Yeah, too bad she couldn't load in and see it for herself. You should know better than to bet against her." Pik knew he was right, but she was competitive. She could never turn down one of Horn's bets.

Horn was their Number One. She was a brilliant researcher and a terrible Echo. She'd only had five successful dives. Horn had solid analytics and programming skills that were key to the team's success. Her skills, though, inhibited the flexibility of mind needed to successfully load into different environments. It prevented her from loading into anything but the most advanced historical builds. Any older environments that couldn't support full self-realization would bomb her load.

"Command here. Can you hear us?"

"Yes," the two said in unison as Trick took the lead being the senior diver. "What do you have for us, Command? It looks like Horn was right, but we're sitting empty-handed."

Most of the environments they explored ended up being some form of game. Broader entertainment was available at this time through holo-dramas, travel, and education-based programming. However, the virtual matrices most likely to survive over time were the ones most invested in, which, even in modern times, tended to be games.

"Copy. We can get you a starter equipment set—but otherwise, you will have to play the game."

This was common. Most of the exploits to employ a god mode on these games had been lost over the centuries. The inception of the Metaverse also net resulted in a wipe of 'nonrelevant' historical data to the current iteration of humanity's regret.

Pik watched as a pistol, a rudimentary, explosive-based projectile weapon completely unsuited for spaceship environments, materialized. Her skimpy outfit transformed into a sexy, torn T-shirt and camo pants that belonged in a humid jungle environment.

"These games are all the same," she shook her head as Trick got body armor and a basic machine gun. His load was completed with the addition of a lit cigar, which fit his look but not their environment.

Their job was to play the game from the drop point. Dying early was preferred as most games would allow resetting to the beginning. They could theoretically monetize the link if they could map out a new game from beginning to end. They would be able to sell a walkthrough to the public in addition to providing a stable, accessible tunnel to the digital experience. For a decent game, an Echo team could set up a service fee, game guides, and even guided experiences for game tourists.

This further funded their research and allowed them to document historical experiences - delving into the archaic roots of their society. Timmic was their historian. He could go on for ages about the relevance of the patriarchal manifestation of a skimpy shirt on Pik's character or the socioeconomic reasoning behind marines smoking cigars.

"Let's roll." Trick's voice had an uncharacteristic grave quality Pik found off-putting.

"That a preloaded phrase for your character?"

"Yup." He grinned at her, knowing she hated the cheesy catchphrases developers of this era couldn't seem to resist.

Shaking her head, Pik put her pistol forward with a two-handed grip.

Game Play Engaged popped up on her heads-up display (HUD).

The environment's ambiance began to change to suit the plot of the story. Panels had taken damage, and sparks crackled and snapped as they hit the floor. A chemically laced, burnt smell permeated the air.

"This is more like it." It was Trick's turn to roll his eyes at Pik. Timmic and Horn were in it for intellectual gain. Junip, the last member of their team, was convinced there was money in the profession, but Pik did it for fun.

A distant scream: "Command, we're engaging. Any last words of advice?"

"Have fun in there."

* * *

Two days later, Pik sat outside the infested freighter's shuttle bay, looking at the last level-up notification.

Maximum Level. Maximum Danger. You have unlocked +200 Armor and Unlimited Clip. Bonus to Regeneration. Bonus to Resistance. You are unable to Level again. Do you want to engage OBLIVION protocol? Warning: You will only get one chance.

Pik hit **No**. Echo's rule on the first run: Don't complicate the run. Just get to the end. No hints indicated what the OBLIVION protocol was, and this wasn't the moment to find out.

Trick watched as Pik examined her inventory and options. "You finally hit max level?"

"Yes." She was going through her boost options for the final boss scenario.

"You accept the OBLIVION protocol?"

Looking at his stubby, shit-eating grin, she said, "No, I declined it. Didn't you?"

He raised an eyebrow in challenge. "No."

"What the hell, Trick? Why? Why break the first rule? Command? Are you picking up on this?"

A dark shadow came over his face. “Command went silent after I chose it.”

Pik hadn’t been worried until that moment. Many games had ultimate hard modes named as taunts to appeal to players’ egos. She’d never known Trick to break one of the base rules of Echo diving.

“Why take the bait? Why execute the OBLIVION protocol?”

He shrugged. “Just one of those feelings. You know, like that mini-game on Jeweled Island-18. It’s going to be worth it.”

“If we just wasted two days, you’re buying me dinner when we get out.”

“Aye, captain.”

One final check, and they were ready. Pik’s load out had undoubtedly improved. She had a melee dual knife build that could gut a face hugger in one swipe. She had two sets of energy weapons: one continuous fire laser that screamed through biomaterial and an Ether Pistol that packed a considerable punch compared to her starter gun. For the grand finale she had a mini rocket launcher. Admittedly a rocket launcher on a spaceship was more ridiculous than any of Trick’s weapons or characteristics. Still, it worked incredibly well against the mega webbed cocoons that would sprout hundreds of mini aliens that could overwhelm them if the cocoons were allowed to burst.

While Pik tended toward multi-situational build-outs, Trick got his name from his gameplay. He tended to settle on a handful of tricks that dealt incredible damage and leveraged faulty game mechanics. For this game, he’d outfitted himself bizarrely. He was a stealth specialist with an overall dexterity-based dodge class. He could deal immense damage with explosives planted in stealth. He also created a compound to poison creatures and wear them down by dancing in and out of range.

Trick either epically succeeded on his own or fell flat on his face. Over the last few years, Pik had learned not to bet against the man.

"Alright, I'm ready if you are."

Pik watched as Trick reached out and hit the button to trigger the door. It slid open slowly, making a whooshing sound. Peeking inside, she noticed sticky webbing stretched across the cargo bay. It pulsed with energy as a scaled monstrosity opened its eyes.

Attached to long webs were what appeared to be the remnants of the crew. Five humanoid mummies shambled forward, eyes glowing in sunken sockets.

"Defilers!" one shouted in a raspy, artificial voice.

The other four mummies took up the call, muttering "Defilers" in an off-tempo chant.

The sixth body was different. She wore garb more akin to Pik, a game player's build. Her voice stood out as wholly confused.

"Where am I? Who are you?" The construct sounded sleepy, like she'd awoken from a long nap mid-nightmare.

"Alright, little sister. It's time to light this thing up."

Pik swapped to her laser build. The beam could deal significant damage quickly and was usually distracting enough to allow Trick to sneak into the shadows so he could begin planting his explosives.

Pik targeted the closest humanoid, flicked off the safety, and started exterminating. Damage indicators began to stack. That's when the screaming started.

The woman's cry was distractedly human-sounding while the shambling horrors screamed in rage. Their glowing eyes pulsed in time with the web, and they responded with their own laser attacks as Pik's target melted. Pik quickly dropped her weapon, dodging to the side as plasma shots crossed the space she had evacuated.

She pulled her pistol. Two shots. Move. Duck.

Shoot.

Headshots were criticals, but they were hard to manage while weaving. Trick hadn't contributed yet. This was normal. Pik ducked again, blonde hair getting singed. The longer Trick had time to move, the more damage he could inflict.

Pik moved closer to the woman. The shamblers didn't move much, relying on range to deal damage. Pik aimed and got a lucky shot. It blew through one's eye socket, finishing off another horror.

Pik paid for it as a plasma bolt slammed into her armor. The pain feedback momentarily took her vision in a flash. By the time the pain ebbed, 25% of her health had vanished.

"Damn, that hurt."

"Are you real?" The woman moved toward Pik's position. "Did they send someone to save me? Mercy."

Pik didn't know how to respond. This generation of games had pre-programmed, artificially unintelligent—or AU—interaction. Pik took an honest look at the woman.

She wore the same dumb armored shirt as Pik. Her brunette hair was pulled back as webbing snaked across the bay, attaching the back of her head to the creature.

Blue lightning began pulsing across the webbing. The woman winced as it hit the back of her head.

"Trick, I think you better hurry up!"

Pik's health dropped again as another bolt hit.

She tagged another horror. Pik made a decision. She rolled toward the woman, taking out a knife.

As she gained distance, she saw tears running down the woman's face. "You're finally here."

Pik said nothing as another bolt clipped her foot. The pain was too real.

"Any time, Trick!" Pik used her knife to slice through the webbing, detaching the woman from the alien's influence.

The woman screamed.

A blast rocked the bay.

Two of the remaining three shambling horrors dropped to the ground, connections severed. Trick appeared on the grotto above the principal alien. He gave Pik the thumbs-up sign as he lined up for his run.

Pik watched as he jumped, energy sword extended.

It was glorious.

Until it wasn't.

The boss hadn't moved yet. But when she did, she moved like lightning.

She spun on spidery legs. Opening up her mouth, she ducked under Trick's blade. The boss grabbed his leg with her teeth and tossed him across the bay.

"No!" Pik shouted.

Trick landed with a sickening crack. His health bottomed out. He was full of tricks, but success was never guaranteed.

Pik swapped her knife out for a final push.

"If you can help, he's got a secondary detonator on him." Trick always saved two sets of explosives. His ego left the second set so he could go out with a bang.

Surprisingly the woman scrambled toward Trick's body.

Pik brought her rocket launcher to bear. She aimed at the last shambling horror, waiting a moment to get the target lock. She staggered as the kickback from firing the overpowered weapon knocked her back.

Fried chunks rained down. Pik aimed at the main event. She only had two remaining shots. Her first shot missed; the beast's agility got the better of her target lock skill. The rocket buzzed past the monster, igniting webbing.

The boss scuttled toward Pik as she tried to reload. Virtual heart pounding. The stakes were a few days of game replay, but it felt like life or death in the heat of the moment.

She wasn't going to make it.

With 25% health left, a glancing blow from the beast would end her.

The rocket slid into place. Pik couldn't raise the barrel in time.

"Got it!"

An explosion rocked the bay. Pik was knocked off her feet as the floor rippled. The boss was launched into the air, engulfed in flames as Trick had managed to tag its butt. The man was insane.

The boss hit the floor with a crunch. Pik eyed it in horror as legs began to right the creature. The blow hadn't been as life-ending as Trick's.

The beast stumbled to its feet. Its eyes were glowing with the same energy as its dead minions.

Pik grinned.

She brought the barrel up and fired.

The stunned creature couldn't dodge quick enough.

You have defeated Iraxinus. Mission Complete. Congratulations.

The print faded from Pik's vision. She sat for a moment. She hated these horror shooters.

"You alright?"

Pik blinked. The AU was still standing in front of her.

"Huh?"

"You alright? Thanks for coming for me."

Pik typically wasn't known for her eloquence. "You're . . . welcome? Wait, are *you* real?"

The woman smiled. "Yeah, I'm the one they sent you to rescue. Brit Montgomery."

Brit held out her hand. Pik took it, humoring the end-game banter. "Pik. But I wasn't sent to rescue anyone. I'm an Echo."

A humanlike furrow of confusion decorated the AU's face. Pik ignored it, moving to Trick's crumpled body. "Alright, man, let's get you rezzed and get out of here."

Pik tapped his forehead, using the resurrection command.

Nothing happened.

She hit it again.

Nothing.

"Command, you copy?"

Silence.

"Who's Command?"

Pik whirled in anger at the AU. "Leave me alone. I'm trying to figure this out."

Pik brought up her party status.

"Pik, is that you?"

"Command, we need an extraction."

She looked at Trick's status. Her vision began to fade as the emergency extraction took hold. Horror filled her soul.

Party

Pik - Health 100/400, Armor: 0

Brittany Montgomery - Health 250/325, Armor: 0

Trick was gone.

Chapter 2

Chaos. Pik loaded back into a base consumed by absolute chaos. Red and yellow lights blinked, alarms were blaring, and her frazzled crew was trying to tame the madness.

"What the hell did you do?"

The quarantine alarm was blaring. If the safety standards were followed, it took ten to twenty minutes to fully reintegrate into the Metaverse. The home network transfer took longer because the system scrubbed an Echo before allowing them to return. The standard protocol had been bypassed.

Pik was wide awake. Completely aware.

Her voice was hoarse. "If you want to get out of this shell, you need to stop Trick from . . ." Her words trailed off as she watched Trick's return load materialize in the #5 chair. Instead of his blue eyes and full beard, what loaded was *her*. It didn't look like her, but it wasn't Trick. She wore his face, had his hair, and even smelled like him, but vacant brown eyes loaded as the woman's consciousness merged into the system.

Junip, the medic of the crew, was shocked. Usually the calmest of the lot, they were in charge of terminations in the event of an anomaly. Junip's eyes were on Pik. She could feel them, waiting for the command.

"Pik, what's your word?" Junip's ordinarily calm voice held a deep horror. They'd never had to punch in a kill code.

Pik looked into the honey-brown eyes of the woman who had somehow been traded for Trick.

Trick.

Flashing lights. The last time they'd had a quarantine emergency, Trick had been the one who talked down the Central Command police—Enforcers. He made the decisions. She'd been angry at the time. Timmic had stupidly touched an infected file on the trip and brought back a bit of a virus. Timmic was always rooting around in the games, looking for *more* than the simple payout. Trick had sat with her in the bunk room, nodding as she vented her rage at Timmic to him. And when she was done, blood pressure spiking in her veins, he just pulled her into a hug.

He hugged her until the rage flipped, whispering, "Timmic's our responsibility. We survive as a team. Each soul matters." *Each soul.*

"Pass. It's a false alarm."

"FALSE ALARM!" Junip shouted to the rest of the crew, relief evident.

Pik unbuckled, jumping to Horn's station. "Punch in the passcode now. It's going to take a minute for Trick to reintegrate."

Horn complied. Pik was conflicted. Horn should have questioned it. They all should have. In the emergency, alarms blaring, they were all too ready to accept Pik's word. Pik could have been infected. This was what they trained for, this moment when things go sideways, to do the *right* thing. They'd all taken an oath when getting their Echo license. They were obliged to move in the greater 'verse safely. The wrong contamination brought back could destroy the entire infrastructure humanity relied on.

"Zelda-Three-Four-Twin-Five. This is Horn. We're clear."

"Link-Five-Four-Twin-Three. This is Pik. Dive team. We're clear."

The clear codes given by Command and the dive team were usually enough. They waited for a tense minute. It always seemed like forever.

One minute became two.

Technically the Home Command could sterilize the lot of them. No permission was needed. It was part of the risk of being an Echo. Pik hadn't heard it happen in the last twenty years but wasn't sure it would have been advertised. Teams sometimes went missing. They might disband and members reintegrate into society so quickly that nobody knows where they went. Or maybe not.

Two minutes became three.

The team looked at *her*, not Trick. Not that woman.

Three minutes became five, and the confirmation came through. "Confirmed Trickshot, stand down initiated. Your analysis came back clear."

Pik let out a shaky breath. They needed to be careful. Post-load observation was pretty typical, even if a team was cleared.

Pik turned away from the speaker. Three sets of eyes, all with an edge of white panic, were glued to her. Not-Trick wasn't functional yet. Thankfully the observers rotated so that no one would notice this as an anomaly in the team's behavior.

Any good team had cues. They weren't just a good team; they were the best. She triple-tapped the console in front of her. *It's not safe to talk.*

"Trick had a bad run-in with the boss. That's all, folks. Let's give him a few, and then we'll debrief." She blinked on "That's all." Spot the lie. *That isn't all.*

They'd developed a code for talking under Home Command's radar. It was one of the early lessons Trick drilled into the team members before he'd let anyone take one step on a dive. He insisted it was necessary, critical even. Pik had thought he was paranoid. She'd never used it until now.

Pik held each of their eyes for a few seconds until she got a nod of assent. *Confirmed.* They were all on high alert but giving the impression that everything was normal. Pik had her team in line. It was time to focus on the woman.

Pik turned back to #5's chair. The immediate crisis was adverted temporarily. Now they needed to figure out if they should recall the quarantine. To figure out how to pull the real Trick out.

Pik got Horn's attention by flicking to the emergency protocol console they had in place. It was a hidden setup Trick had Horn install when they were first getting started. It included an artificial looped feed to keep Home Command off their backs. It also had an emergency sterilization procedure that could be used outside of a quarantine. A team of Echoes had to have deep trust for that particular kill switch. Sterilization was just that. In the Metaverse, one could theoretically live forever or choose reincarnation for variety, but actual sterilization deleted your matrix completely. That power wasn't lightly put to a team you didn't completely trust.

Horn shifted over and began setting up the shift of Central Command's attention. It would take hours of work. One had to do it slowly, let their algorithms normalize over small changes until the whole feed was migrated.

Pik stepped over to Trick's chair, putting on her best fake smile. Her acting was terrible, but she figured it wouldn't matter. She wasn't good at showing facial emotion anyway.

"Hi, Trick"—with an emphasis on Trick. "You got shot there at the end of the delve pretty hard. It looks like it may have triggered the quarantine protocols. We've got them off, but we'll be under *observation* for a while. You picking this up?"

Not-Trick gave a convincing nod. "Yes, ma'am." It was Trick's voice, but not his words. He'd never say, ma'am. He wasn't brought up with manners. Horn was convinced the man was raised in a monastery—all zen and focus, with a feral denial of the niceties of polite society.

"Best you not talk much while you reintegrate. Don't want your brains more scrambled than they already are." Pik feigned nonchalance as she turned to Junip.

"You keep an eye on . . . him." The hesitance on the

"him" was so slight, only for Junip's ears.

Junip nodded. "Yes, ma'am." They signaled that they caught Not-Trick's misstep.

Pik turned to Timmic. "Alright, let's start downloading the feed and examining the run. See if we've got anything worthwhile. Personally I don't think there's much there. Another alien horror survival on a ship."

Timmic made a disgusted sound. They'd been running dry in their delves lately. Alien horror survival games were a cliché that stuck in humanity's psyche. Possibly one reason exploration went inward instead of outward on the bend of history. One didn't have to fear the alien horde when complete control over the Metaverse was in the hands of humans.

Suffice it to say modern alien-takes-over-spaceship games were much more sophisticated and varied than this ancient example.

"Nothing useful at all?" Timmic asked, glancing at Not-Trick. "I have a hard time believing that a game capable of triggering a quarantine would be that useless. Let's start at the top with a detailed A-level progression."

Pik nodded wearily. She cracked her knuckles, one by one. It was an old habit she'd used as a kid to relieve tension. An A-level progression would take a while. It was the top introspection for any delve. She'd go through build, layout, stats, game progression, and detailed footage with Timmic for the next six hours. Long enough to get them to Horn's blackout so they could talk about what was going on. In reality it was smart. They would be focused on the boring details, not the anxiety of what happened. Not-Trick wouldn't have much room to say anything to anyone. Their cover would be safe.

Pik still wasn't sure it was the right move. The woman sat in the #5 chair calmly. She looked around at the environment cautiously. She was obviously trying to figure out where she was without giving it away. Junip observed her movements, silently taking notes. They were on high alert.

Who was this woman? Why had the system swapped Trick out for her?

"You following with me? What did you load as? Why do you think the rest of us bombed our initialization?"

Focus. Pik had to focus on the moment. The decision not to blow their team out of the proverbial airlock had already been made. These folks were her family. Trick's family. She'd keep them alive.

"You three didn't load because of your lack of agility. Trick and I loaded into preset characters without any customization. You'll see here when we bring up the data recording."

She pointed, and Timmic couldn't suppress a laugh. "You were a blonde bombshell? And Trick had to smoke a cigar the entire time?"

Even Pik smiled. "Yeah, I know it's hard to imagine. All I could pick up from Trick was some basic face customization, but I'm not sure I even had that."

The woman unbuckled from her seat and moved to sit down next to Pik and Timmic. Pik tensed. She hadn't noticed the woman moving. Not-Trick's face had started softening, and his beard wasn't as defined. She'd have to get Horn started on a layover if the woman made too many more strides in reverting to whatever she perceived as her own identity.

"You didn't look like yourself at all," Trick's voice said.

Pik tried not to hush her. Timmic stared at her mouth for a second. They both had to take it in stride. Central Command was still watching. If Pik was honest, this was the best course to continue forward with the farce.

"That's you all the way," Timmic interjected. "You flow like water."

Into whatever form was needed. Now Pik's team

needed her to be the one in charge.

"So we loaded in mid-game." Pik kept her walk-through heavy on the detail. The guns, the corridors, the acidic goo they encountered, every detail she could dredge up. Not-Trick helped, piping in with more information about the ship that she theoretically lived in for centuries.

An A-level progression didn't need this much detail, but they were all effectively stalling. After the third description of what it felt like to be hit by an acidic goo explosion from one of the alien's web traps, Horn finally stopped them.

Her tight voice cut through it all. "We're masked. What the hell happened in there, and who the hell is this?"

She had pulled the emergency kill switch out. They'd programmed it to look like an ancient gun. Junip initially had loved the drama of the look. No one ever expected to have to use it.

Not-Trick dropped the fake interested smile, her eyes going dark. Her face lost a bit of its masculine edge, and Trick's red-brown hair lightened.

"Hi everyone, my name's Brittany. Brit for short." They looked at her curiously.

Pik interrupted, "Brittany Montgomery." Brit nodded.

Timmic whistled. He knew what that meant.

"Is that a . . . what was it called? A surname?"

"My last name?"

Timmic filled in the blanks, his historian instincts kicking in: "Surnames, last names, went out of style in the twenty-second century once birther laws were in place to limit population growth."

Pik knew the game was old but didn't realize it was *that* old. This game was pre-Meta, back when they had entrapment issues, and a horrified realization came across her from a long forgotten history lesson. "Was that a gladiator game?"

Brit used Trick's face to give a confused frown. "Gladiator game? Not sure what that means. I joined it to win for my family. If I won, we'd have been set. My mom was sick. We didn't have any other way to help her. It was a long shot. I didn't win."

Pik's gut twisted. Trick was trapped in one of the late twenty-second-century death games. When society grappled with virtual versus real-life consequences, they created game shows where real-life risk and reward were enforced. They dubbed it a modern gladiatorial fight. Brit had been trapped in the game for almost four hundred years.

Junip dropped the kill switch, putting a voice to their collective thought: "How are we going to get him back?"

Chapter 3

Family. Trick was family. Pik hadn't realized how close they had all grown over the years. Trick was older than the rest of them. He was hitting his seventy-fifth year the last time they'd talked about it. Usually, at seventy-five, a person had become exhausted enough with the world to look into a reincarnation protocol. If the person chose to stay, they would officially receive an "elder" designation. At the time, Pik worried about what the team would be without Trick if he chose to reincarnate. She'd broken one of the golden rules. She'd asked him about his future.

Pik remembered the conversation like it was yesterday. She'd failed a big mission on a delve and was nervous about taking over the crew. "You're not leaving us anytime soon? You'll give me plenty of notice, right?"

He'd smiled at her. The laugh lines around his mouth creased with practice. "No worries there. If I have my way, we'll be a little family for a long time, Pik."

The team had few wins at that point. Horn hadn't joined them, and they kept running into bad loads. "Why not? You're already an elder, right? You'd qualify."

Pik had been beating herself up. They'd found an interactive puzzle game requiring the gamer to solve intricate puzzles physically. It was going to be a hit. They all knew it. Pik had been the last to leave the dive, responsible for pulling the code with her, and her trace hadn't worked. Upon review later, they discovered that she'd failed a step in her monthly maintenance routine that had caused the error. A mistake she'd never repeated since.

Trick had looked her in the eye, something he rarely did. He was never a front-on type of leader. His style was to hint and smile and discuss. "The reincarnation protocol is for folks who are bored and disconnected. Boredom is for those that lack imagination." His eyes were particularly piercing. "And I'm building connections."

Pik had scoffed in that moment. Folks rebooted their existence for a variety of reasons. Trick had seemed naive at the time, but here they were. As the team looked at each other for answers, no one considered abandonment an option. Connection indeed.

"We can go back." Junip was leaning on the alert panels, their brows knitted together with worry.

"And get trapped ourselves? Besides, Pik's the only one that successfully loaded." Timmic paced the Command Center, practical as always.

"I can try to load a bot with a trace." Horn watched Junip's face as she tried to instill some hope.

"A bot wouldn't survive three minutes in that environment. Certainly not enough to find Trick." Pik shook her head. Half measures weren't going to cut it.

"We could get Home Command's help. They've got more resources." Junip's final suggestion had them all rolling their eyes. "I know, I know. It's stupid. But we've got to do *something*."

The need to do something sat heavy with them as Horn sat with her head in her hands saying what they all knew about Home Command. "They'd just quarantine the lot of us. Even if they did have compassion—and they don't—it would be game over for Brit."

Brit's eyes went wide. So far she'd just sat silently in Trick's body, watching the group. It was creepy—a mimic sitting in their midst.

"I'm not sure it's not the right move to quarantine Brit anyway. How do we know her matrix would be stable in our modern environment? The code that put her in that game is *old*." Horn tapped the screen in front of her as it scrolled through an archaic programming language Pik didn't recognize.

Pik tried to resist looking at the interloper but

couldn't help herself.

"Hey, I didn't exactly ask to be pulled out of the game in exchange for your friend. I'm just as much a victim as he is." The panic in Brit's voice was evident. It sounded genuine.

Junip, as expected, spoke up for Brit as an uncomfortable silence built, "We can't quarantine her. We can't pretend we don't know what Home Command would do to her." Horn, ever the pragmatist, was about to object before Junip continued, "Besides, if we admitted where she came from, there's no way they'd let us back in to rescue Trick."

Each of the crew members paused their reactions, contemplating Junip's truth.

This wasn't a complete rejection of dealing with Brit. It was a stay of her fate. Pik watched Brit think through her situation. Brittany Montgomery might be from a long-gone physical era of humanity's existence, but she wasn't a fool.

"I'm willing to help get your friend back. Send me back in, and I'll do whatever I need to. Just, please, don't lock me back up. I want to live." The plea would have moved Trick.

"I have seen Brit. I hear her. I will not be a part of yeeting her out an airlock." Horn lifted her head in surprise at Timmic's words. His clear eyes looked right into the programmer's soul. They came to an agreement. There were moments for regulation, and there were moments an Echo team had to do what was *right.*

Pik nodded slowly, watching her team come to a consensus. For now, she could use the woman. "Okay, so how do we do this?"

The two Echoes looked at her, stumped. Junip was relieved. However, none of the ideas proposed so far were viable. At the end of the day Brit told the truth that Pik had already concluded: "We have to go back in."

Immortal beings rarely confront mortality, even those who routinely watch folks reboot themselves. Pik's last incarnation had chosen to get rebooted into a family. And Pik had started her journey as a child. Her parents had long since left. They could be one of the three Echoes sitting before her for all she knew. Existence in the Metaverse was weird like that.

She was the one that was going to be risking her life, her existence. Brit didn't have a choice. Not really. Pik was the one who could get just as stuck as Trick—or get corrupted and lost.

Pik's artificial heart beat with excitement. She was going to *do* something that mattered.

"We all go," Horn's voice cut through her heroic introspection.

Junip and Timmic were nodding like fools.

"Why? How?" Pik was pulled out of her one-woman daydream by Horn's statement. None of the other team members had loaded the first time; she was Trick's only hope.

"We use the sub-verse and branch from the trunk," Horn stated her insanity calmly. Pik had never met a programmer as tuned into the Metaverse code as Horn. If she thought it could be done, it could. The woman never overstated.

"Would that work?" Junip, the least technologically trained in verse navigation, asked.

Timmic nodded. "Of course it'd work to get us there. *All of us.* But we wouldn't be able to return."

Pik's beating heart shot into overdrive. She was willing to sacrifice herself. She wasn't ready to put the whole team on the line. "No, Brit and I will load. You three will stay here."

Horn touched Pik's arm. "Not this time."

Their crew was tight. They'd grown close, working daily as Echoes together for the last ten years. Trick was their linchpin. He'd chosen each one of them and plucked them out of obscurity. He made them family. Pik didn't blame them for wanting to risk everything to save Trick. It didn't mean it was the right decision, but she understood their instinct.

"What in the hell are you all talking about? What is a sub-verse?" Trick's voice cut through the tension. Brit sat, frowning at the lot of them.

Horn tried to explain, "My proposed solution has us breaking off from the Home Command, from the main code of the Metaverse." At Brit's blank look, Horn continued, "You had submarines back in your time, correct?"

"Of course. You don't?"

"Not in the literal sense, no. But look, we'd basically take a submarine and attach it to the game you originated from. The five of us could then physically load instead of trying to port our consciousness into the game."

Timmic piped up, "It would likely destroy the stability of your game, but we could pull Trick out and leave."

Pik couldn't let them do this. Best case, they'd be marooned in the middle of a game, worst case they would be permanently deleted from the Metaverse. "The problem is, the main system wouldn't ever let us rejoin. We'd be stuck externally. Or worse, we could lose cohesion and defragment."

"You don't know that." Horn obviously thought she was being overly dramatic.

Pik wouldn't let them turn away from the truth. "No one's ever returned."

Junip, of all people, picked that moment to add their two cents. "So it's an unknown. That's our bread and butter. It's a risk every time we hook up to a new environment."

Junip, the imp, dared to be excited. As the #3, they loaded more frequently than the other two, but not as often as they wanted. Their specialty as a medic meant they were skilled in re-knitting a person's matrix back together when the environment had damaged it. They were also responsible for the psychological survival of the group after traumatic events.

"Absolutely not. It's too risky." Pik was adamant.

"You're outvoted, Pik." Horn gave Junip a lopsided grin as she declared victory.

Pik brought steel to her voice. "This isn't a democracy; I'm in command."

"Actually, you're not. Trick hasn't been declared lost," Timmic pointed out. Pik gave him a look of betrayal, she didn't like the rules being used *against* her.

"Timmic, how can you support the idiocy of these two? You know this goes against our established recovery rules." *You always follow the rules.*

"Trick's first rule." Timmic had stopped pacing, resolve in every line of his face.

Never leave anyone behind.

Trick *had* been successful. He had melded them into a family. Whether Pik liked the result or not, she could see it in their eyes. There wasn't an argument that would dissuade a single one of the crew members.

"You. The lot of you. Are insane." Pik dropped her eyes in defeat.

"That sounds like a yes."

Pik nodded. She was trying to hide her own emotions. She would have gone in alone. She would have done it. But deep down there was a sprinkle of relief that the team had insisted. She hated herself for it. If they were going to be doomed, it would be together, and it'd be her fault.

"Let's get to work. How much time do we have left on your block?" Ever the professional, Pik wasn't going to let their argument waste any more time. They'd come to a consensus, and they had limited time to execute.

Preparations went underway. Timmic and Horn were busy gathering the information and resources the team would need once they departed the core. A digital existence had its advantages. One had to find food and water in all the old games. Pik couldn't remember the last time she pretended to eat. They needed a download of the core data stored in the Metaverse—human history, combined with a library of reusable code blocks. They might have a chance if Horn could set them up with a thousand different options to traverse the unknown.

Pik's parents had been involved in the reenactment lifestyle. That's why they'd chosen to have a kid, and she'd been raised on three empty meals a day. When they still existed, she'd have dinner with her parents occasionally as an adult. She watched them age over the years. They wanted their existence to be the whole gambit of physical life and had written in an aging protocol.

In a world without death or parents, Pik had the unique experience of both. She dreaded the day Trick chose to move on to his next life. Part of her couldn't imagine Junip, Horn, or Timmic moving on before her. It happened. Sometimes someone relatively young would drop off from life. She just blocked out the possibility.

Facing the odds of permanent erasure should have been terrifying. Horn was busy downloading code, Timmic was seeking relevant documents, and Junip was checking her repair protocols. Brit didn't even know what they'd be risking. Something was calming in the group's movement. Their business gave the calm appearance as though they *had* this. It was an illusion. Pik wasn't fearful of her own erasure. She was afraid of being responsible for the group's. To watch her family get erased because of her poor decisions.

She'd never been tempted to restart her life. There was too much to explore. Too much to do. She'd made peace, though, that it would be a choice eventually. Pik would move on someday, and her essence would be reborn into the Metaverse. What they were about to do, however, risked everything. No moving forward. The end of the line. They were gambling it all.

Brit repeated herself, “What do I need to do?”

Pik blinked, thoughts interrupted. She blurted out what she hadn’t had time to ask: “Are you really from the twenty-second century?”

Trick’s face gave her a winsome smile. “Yeah. I can’t believe it’s all gone. Everyone I knew. My mom, Aunty Bev, my . . . my daughter Jada.”

It never occurred to Pik that this woman would be a mother. “What was it like?” She wanted to ask “What was being a mother like?” but the rudeness of it stopped her.

“I’m sure you have simulations that do my world justice.” The woman blinked back tears.

Pik hesitated. This was Junip’s territory, this emotional trauma, but the medic was suspiciously absent. Pik looked over and saw them with Horn, two heads buried in a console across the Command Center. Pik got the distinct impression, as she caught Junip glancing her way, that the medic was waiting to see how she’d handle the situation by herself. “We do, but we have no one to tell us if they’re accurate. What was it like to give birth? To eat real food? To sit in a sunbeam?”

It was perhaps unsympathetic to ask about something as simple as sunbeams as the woman mourned her daughter. In Pik’s mind, distraction was a good salve for trauma.

“My cat, Lollie, loved sunbeams. She was a calico, and she’d always be on the couch in the afternoon, lying in the sun. Before I had Jada, I’d lie there with her once in a while and take a nap. The warmth on my face.” Brit’s voice had a wispy quality, her eyes far away in the memory.

Pik tried to imagine it. They could create a simulation of any of the historical holographic captures of the world. They could create new worlds and new existences. Everyone still missed Earth. Junip insisted it was a form of displacement. This hunger for *before*. It gave them all jobs as Echoes to seek new experiences from humanity's history.

Nothing they'd ever found could replicate a nap on a couch in a sunbeam with a cat.

"That sounds nice."

"It was." Brit, wearing Trick's face, went silent. Even Pik, who was poor at reading human cues, understood that the woman needed a moment.

With a smile and a nod of thanks, Pik left Brit to her thoughts. She returned to her own station as the woman stared off blankly. Pik's mind drifted as she began identifying the files she wanted to bring with her. There would be time to quiz Brit on the nature of reality. It's a shame Home Command would have sterilized her existence. She could have been a vast resource of new knowledge and transformation. Instead she would go on a suicide mission with Pik's family.

Chapter 4

"So explain this to me one more time."

Horn sighed. She was thorough, but Pik agreed with Horn's unspoken assessment. It didn't matter how often they explained the mission parameters on this one. It was too far out of Brit's scope of understanding.

"Look, Brittany. Brit. I don't think we're talking the same language. At this point, I don't think you can understand the details without spending a lot more time than we've got. At some point, Home Command is going to get suspicious." Pik watched as Horn's frustration softened. "I know we're strangers, but you're going to have to trust me. Trust us."

It had been a day of preparing, explaining, and theorizing. Trick's physical pattern had slowly given way, and now Brit looked like herself. Pik knew the woman was intelligent, but there were centuries of technological advancement between them. "I've been in stasis for a long time—I get that. But what I do remember is my training on integrating into the game. When you import, it's crucial to go slow, or the fragmentation factor becomes too big." Brit paused. "It's hard to trust anyone. It's not just you." Pik noted that Brit touched Horn on the knee.

She didn't understand the gesture. Pik didn't connect easily—certainly not romantically—and definitely not within a day. Perhaps she misread it. Trick frequently told her she wasn't good at human relationships.

"Fragmentation factor hasn't been a problem in four hundred years. When we integrated our cognitive matrix with the Metaverse, fragmentation stopped being an issue." Pik could tell Horn was trying to be patient, but she was starting to snap.

"Yes, but we won't be visiting the Metaverse, will

we? We're visiting *my* world, *my* technology." Brit had spent a good portion of the last day telling them about Infestation, the game she'd been stuck in. She was determined to be useful, to give them the knowledge they needed to be successful. Pik knew her crew, though; they'd logged a lot of simulator experience, but the real world load was going to hit them hard.

The woman could be stubborn. Pik hadn't seen anyone stand up to Horn on technology integration in a long time. She silently observed.

"True, but we solved the integration barrier when we created the Echo profession. Our technology has adapted to these old interfaces. Compression happens before the load," Horn told her politely, giving a smile that was all teeth.

"Right, that's why you lost your captain to Infestation. That's why this whole place is worried about quarantining the lot of you."

Pik winced at the gut punch.

"She's got you there, Horn," Timmic called from the other side of the Command Center, not being able to resist emphasizing a weakness in his intellectual rival's logic.

Brit pressed her position, "Besides, from what I *do* understand, you're not going to be leveraging the Metaverse capabilities to interface with my game. You're going to be—what did you call it . . . manually inserting us into the game? Didn't you say yourself that this could introduce instability?"

Junip whistled. They clashed with Horn the most on strategies, holding opposing philosophies. Junip always opted for the safest option, and Horn rarely had patience for such suggestions. "Maybe we should listen to her. There's a reason half the team bombs their loads. Loading up slower isn't going to cost us anything."

"But it does. Imagine that Brit's game is actually a

starship floating through space that we're trying to dock at with our starship." Horn looked at Timmic. "And no, we're not the Enterprise. We're not docking in the middle of space. We're trying to dock in the middle of an asteroid belt. If any of these other programs hit our capsule, we'll be sucked into some other reality before we can even get to Infestation."

"What happens after we rescue Trick?" Pik couldn't help but ask. Rescuing Trick without a next step wasn't a rescue at all.

Reality was starting to set in, and it was uncomfortable.

Horn sighed. "We figure it out. We figure out how to port ourselves back."

Pik was angry. "No, we don't. We will be stuck. This is why I should just go myself."

"Trading you for Trick isn't a solution."

"We love you too." Junip's soft voice interrupted the argument. Junip used that word often: love. Love got you in trouble in the Metaverse. When Pik's parents had moved on, she'd been about to make the same decision. It wouldn't have disappointed them. They were already gone. She'd been so alone when Trick found her. He'd given her not love but purpose.

"After we rescue Trick, we find Elysium." Horn raised her hands in defeat. She'd kept that piece of information to herself.

"The farmer game Black Cat discovered last year?" Pik asked, eyebrows raised. Black Cat was one of the top Echo crews, much more financially successful than them, as though that was the point. They'd gone unusually quiet in the last year, and Trick had his suspicions.

"Yup, we load into Elysium and then return to the Metaverse. That's why I've put Timmic on setting up a trace to Elysium so that we can find it."

It couldn't be that easy. Pik was about to say so

when Horn caught her eye and gave a quick shake of her head and a glance at Brit. Superficially, Elysium was a good choice, but Black Cat had gotten swallowed up when they converted Elysium. Officially, they retired. Unofficially, no one knew what went wrong—but that *something* had. Something had caused the premier Echo crew in the Metaverse to simply disappear. Horn had pulled Pik out of more sticky situations than she could count. If Horn had a reason she didn't want to explain, Pik would trust it.

"Alright, Elysium it is. It wouldn't be the worst if we had to live out our lives there. Blue skies and welcoming yokels."

"Look, I'll agree to a slow load, but only if I can accelerate if we bounce into an infraction." Horn acquiesced. Pik was surprised.

"I have no idea what you mean by an infraction, but I'll take a slow load," Brit sounded relieved. Pik had heard horror stories about issues of early upload technology, nothing made those stories more real than Brit's terror.

Horn, always willing to sit for an extra minute to slowly explain what was happening, opened her mouth, only to have Timmic stop her. "There's chatter. I think Command has figured out we looped them."

"Time's run out, folks. Buckle up." Pik buckled into her station taking command.

"Are we ready?" Junip nervously croaked as they sat down in their #3 chair.

"We're going to have to be. Get ready for free fall. Three," Pik answered. They were going to have to dive quickly if Home Command was paying attention.

Pik glanced across the group. The white and black text of their monitors reflected on the Echo's faces. Trick had outfitted their Command Center with steel panels and plastic buttons, LED screens and pleather seats. Pik could even see her locker in the back of the room with a cotton tag frayed from age with her name penned on it. This was her home. Timmic was snapping the safety harness on, a frown of concentration on his face. Horn's fingers flew across her keyboard as she made last-minute adjustments. Junip's features were unworried, their trust in their teammates complete. Pik took note of Brit's face, the woman looked . . . *hungry*.

"Two."

Pik closed her eyes, breathed out, and took one last look at her pseudo-family before she killed them. Timmic had finished buckling in and was looking at her, horrified.

No, not me.

"One."

Brit.

The world punched Pik in the gut. Existence scrambled as gravity gave up, and her stomach occupied her throat. Light elongated as the blinking buttons on her dashboard flared. This was wrong. Loading into a new environment took seconds to determine if it would be successful. If a load failed, an Echo could get a hangover and, worst case, a reactive migraine.

Timmic and Horn shouted at each other, hitting controls as they tried to split reality from the Metaverse.

"Command has a hook!" Horn yelled.

"I don't care if they trace us as long as we can split." Pik tried to keep her voice calm.

"I've lost the trace to Infestation." Horn's voice held an edge of panic. Her fingers flew over the buttons. Everything screamed in Pik's head.

"We're loose." Pik hadn't sat idle; she'd been jettisoning the core code of the Command Center in an effort to lose Home Command. "Come on Horn, I'll keep us stable but you've got to find Infestation." Pik was sick. The agility that served her well as an Echo meant she was stretched and spun and flipped in the space between the Metaverse and their destination. Horn, Timmic, and Junip had solid definitions of self. This was why they frequently failed their loads. Pik was not okay.

"I can't take it." The voice said in a metallic screech. The stretching, the *twisting*.

The voice was her voice.

"Hold on, Pik."

A cold hand grabbed her arm.

A dull, hollow voice whispered, "Just let go."

Pik turned her head.

The lights went out.

Her arm burned. The light flickered. She was no longer on their sub-verse. Pik sat up, headache throbbing behind her eyes.

"Junip?" A burnt ozone smell permeated her senses. She found herself lying in a dull, corridor as the lights flicked on. She was back on the Atlantic, the spaceship of Infestation. Looking down, her body was her own, except for the commando load out.

She brought up the player interface options, tweaking them so her HUD displayed life, stamina, ammo, and some quick slots for her inventory. She and Trick had played through most of the game their first time through. They'd loaded mid-game, but Trick was a completionist and had made them backtrack to the beginning. Suffice it to say there shouldn't be many surprises.

Her health was at 25%. That wasn't a good start. She mentally brought up her starter pistol. This game was an authentic relic.

"Timmic! Horn? Junip?!"

The only response was a distant skitter.

Pik stepped forward, her five-foot-two frame hugging the floor as she crept along, gun extended forward. She caught her reflection in a metallic panel. She smiled, looking at her signature blue-streaked hair and high East Asian cheekbones. Pik was clad in her personal Echo armor, leather molded to fit her body. She was equipped with electronic bracers and the quality black boots all Echos deserve.

Game Play Engaged popped up on her HUD.

She loaded with thirty rounds. The first goal would be to pick up a more sophisticated gun and some extra ammo in the first weapons locker.

The second goal would be to find everyone else. They weren't as prepared to survive in the environment. Pik wasn't going to contemplate what would happen if any of them died in the game.

If her memory served, there should just be two smaller aliens and an exploding web on this level. Pik peaked around the corridor. An acid spitter stood in the hallway, green goo dripping from its maw. She would have cursed if the thing wasn't sensitive to sound.

The lights in the hallway glowed red.

Where were the differences coming from? The color scheme had been blue and black, with bits of green alien goo. And acid spitters weren't supposed to emerge until the second level.

The alien turned. Pik ducked back behind the corner and took a breath. Taking a trick out of Trick's book, she visualized the movement: breathe in, move in position, breathe out, aim, and fire. She took one more look at the alien and went for it.

Move, pivot, aim, shoot. Headshot.

The creature slumped with the critical hit.

An explosion of carapace and organic matter splattered the hallway. A scream broke the silence Pik's violence had brought. She turned to find a second acid spitter had crept down the corridor behind her. A trill of terror shot down her spine as it cocked its head back to disgorge acid in her face. She slammed her hand quickly on the activation button for her personal shield. She'd hoped to save it for later in the game.

The hum of the shield was welcome as acid splatted

against it, popping and evaporating. She flicked the shield off as quickly as she turned it on, shooting the alien through its maw in a one-hit kill. Her assumption of a kill was quickly punished as serrated teeth chomped down.

Ten percent of her health flashed away as she cried out in pain.

Pik reflexively shot the beast in the head again. This time, it sunk into death.

"What the hell?" A scream of alert sounded from further down the hallway as a third acid spitter came running her way.

Aim—double tap. The first bullet hit, the second missed, and she was stuck in a reload action. Even physically present, the game imposed rigid limits on players during specific activities.

Shit. Shit. Shit. The acid spitter was on top of her as the reload function finished. She had to flash her shield again, draining it by another 5% to give her enough bounce to bring her gun up.

Bang!

Breathing heavily, she looked down the hallway, trying to identify further threats. When none appeared, she retreated and brought up the menu.

Pik didn't need the confirmation, but she needed a moment. The dread was already seeping deep into her soul. Confirmation didn't change anything. She was playing on hard mode—death mode—and she knew it.

Brit had talked about the game "show" she'd been on: Deathgate. A contestant was loaded with a team of five and gambled your lives against potential reward. Folks did win. That's what made it so attractive to someone as desperate as Brit. It wasn't easy though. Folks would study and train for weeks leading up to their challenge, and even then there was only a 40% chance of success.

Here, Pik had only one trial run.

She was an Echo. This was what she did. It was

possible to survive. She shoved her secret doubt of impossibility to a tiny ember. She chose to believe it was possible.

With the first corridor clear, Pik crept down the hallway, listening. Most of the aliens made sounds that could be picked up on: the skitter of multiple claws hitting the steel of the floor, the soft squelching as slime-encased venom slugs felt out their environment, even the soft hiss of reptilian skin had its whistle. The only silent killers were the explosive acid traps in the webbed areas. She wouldn't have to worry about those, hopefully, until level three.

After taking care of four more spitters, Pik was getting desperate. She'd ducked into a locker almost out of ammo as a fifth spitter marched down the final corridor to the armory. Sweat trickled down her face as she watched through the ventilation slots in the locker. The alien was so close she could have reached out and touched it. Pik held her breath as it paused, the slimy-tusked head swinging toward the locker, slitted nostrils flaring. The spitter's breath was acrid, bitter. It made her eyes water. Pik waited, tense, ready to move. The alien swiveled its head and marched its six bug legs down the hallway. Each tap was sharp on the cool metal of the corridor.

Pik counted to ten, waiting until it turned the corner. She'd have twenty seconds until it pivoted and returned. She quietly lifted the latch and moved, doubling down on stealth when she realized there wasn't enough ammo to get to the armory. This effort wasn't about blasting her way through the alien horde but sneaking her way through, undetected.

Pik crept quickly to the armory door, which slid open quietly. Rows of guns sat latched to the walls. Pik grinned at the array of choices in the room. Quickly she stepped in, letting the door close. She pressed her forearms to the charging port, filling the charge on the two personal arm shield units. And she waited as the counters ticked up.

Meanwhile she began planning her attack as she eyed the energy grenade case, the stacks of medkits, and the rows of guns.

Chapter 5

If something had held steadfast in her experience, it was that beginner difficulty levels were about firepower. Load up on ammunition and blast your way past all the creepy crawlies. Hard mode and all of its incarnations were the opposite. Attempting to blast through the unending horde of monsters sent your way was equivalent to a death wish. The game developers unerringly wanted the top-tier gamers to use strategy, stealth, and guts to navigate to the end. Unfortunately they also often wanted gamers to expend lives as well.

Pik didn't have any lives to give. She didn't know what would happen to her if she died on this load, but she knew it wouldn't be good.

She stacked her character attributes up. Quickly, as she dug through the settings, she found herself blessed with some of the alt capabilities an Echo typically had, like an unlimited inventory, which allowed her to loot most of the armory. While helpful, she carefully cataloged the items in her scratchpad, another Echo enhancement. Rarely did these games give you time to dig through a backpack to find the right weapon.

Pik had two pistols: one an automatic and one with a zoom. She also looted an energy rifle, a small rocket launcher with limited ammo, several variations on assault rifles, and the rare spawn, a low-grade sniper energy rail gun.

Trick had gotten the energy weapon on their first game halfway through and used it very effectively. The gun could see and shoot through most walls. Incredibly useful, she could already imagine a couple of scenarios she'd need it. As with all guns that are too good to be true, it had a minimal charge, and recharging ports were usually heavily guarded and few and far between. The ability to peer through walls to see what was coming, however, stayed useful even after it ran out of energy to shoot.

The acid spitter made another round. The top of its head plate could barely be seen crossing the high windows on the door to the main hallway. Thankfully it wasn't tall enough to peer in, and the automatic door mechanism didn't trigger for non-humanoid life.

It was the small, illogical things in these games that saved the day. Pik took a deep breath, waiting for the acid spitter to cycle through again. Their vulnerable spot was behind the main face plate, which meant sneaking up from behind. Even then, a bullet wasn't usually a one-hit kill.

Pik waited for the green carapace of the beast to trot by and then she gripped the rubber hilt of the blue "Cosmic Sabre," the melee option for the early gameplay. She thought the name was a bit overstated. She wasn't as adept at the melee game for space shooters, but it was the best bet at getting a one-hit kill.

Pik's thoughts were interrupted as the telltale skitter of its talons against the floor heralded the spitter's passing. She counted as she watched the head of the alien pass.

One.

Two.

Three.

The door slid open before the creature fully recognized what was happening. Pik slid the blade smoothly below the plate of its skull, neatly severing the spinal column.

It was over in seconds. Pik glanced down at the critter, almost feeling bad for it.

Almost.

Cosmic Sabre in hand, Pik stalked down the hallway to the shaft that would take her to level two. Three reapers later and the anxiety tampered down by her trip to the armory came back. She wasn't worried so much about herself. She'd done this type of gameplay before. Timmic, Junip, and Horn, however, had only done this in simulations. Never when their lives were on the line.

On her third mission as an Echo, Pik loaded solo. She'd been dumped into the middle of a quagmire horror game full of gooey zombies. The reward for dying in the gory thriller was a complete game restart.

Pik had been trapped in the zombie apocalypse for weeks, memorizing floor layouts and monster patrol patterns. Afterward she'd considered giving up the Echo profession completely. Junip had spent days with her then. Hours upon hours of distancing therapy to build a mental wall between herself, the experience, and her perceived failure.

Junip, about as helpful as a kitten in a fight, had also been force-loaded into this hardmode nightmare. Pik grew more worried as she experienced each layer of the game. She hadn't encountered a single trace of her friends. It was all she could do to put their fate from her mind. She had to concentrate on the game, or she wouldn't be of use to anyone.

Based on Pik's first load, the next sequence would be challenging. A nest sat between her and the second-floor boss. On their last run, the nest had been worse than the boss. Which, in her estimation, meant they'd missed something. Trick had accidentally stepped on some webbing and triggered the entire horde of reapers to attack en masse.

Pik paused, noticing threads of silvery white webbing along the walls. Pulling out the rail gun, she scanned the adjoining knuckle where three hallways met. She squinted through the scope, seeing dozens of creatures—too many to fight. Using the rail gun's scope to scan the sides of the hallway, she sought an alternative route. There had to be a way around the nest.

Down to the right, a tunnel glowed faintly; an air

vent ran parallel to the main hallway. She traced its path with the gun, verifying that it completely bypassed the knuckle and, as far as she could discern, kept no creatures in it.

That wasn't a guarantee. The gun wasn't sophisticated enough to detect webbing. Pik sat for a moment, contemplating the ventilation cover. An invasive thought shot through her brain: the cramped condition of the vent pressing down on her as she fought for her life as the horde in the nest assaulted her in the tiny space. Her skin crawled at the thought. She took a deep breath, trying to let go of the fear.

Pik could almost hear what Trick would have told her. *Nothing risked, nothing gained.* Half of his plans fell flat, but the other half worked epically. She tucked the rifle back into her inventory, pulling out the automatic pistol. It was better suited for close quarters.

It took seconds to unscrew the vent cover, and before she knew it, Pik was on her hands and knees, crawling through a tiny air shaft barely big enough to fit in.

Reapers were spider-like—if spiders were the size of a St. Bernard. They sat on six legs, instead of eight, and covered their webbing in a sticky, regurgitated slime. Of the creatures in the game, reapers were the most intelligent. They'd set trip wires to sound alarms and trigger nets or acid traps. They used their cocooning ability to set up remote bombs. The final boss was some reaper mutation that could mind-control its victims into attacking friendlies.

Pik thought about all the bits she knew about reapers as she slowly crawled past the nest. It was an insane habit, according to Junip, to focus on the thing you were afraid of to calm down. Junip would have told her to feel the cold metal beneath her hands. To take deep breaths and count as she exhaled. But a deep breath would only remind Pik of the claustrophobic stuffiness that came with this crawl.

Reapers were intelligent and blind. Instead of eyesight, they used their complex webs to detect intruders. Trick had guessed that they also possibly had an overdeveloped sense of smell, as they frequently lifted their heads and inhaled when not in combat. It was as though they were checking if the prey was downwind. They had family groupings of three to four, although she and Trick did fight one nest of over twelve. The two had argued about whether it was three overlapping nests or one big colony. From the view she'd gotten from the rifle, it looked like one large colony. The one she was slowly crawling past held twenty-five of the creatures. Not all were full adults; nonetheless, it was an intimidating group, to say the least.

The clatter of claws broke Pik's mental stream of reaper habits, and she forced herself to suppress a scream. She held her breath as the clack of a claw sounded somewhere behind her. The tunnel was so narrow she couldn't even look back. She tried to convince herself that there was no way the monster had sensed her. If it had, it would have already been on top of her. They could skitter down the narrow shaft much quicker than she could crawl. She just froze, held her breath, and hoped it would lose interest.

Reapers were blind but could down their prey with a very accurate acidic shot. The acid was a gluey slime that was almost impossible to remove. If one pawed at it to try to remove it, it would slowly eat through your fingers. Two opposites were effective in eliminating it: fire or water. If you could douse the hand, the acid concentration would dissipate into an inconsequential goo. An alternative was burning it; however, you'd get burnt too. In the first run Pik had chosen this option once. It was more pleasant than getting digested alive, but just by a hair.

The clicking was still growing closer. Pik's theory that the creature did not know she was here may be correct, but that wouldn't stop it from stumbling upon her witlessly.

She had to move. She crawled forward as quietly as she possibly could. Reapers didn't have keen hearing, but if she bumped the thin steel lining of the air duct with her flashlight, they would discover her immediately. Pik had already stored the pistol in her inventory; she could bring it out quickly enough, and it only slowed her down. Hands in front of knees, she held onto the flashlight in her mouth, light bobbing drunkenly in front of her.

The light illuminated an opening into a larger shaft. An air exchange. If this mirrored other areas of the ship, there would be an exchange with several large fans that helped to direct air. Sweat trickled down Pik's face. It was hot in the shaft. Unusually so. She could still hear the tick of claws on the vent floor. Scoping ahead, she saw that she could turn left down a side tunnel and return to the main hallway, hopefully bypassing the reapers completely. Or she could kick in the slatted vent covering of the air exchange room and take advantage of plenty of space to deal with the pursuit.

Pik couldn't turn her head to see how far away the reaper was, but she suspected it was much closer than was healthy. Not sure if she could return to the hallway before she was overcome, Pik decided to fight. She reached the air exchange vent and went to headbutt it open, not caring if the creature behind her heard the noise; they were destined for confrontation anyway. The cover gave way quickly—too quickly. She tumbled out into a large, cylindrical room with several rotating blades stopped up, tangled in webs.

"Shit."

She mentally fumbled for a gun, any gun, as multiple reaper legs moved, twisting their bodies so their open maws faced her prone body.

"Shit, shit, shit."

The hairy legs of the creatures descended the webbing. She counted eight—way too many to handle on her own. The one behind her began to push through the vent. It was a juvenile, she realized, the size of a house cat returning home to its family. Pik brought up her gun, reaching in her inventory for an automatic that could spray out damage. The eyeless reapers seemed to regard her, taking a moment to decide whether she was a threat.

The snap of her magazine loading into place was enough. Chaos descended as creature after creature plunged from the ceiling. Pik opened fire, belatedly realizing her mistake. She was functionally only a few feet away from the nest in the hallway, and the shots reverberated everywhere like firecrackers. Panicking, Pik brought down two monsters. The juvenile latched onto her foot, teeth gnawing on her heel. It was too young to have developed the acid-spitting ducts. The thought floated obscenely in her mind as she aimed, fired, aimed, fire.

Pik gave up aiming. The staccato sound of her bullets in the enclosed space gave her little comfort as reaper after reaper began pouring from the vent she'd been cautiously navigating just moments before. Her last thought as a glob of acid pelted her face was of Trick. She hoped he was faring better in this godforsaken game than she was.

Pik's vision blurred as the gun fired. The acid had begun eating at her eyes. No pain dampening on hard mode. Her finger locked onto the fire trigger even after losing consciousness, and the rifle fired until the magazine ran dry. The world didn't fade to black, just her consciousness.

Chapter 6

Consciousness was a dream. Pik floated along a river, lying on her back, getting tossed by rocks and foaming water. The rapids splashed water over her face, but she wasn't afraid of drowning. The blue sky held few clouds as the warm water cradled her body. She floated as though she was unsinkable. She shot down at an angle as the river gained speed, narrowed by a canyon, bouncing along immortal in the bubbly water. No pain. Pik laid her head back, enjoying the ride. No consequences.

"Stay with me, Pik," Trick's voice floated along with her like a mirage as the sense of a cold washcloth dabbed at her forehead. Pik frowned for a moment. There was a reason Trick shouldn't be taking care of her, but she couldn't remember why.

"I'm fine; leave me be." Pik just wanted to drift in the sunshine. Trying was too much effort. Trick didn't respond, and somehow Pik knew this was right.

The sunshine on the river felt good. Her mind drifted to the day they'd met. She'd had ups and downs during this iteration of existence, but that day was the worst in memory. That day, long ago, Pik's parents had told her they'd planned to move on.

Pik had been eating dinner with her parents, the way they did every weekend. Her parents had been tiptoeing around something the entire dinner. When they finally told Pik, she stood up abruptly, knocking her orange soda all over the table.

She remembered yelling at them, "That's a permanent solution to a temporary problem!" They hadn't cared. They moved on with their reincarnation, unmoveable in their choice.

Looking back on her life then, the Pik who existed

today would consider herself a failure in all aspects of her life. She had loved her parents, and this was unusual in a world that didn't provide parents to love. She'd been living with them, a rare triad not based on a polycule. She'd lived in their basement, focused on whatever whim she fancied at the time.

Pik had always been a game player, quickly devouring the latest Echo find. It hadn't mattered what type of game. They were all worthwhile in her book—probably part of what made her a great Echo.

Her parents had been pushing at dinner. They'd go through these phases where they encouraged her to "find herself." Or seek out friends. She had some online friends but hadn't seen the point of making friends "in real life" when real life was a digital existence. They'd pushed her to find something in school to latch on to, but there weren't any real jobs outside the system admin support roles. Not like the ones she'd read about in the history books.

Pik wasn't inherently creative. Her school art projects, game programming attempts, writing, and tone-deaf amateur music composition were inevitably bottom-tier. History was the only thing she'd found mildly interesting in her assimilation schooling.

History was funny, exciting, and unlimited. But it was not something she could wrap a future around.

The thoughts about her parents paused a moment as a bird flew between Pik and the sun, great wings extending, blocking out enough of the heat to be noticeable. She squinted at it.

"Honey, we have something we want to talk to you about." Her dad's voice was soft. He was never that soft unless it was serious. Pik's body immediately clenched up in anticipation of what he would say next. She'd sat in a cushioned chair at their well-worn kitchen table. A place where she'd spent countless hours finishing homework or conversing during their obligatory family dinner. Decades spent tracing the lines of the table's grains with her fingers.

Pik's mom made it worse. "Don't worry. This is a good thing." It was a lie. Her mom's left eye always twitched when she lied. The words were so honey-sweet. The last time they'd ever gotten close to this sit down had been the day Pik's cat had walked into a dead zone and defragmented.

Her dad began speaking again, but she'd disassociated back to the day they told her of Regina. Her black and brown fur was gorgeous in the sunlight. She could still remember the cat's soft purrs.

"What do you think?"

"What?" the word bubbled out of Pik in panic. Her mind raced to pick through the words he'd spoken.

"We think it's time. It's been a couple of centuries for us." Her mom's voice was unnaturally gentle. She reached forward to caress Pik's face like she'd done when Pik was a kid. When they still cared about things like a kid, like kindness.

The words between them solidified into something tangible: "So you're leaving me?"

"Not right away. No, not until . . . not until you're ready." Pik's dad had always been the one who compromised. He'd never intentionally hurt her if he could help it. Except he was. Her mom was generally the colder one, the logical one. She had frowned at her husband; he'd gone off-script.

Desolation had opened up like a crater in the pit of Pik's stomach. Empty.

She tried to focus on the present now: the sunshine, the river, the heat on her skin. The hawk persisted. It floated in the air, tracking her progress.

She opened her mouth to yell at the stupid bird. Water rushed in immediately, causing her to choke. She felt like she was drowning.

Rage filled her. She couldn't drown. They couldn't

just leave.

"You're just going to leave me?"

"It's been decades, Pik. We haven't just gone up and left." The coldness of her mom's words enflamed the rage.

"You brought me into this world empty. I didn't have the advantages all of the other “kids” had. I had to learn to walk and read, and I stumbled across subject after activity that I couldn't compete against my peers because I wasn't a peer—they were gods. And now you're just going to leave? Leave me to do what? To be what? To do what?"

Her mom's face twisted in anger. Pik was used to that. The tears in her dad’s eyes—that had been new. That had hurt.

"Look, honey, I know this isn't easy. We've delayed our rebirth cycle for a long time. If we wait longer, we'll risk defragmentation."

That wasn't necessarily true. There were ways around defragmentation. The oldest continuous consciousness was approaching four hundred. The two of them were sitting neatly at a hundred and fifty. They didn't want to stay.

She wasn't enough for them to stay. Her mom's experiment was over.

Her mom hit with another tidbit: "Besides, you choose to be born with a fresh start. Your previous incarnation did this to you. It wasn't our choice. We just embraced your peculiarities."

"Your mom is trying to say that we've never compared you to your peers. We've loved you unconditionally. This decision has been hard and really isn't about you, Pik. It’s about us."

And the conversation had effectively ended. Pik knew that they hadn't seriously considered her for years. If she'd been really honest, she hadn't considered them either. She'd just gone about her life thinking that nothing would ever change. She'd float from one game, one dinner, one vacation to the next.

It'd been a hard day. Their decision had already been made, and no amount of anger or eventual bargaining or negotiation would change it. Her parents decided to move on to their next iteration, and their rebirth would be anonymous. None of them would know or recognize each other. Pik would be alone.

She'd closed her eyes at the memory. Something wet and slimy hit her face with a splat. Surprising since she was still floating down the river.

Pik wiped the bird turd out of her eye. "Defragmentation take you too." She waved a fist ineffectually at the hawk while her other hand pushed the putrid mess out of her eye. The white poo was sticky, and it stung.

She'd left the house that day, that minute. Pik couldn't stand sitting at the kitchen table she'd grown up at, where they'd been a family.

She'd changed everything. She walked away from the life she'd known and straight into one she'd only vaguely dreamed of. In hindsight, her parent's actions had the direct effect they probably wanted. Their decision to move on forced Pik to decide where she wanted to go, what she wanted to do. In one moment, everything changed.

Another bird joined the first one, further blocking out the sun. They flew at different heights, wings overlapping—another hawk.

"You should talk to your parents before you enter training."

Trick had volunteered as an Echo trainer for a cycle. He'd done it to evaluate recruits and to pick up new folks for his own crew. Later in life, Pik had done the same thing. It's how she'd found Junip.

"I don't have anything to say to them."

"Trust me on this one, you do. Talk to them. If you don't, you'll regret it the rest of your life." Trick's words were honest. He, this stranger, had managed to cut through the angry fog Pik had stumbled through. In the end she'd grudgingly made an awkward peace with her dad. She still hadn't completely forgiven her mother to this day.

Pik allowed them to explain their memorial to the only person who cared. They left their house to her, even if she had no intention of setting foot in it. They told her they loved her.

"It's more than most get these days," Trick offered, but nothing he said could squelch her grief.

In the end, Pik had managed to choke out her love, even to her mom. The lump in her throat was an attestation to her feelings. They'd hugged. And it was over. They'd chosen to walk into the unending forest, and Pik had stood with Trick by her side. He didn't know her. He didn't have to come, but they watched together as the two figures, the only two people in Pik's life who meant anything, walked into a sun-dappled eternity.

The heat was no longer hitting any part of her body. A fourth bird had joined the other three, and her fury began to build. What right did they have to interrupt her sun? Her peace?

Trick had placed a hand on her shoulder, steering her away from the eternal forest. It was said that if you stared at it too long, you, too, would find your feet making their way toward eternity. If you did that without making preparations for your consciousness, for your soul, you would be lost forever. If you didn't preset the future, you'd be deleted.

"Follow me. We have much to teach you. It's time to get started on what's next."

Pik took one long look at the forest. A cloud passed overhead. The coldness of the lack of artificial heat made her shiver.

"Do you think they made the right choice?"

Pik had remembered this moment. It stuck with her.

It was rare to find someone so confident about the afterlife.

"No."

The simple word had conviction. She'd never been brave enough to ask him to elaborate, never poked the completeness of his answer.

"But you are making the right choice. I have a good feeling about you." The scruffy man had gently led her away from the sun. "It's time for you to wake up."

It'd been the first time anyone had ever thought she'd be good at something worthwhile. Trick had saved her that day and every day since. She frequently didn't understand his motives, why they'd go on some delves and skip others, why he didn't care about the payout, why he'd always been morose when team members chose to leave. But none of it mattered. He'd provided a map. Even if the destination was ill-defined, Pik had needed a journey.

"It's time, my little hawk." Oh, that's right. How had she forgotten he used to call her that? Not anymore. Now they were effectively equals, running their team together. He wasn't her teacher or even boss. He was her partner in the journey.

She opened her mouth again, struggling to ask what it was time for. The hawks swooped down and plucked her from the river.

Pik gasped. She woke up in a box. An old-fashioned coffin. What they had before the unending forest. The top was plexiglass, and she watched as a reaper skittered across the top of her box. It didn't seem to recognize her existence. Her right eye burned. She remembered the acid bath it had received and decided not to complain about the pain. She could see.

Her breath, her very alive lungs, fogged up the barrier between her and the bottom of the reaper. It moved onward, and as the feeling returned to her appendages, Pik moved her hands, tracing the box's lining. From all appearances, she'd dropped below the vent in a shallow grave and had been sealed off from their attacks. None of it made sense.

It's time for you to wake up. Had that been Trick? She didn't smell his lightly spiced cologne or his herbal soap. She closed her eyes, trying to bring back the river—the fever dream.

The clack of another set of claws on the roof of her box snapped Pik back to reality. It was time to move again—the why could be solved later.

Chapter 7

Horn had never been one for yoga. She'd been more comfortable in front of a computer than practicing some of the acrobatic maneuvers that made Trick's gameplay famous. When she loaded into a game environment, which wasn't terribly often, she mostly crept around, resorting to stealth and hacking. She was the brains. Everyone knew it, except Timmic, perhaps. But he was an ass.

Adaptation is the heart of the Echo profession. Horn was all zeros and ones, logic, cause and consequence. A burble of bile crept down her throat, the transfer protocol had warped her perception and the game's parameters were not settling onto her well. She hung upside down, cocooned in some sticky, downy substance. Horn tried to shake her head, but the webbing prevented her from doing so. Suppressing the urge to puke, she tried to take a deep breath and almost choked as filament streamed into her mouth. She spat and coughed.

“Is that someone? Is someone alive?"

To her credit, Horn didn't sigh. The only person that voice could belong to was the one person she had no desire to collaborate on a self-rescue with: Brittany Montgomery.

"Yes, it's me, Horn." She wasn't completely able to keep the disappointment from her voice.

"Ah, hi, it's Brit." Brittany also seemed not to be too enthusiastic about her partner in crime. "Can you see anything? Have a plan?"

Horn scrunched up her face around the tangle of weave. Why did *she* have to have a plan? Very rarely was she ever the one to do the rescuing. "No."

Horn swung a bit in her cocoon, wiggling around to try to get a hand free. The fibers were soft but constricted if she moved too much. Panic sank into her mind. She couldn't move, not enough. She tried to calm herself. She visualized her favorite ancient sports game to watch: hockey. Mentally she replayed the championship game, the women flying across the ice, Montreal winning. Her breathing slowed.

"I can't move." The panic in Brittany's voice knocked her out of the calming exercise.

"I am having difficulty too. Let's take a moment. How are you oriented?"

Brittany's breathing was rapid, frantic.

"Take some slower breaths. We will get through this, Brittany. I have every confidence in us." Horn didn't, but she followed Timmic's advice about faking it.

"I just—I can't be trapped again," Brittany squeaked.

Horn tried to imbue her voice with all the confidence she didn't have. "You won't. We aren't. Just take some breaths so we can logically think this out."

Horn waited. Listening. She wiggled her fingers, trying to reach anything valuable in her pockets. Slowly, centimeter by centimeter, it was possible. The fibers seemed alive. They didn't register the slow movement. But if she rushed, the fibers compressed instantaneously. She wasn't the most dexterous on the team with her thick, heavier frame, but she was making progress.

She became lost in her experiment but then snapped back to the hyperventilating refugee from a lost era. "Brittany, you must slow your breathing. It's constricting you because the fibers are reacting to your movement. It will squeeze you to death if you don't calm down. The faster you move, the more it squeezes."

Brittany gave out a shallow squawk, and, thankfully, her breathing did slow. Eventually a calmer voice spoke, "You really are terrible at calming someone down, you know?"

Horn rolled her eyes. In the Metaverse, when

Trick's features had faded away, they'd gotten to see Brittany's true form. She'd been young-looking with blown-out hair and fine features. Young, but with eyes that looked like she'd survived something. Horn didn't expect Brit to be so emotionally delicate. "It worked, didn't it?" They hung in silence for a moment, Horn's fingers finally stretching into the pocket of her military pants. Fumbling around, she found nothing. "Damn it, my pockets are empty."

"Why wouldn't they be?"

Horn still felt ill. She wasn't sure if it was from Brittany's insipidness or the upside-down headache that was complimenting the nausea. "I was hoping for a starter knife to cut us out of these webs."

"It wouldn't be in your pocket. It'd be in your inventory."

If Horn could have smacked her forehead, she would have. Of course it'd be in her inventory. She was in *a game*. She didn't want to admit she had no idea how to check her inventory, so she countered with a question.

"Do you have anything useful in your inventory?" Meanwhile Horn squinted her eyes and thought *inventory, bag, sack.* Nothing happened.

"Nothing offhand. This game is stupid. It'll only call up what you think from the inventory. It's hard to tell what's in there otherwise. So far, I've only brought up a pistol successfully, but I'm as likely to shoot you as anything else."

Horn thought about it. *Knife, sword, machete, pistol.* The webbing stretched around her right hand as a pistol appeared. It was small, and Brittany was right. It wouldn't do a damn thing against their efficient prison. It seemed wrong, though, even for ancient game designers, to put together an inventory system that worked so poorly. Horn reached for the methods she was much more familiar with than physical weapons; she opened up the system menu and began rooting around in the settings.

"Horn, you still there?"

Horn blinked. "Yes, of course. Why wouldn't I be?"

"You've been quiet for twenty minutes. What are you doing?"

"If you'd give me a moment, I'll solve this inventory problem. I found the root function that controls the inventory, and I'm attempting to edit it to give me an adaptive pop-up listing all the things contained within it."

Brittany's voice trembled, "Y-you can d-do that? How?"

Horn inserted the code she wanted for the hot control function of the inventory command. Instead of producing the hidden error that the game had been designed for, she'd bypassed the error and put in a graphic with named boxes giving details to everything included within. The solution was admittedly easy, but in this situation she'd call it genius if she weren't so humble.

"I just turned on a visualization for my inventory. I can assist with yours, too, once we get out of here." Horn's inventory screen popped up. She examined it, searching for anything useful. Pistol. Rope. Torch. The torch might be helpful. Basic Rifle. Flash Pop. Cosmic Knife. Multi-functional Key.

The Cosmic Knife sounded promising. As she thought it, a cold handle appeared in her left hand. "Perfect! Think about your Cosmic Knife!"

Muttering came from the other cocoon. Horn ignored it as she started sawing with the Cosmic Knife. It would take a while to get through all the filaments, but even a few seconds made a difference. The webbing shied away from the knife, almost alive.

"I don't have a Cosmic Knife. What is that?" Brittany interrupted her progress.

"Give me a moment." Horn didn't feel the need to elaborate as the knife's progress sped up. The strands began to fall away en masse.

Horn fell to the ground hard, her broad shoulder slamming into the deck. Blanketed in viscous goo, strands of webbing coated her short hair. She removed the sludge, blurring her vision, reveling in the ability to move. A deep breath later and she was ready to free Brittany.

"Okay, wiggle or say something." Horn squinted. "I can't tell which cocoon is yours."

She was in a large room that was dimly lit because it had been completely overtaken by disrepair and the cascading webbing that coated every inch of the room. Even the "floor" she'd fallen onto was some sort of spider's cargo net. Bouncy and forgiving, the net didn't give her confidence that freeing themselves from the cocoons was the last step in escaping.

Five chrysalides surrounded her, but as she moved closer, the one containing Brittany was unmistakable. It frantically swayed from side to side, and the woman continued in her panic, alternating wails and gasps.

"Calm down. I'm cutting you out now, and I don't want to cut either of us."

Horn couldn't tell if Brittany hadn't heard her or was too far gone. She hit the sack hard enough to make Brittany let out an oomph.

"W-what'd you do that for?"

"I told you, calm down."

"So you hit me? That was going to make me calmer?" Brittany's voice rose, the hysterics quickly starting again. Thankfully, for both their sakes, cutting through the sac with the Cosmic Knife was much simpler from outside the cocoon. With another swift strike, the webbing parted, and instead of dumping Brittany out in an unseemly gooey pile, the woman, typical of her sort, took a gasp of fresh air and calmly stepped out of the slit. She'd been hung up right-side up.

Horn didn't hide her annoyance as the headache

she'd earned tumbling head first into the webbed platform throbbed.

"You actually did it." Brittany was pretty surprised. This pissed Horn off more. Of course she'd handled it. She whirled through her inventory.

"What's next? What are you doing? Why are your eyes lit up?" Brittany stood, lips thin, studying Horn.

"I'm looking at my inventory. I need to find a trick for us to use here." Horn tried to ignore Brittany's judgment. Her shoulder was hurting, her head ached, and her stomach was still rebelling.

Brittany's forehead knitted together in confusion. "For what?"

"Look up." Horn kept her voice calm, flicking through different options. Logically there were spiders above them. Something wrapped them up for a late-night snack. Horn may not have been loaded into too many games, but she'd watched enough footage of Pik to know what was coming next.

Brittany looked up, squinting into the dim, web-covered ceiling. Wall-mounted paneling gave off a muted light. "I don't see anything."

Horn glanced up, surprised. She didn't see anything either. She returned to her coding, unable to shake the feeling of being watched.

"Wait, do you hear that?" A tremor crept into Brittany's voice. Horn focused on a low insectoid clacking sound. "Oh god. It's a horde of reapers." Horn followed Brittany's eyes up to the corner of the room where spider-like aliens began pouring out of a large ventilation shaft.

"Can you check to see if you have any grenades? You played this game before, right? You've got to know what the deadlier weapon options have to be." Horn looked at Brittany, frozen in fear. "Snap out of it, we *can* do this. You've fought these before. Based on their profile, they hunt based on feel and sound?"

To Brittany's credit, she nodded.

Horn had no grenades, but she was reasonably sure she could rig an explosive. The question would be whether it would take the two of them with it. She began pulling out a pulse rifle, the Cosmic Knife, and a starter pistol. None of them were impressive by themselves. Horn removed the pulse rifle's power pack and put the body back in her inventory.

"You've got to have a pulse rifle. Take it out, and hand over the power pack."

Brittany didn't ask questions, a minor miracle. Horn used some fibers and goo from the cocoon to wrap the two power packs together, attaching a fiber she could swing the packs from. Lost in her build, as she tested the sturdiness of the fiber holding it all together, she completely missed Brittany talking.

"I'm sorry, what did you say?"

"I do."

Horn ran through her short-term memory, but she couldn't imagine what the woman was referring to.

"You do what?" Horn couldn't hide her annoyance. Over a dozen monsters were weaving their way down the latticework of webbing. All she had was a pistol, a knife, and whatever makeshift explosive she'd just concocted to stand in their way.

"Grenades. I have grenades."

That statement cut through all of it. "Grenades?" Horn emphasized the *s*. This woman had more than *one*?

"Yes, I've got a couple dozen. They may have loaded with my old gear."

Horn's mouth was agape as she raced through the possibilities. They might have a chance. Just maybe. Lifting her eyes above, she saw mandibles and claws. A plop of gooey saliva hit her in the face, and she cringed as she wiped it away with a hand. A plan began to form.

Then all hell broke loose.

Chapter 8

Horn picked up her Echo call sign early in her career. No team she'd ever been a part of would have argued her technical value. She knew she was a brilliant programmer; she had a way of seeing the code and manipulating it on the fly that was unparalleled in modern Echo circles. Until she'd joined Trickshot, her current team, she'd always felt excluded. The hotshots didn't appreciate her inability to load, and she'd never been considered popular.

Brittany had thrown half a dozen of the grenades she'd found in her inventory at the descending Reapers. The woman hadn't considered what types of grenades she was throwing, so although there was a frag grenade in the toss that significantly damaged the descending horde, there were also several flash grenades and something called a Razzle Dazzle. Horn couldn't really see anything in the environment, but her HUD popped up with several statuses:

Horn, Health 225/275, Armor: 0, Conditions: Blinded, Deaf, Mirage.

She didn't exactly know what Mirage meant but assumed it wasn't good. Everything in her vision was white. A phosphorus-like fire had burned out her vision. The deafening silence fed her rising panic.

Horn's first loadout as an Echo had been on another team. They were exploring a puzzle-based game that required a particular interface. Her old team had left that bit out as a joke. So she'd sat in a digital limbo with no sensation for six hours as the rest of the Echoes completed the dive. Those six hours had been an eternity. The group had claimed they just thought her load failed, and that's why they hadn't pulled her out.

That's what they claimed. But she knew better.

Horn had left that team when she returned to reality. Traumatized and angry, she'd needed years of therapy to be a functional human, much less an Echo. Junip had helped get her back on track. Trick's steady hand as the team captain also hadn't hurt. The man had patience.

Horn pulled up her status again, not being able to stop the impulse:

Horn, Health 225/275, Armor: 0, Conditions: Blinded, Deaf, Mirage.

The Deaf condition had started to blink, giving Horn hope that the status would end soon. She stared at the blinking letters, her lifeline. Horn wasn't completely alone or disconnected if she could still see her status in the HUD. Deep breaths. Horn prayed to the computer gods to take her debuffs away.

"HORN, CAN YOU HEAR ME?" Brittany's voice was that of an angel. Loud, harsh, panicked. Horn grabbed the sound with all she had.

"YES!" she shouted back in case Brittany was incapacitated as well.

"We need to do something. That cocktail I threw stunned the reapers, but they're already waking up."

Horn reached out to her best guess of where Brittany was located. Her hands felt something cold and clammy. For a second, she shuddered. What she grabbed didn't feel human. She swallowed a yelp, realizing it was a chunk of a reaper she'd grabbed.

"I can't see. You blinded me. How many are left?" Brittany didn't have the same debuffs as Horn. The woman's hand slid into Horn's, and comfortingly, it squeezed. Brittany must have picked up a bit on her panic. Thankfully, Horn's Blind condition started to blink, indicating the debuff was about to expire.

"Almost all of them appear to still be alive. I think we're on hard mode. Otherwise that should have taken out the lot of them."

Horn's mind raced. Trick had picked her up after several failed attempts at joining other teams. Minimally she'd been ready to leave the profession. Horn had even contemplated reincarnation as a way to escape the memories. That first experience damaged her ability to load into the verse. Every time she tried, she'd tense up and inevitably get a "failed load" notification.

Trick had sought her out as a recruit. He'd seen her worth, even when she didn't. He'd convinced her that she was valuable to his team. Junip ensured she had a home socially too. The ginger minx was relentless in including Horn in banter and off-hour plans. Trick had told her she was the best "backseat driver" a team commander could ask for. Her ability to manipulate the environment for the Echoes that could load was invaluable. Most teams couldn't see past her load failures. Trick made it clear that he was grateful for her area of expertise and never held her failed loads against her.

"I can try to turn that off." Horn's vision had started to return. The Mirage effect, however, was in full force. All of the shadows and brightness blurred the edges. Movement followed slowly with a cascading light that eventually settled into place. Her stomach lurched if she tried to focus too hard on it.

"You can what?" Brittany appeared to be rummaging around in her inventory, searching for more grenades.

"I think I can turn hard mode off. Let me try before you blind me again."

Horn went over and touched one of the webs connecting the reapers. She concentrated on bringing up the editor interface, which she'd used to change how the inventory functioned. The code unfurled, and she began skimming it, looking for the difficulty setting line.

"Any time would be helpful, Horn. They're going to be on us in a few seconds."

No one on her team would have recognized Horn in that moment. She scanned the code, coolly identified the right line, made the edit, and calmly executed. She was in control. This was her realm. The change shimmered up the webbing and entered all of the reapers it touched.

“Done!” Horn looked at the code take effect. It was done for this group anyway; the game overall was still classified as ‘hard mode.’

Brittany opened up. Her pistol fired over and over. Reaper heads exploded as she got head-shot after head-shot. With the reduced health, they fell to the weapon fire much easier, but it still wouldn't be enough. The woman's aim was phenomenal, but there were just too many reapers to take out with the handgun. She was about to run out of ammo if Horn's calculations were correct. Horn didn’t bother drawing her gun; she was a terrible shot and it was time for plan A.

The programmer pulled out the plasma rifle battery packs. "Hold your shot. Shoot these once they hit the webbing."

Horn threw the batteries as high as she could to get them to stick in the webbing near the largest mass of reapers. The battery packs did a wide arc, hitting silk strands and bouncing off.

"Oh shit." Horn watched as they rebounded off of the mesh and started somersaulting back toward the two humans. Brit fired immediately.

For the second time in the load, Horn went blind. This time, it was followed by a full-body burning sensation. She hit the floor and started rolling. She’d hoped the plasma batteries would ignite the room and send most of the reapers to their fiery deaths. What she hadn’t expected was the batteries to explode as they tumbled down at her and Brittany.

Ironically, the Mirage condition started blinking.

Horn had given up on being an Echo. She'd trained for it; she'd studied the history and procedures for it for years. That first experience had damaged her. They called her Horn because she was the first to sound the alarm when things began to degrade. The first to pull people out. The first to run if she had managed to load in the first place.

The burning hurt, but it felt good. She knew it wasn't life-threatening. Her health on her HUD had ticked down a bit, but nowhere near enough to endanger her life. For the first time, the very first time, she felt it. She felt what it was to be an Echo.

Horn reached out in the direction she'd last seen Brittany. Her hands scrabbled against the spongy floor, scorched lattice bits and reaper raining down upon them.

She found Brittany's hand and clenched it. "We did it!"

"WHAT? I CAN'T HEAR YOU."

"WE DID IT!"

And in a softer voice, too low for Brittany to hear, "I did it."

Chapter 9

Pik had waited patiently to pry herself back into the active game. The reapers paced above her in her box, one stomping over the hiding place every ten to twenty seconds. She couldn't believe how dumb they were. Artificial intelligence was a joke. More like artificial unintelligence. They were completely oblivious to the player hiding right below their feet.

Her estimation of their stupidity grew as she took action. Pik raised the plexiglass top of her coffin, prepared to fight the creature that had just walked over her. The reaper marched onward. It stopped briefly, tilting its head toward her, looking confused. It even sniffed the air, talons clenching and unclenching as it snapped its maw alarmingly. Then it simply turned back on its route and continued forward. Pik stood dumbfounded, prepared to launch into an all-out defensive attack.

Her preparedness wasn't in vain, though, as the reaper marching up from behind her had no trouble telling that she was prey. Pik whirled, the plexiglass falling against her back as she brought out a pistol in one hand and her Cosmic Knife in the other.

"You want some of this?" The question was ludicrous. No one wanted the smelly, gooey, and viscera-splashed version of her. The creature didn't pause in its head-on assault. It had caught her scent and was moving straight for the kill.

Thankfully the only reapers that fit in the ventilation shaft were small and underwhelming juveniles. This one had to have been deprived of oxygen as a hatchling as it lunged forward directly onto her already extended blade, impaling itself. Pik didn't know what to think of the stupidest maneuver she'd ever encountered in a monster dive, but she decided to take the gift for what it was and move on.

Pik turned around, pushing the plexiglass forward. If the reapers couldn't penetrate with their gaze, it could be the key to her team's survival—an awkward invisibility cloak.

Moving forward could have been faster. Each time a reaper returned on their path in front of her, they'd hit the plexiglass, turn around, and leave. Pik wasn't against breaking the game mechanics now and again, but this almost seemed unfair.

The only thing that kept her from examining the whole situation closer was Trick's voice in her head: *Never debug the gift code in your simulation.* Pik went with it. She had to turn and fight the monster creeping up behind her every twenty to thirty seconds. Easy enough, they came one by one. The hard part was dragging the plexiglass behind her. The tunnel she woke up in was bigger than the one she'd passed out in. She could make her way forward in a crouch, but it was awkward.

Sweat dripped off her nose as she arrived at the termination of the shaft. She set the plexiglass behind her to turn away any further reaper patrols as she examined the slats of the large vent cover in front of her. She pressed her face up to the cover but couldn't see into the next room. The vent was clogged by a black, ashy substance.

It had begun to heat up. The plexiglass was hindering the air exchange, and the temperature was approaching sweltering in the vent. Pik wasn't optimistic the next room would be empty, but it was time to brave the unknown before she cooked. She'd lost her energy rail gun when she'd effectively died. There was nothing useful in her inventory that she could recall from her memory.

For a moment, Pik felt a pang. She missed Horn and her instantaneous solutions. The woman was a wizard who could send you boons through the trace connections back to

Command. Pik wouldn't want to be in a firefight with her, but no one equaled her skills in utilizing preprogrammed capabilities or solutions built on the fly.

Pik had procrastinated enough. The heat was unbearable, and the black ash had started to tickle her throat. She wiggled her body into position. No small feat in the tiny space. Timmic, Trick, and even Horn would have had trouble moving around in the space, but her petite body had no problem. Bracing her arms against the side of the shaft for leverage, she kicked the vent cover off. The cover sailed through the air, and she winced when it clattered on the floor loudly. The sound reverberated into the shaft. If there was a monster in the next room, they knew she was coming.

With resignation, Pik hurried forward, pulling the plexiglass behind her, bending down to check out the room only to find two familiar faces with shit-eating grins staring at her.

"Hey Pik! Your rescue's a little late this time."

Pik stared agog. Horn stood in the middle of a slew of charred chunks that must have been reapers at one point. Standing beside her was a sunburnt Brittany Montgomery.

"You know, Horn, when you plan a barbeque, you're not supposed to light yourself on fire."

Horn laughed. Pik took a snapshot in her mind of the moment. In the years they'd adventure, she'd only seen Horn laugh a few times, and it'd never been on a dive. Horn was brilliant, but on dives, she tensed up to complete uselessness. This laugh was a deep one, spurred by something Pik didn't understand.

Pik reached back, snagged the plexiglass, and jumped. The ground rose, and she hit with a splat, landing firmly on a barbequed reaper.

Brit looked unimpressed, wiping bits of goo off of her face. Horn offered a hand up, used to Pik's antics. "Mind if I make some adjustments to your interface?"

Horn's question was quintessential Horn. Pik's long-term teammate was charred, eyebrow singed, face red, and her short brown hair stood up as though it'd survived an explosion. The woman had survived hell, and all she wanted to do was fix Pik's interface.

"Uh, sure. Hey, are you okay?" Pik's question caused Horn to look up from her work.

"I'm good, better than I've been in a while. You?" Pik looked down at herself; her gear was pristine, and whatever had landed her in the coffin had reset the wear and tear on her body. The contrast between the two couldn't be bigger.

"I'm okay, good even. Thank the Metaverse you're fixing my interface though. If I had to suffer through the stupid preset interface a moment longer, I'd lose it." The two Echoes connected on the mundane as Horn adjusted Pik's settings.

Horn's eyes looked distant. "Please accept the request."

Player Horn has requested to change your settings, inventory, and command functions.

Warning: Giving access to these player abilities can be harmful if you do not know the player. Do you grant control?

The warning was necessary but didn't cause Pik to hesitate in granting Horn access. She'd given Horn all the keys to her player queendom long ago. Horn had taken many games from impossible to easy with the adjustments she made. Pik began to smile as an inventory option popped up in her HUD.

Pik mentally hit it and brought up a bottomless list of the items she'd raided from the armory. Unfortunately this confirmed her lack of an energy rail gun. Before beginning the sorting process, she queried the two, "How armed are you both? What do you need?"

Horn gave her an odd side-eye. "I've got almost nothing. A low-level knife and a pistol with no ammo."

"That's terrible. How'd you manage that? You've got less than the starter gear."

"I know. I loaded in a cocoon. I'm sure there's some game logic that took most of my gear."

Pik had to chuckle. "You were voted most likely to load captured. This tracks."

Horn ignored her.

"How about you, Brittany?"

Brit was standoffish, her arms crossed in front of her chest, eyes watching her. Pik wasn't fazed. Brit stood nearer to Horn. Whatever ordeal the two had survived had brought them closer. "I don't know what I have. Some grenades. A pair of sunglasses." With the word, a pair of aviators snapped onto her face. Utterly useless in a ship environment, but stylish? Pik didn't know what passed for style in Brit's century, but the glasses were oversized and a couple of centuries out of style.

"Did Horn not do the inventory magic for you?"

Brit's eyes hardened. "No." She didn't elaborate. When Pik looked at Horn, she gave a short head shake. Horn reached out and pretended to fiddle with Pik's personal shield device. Her hands brushed Pik's arm and a message popped up on her HUD. In this game, the chat function required physical contact.

Horn: We'll talk about it later.

"Okay, well, I'm going to assume you're not much better equipped than Horn here." Pik began sorting through her inventory: explosives, hand-to-hand, guns from automatic to pump action. She started dumping weapons into a pile. For now, she just dumped the ones she had in excessive numbers. Sometimes, like with the machine gun, any number above zero was too many. She figured she didn't need more than three cosmic swords. She only had two arms, but a third sword would be helpful if she snapped one.

Horn had programmed them all to have an unlimited inventory enhancement. It was her standard procedure. None of them liked to leave loot or options behind. So, when Pik'd gotten to the armory, she'd emptied it, even down to the furniture. Digital existence had some perks. It made a castle's worth of inventory a reality.

Brit's eyes grew wide as she watched the growing pile of weapons.

Horn grinned. "You don't do anything halfway, do you? Please give me your shield. I want to examine it."

Pik complied. One didn't second guess their stout tech goddess, even if the shield was her prized possession. She flicked a few last bits around, set her quick loads, and looked up to find Brit distastefully picking up a Cosmic Sabre.

"You put the pointy end in the monsters." Pik had somehow rubbed Brittany wrong but couldn't figure out how. So, she did her best Trick impression and tried to deflect with humor.

"Yeah, I know. I just have never liked the melee builds. I'm a 'launch attacks from afar' type of player. But when we were cocooned, I would have paid a year's wage for one of these. Anything to cut through the webs." The sword disappeared into Brittany's inventory.

Pik watched Brittany shuffle through the pile. True to her claimed build, Brit mostly added longer-range options to her inventory. In a few instances where only one or two of a specific gun were available, she'd stop and consult Horn to see if it was something she'd want. Horn unilaterally turned everything down. She wasn't a combat specialist. Anything Brit was familiar with would be better in her hands. Horn would do poorly with almost anything they handed her, except maybe a rocket launcher.

The only thing that Brittany didn't skimp on were the grenades. She didn't even ask Horn's opinion. She just picked them all up and stored them away. Pik had an idea of what happened to all of the reapers before she arrived.

"Brit, did you have the same experience as Horn?"

The girl blinked, surprised to be further quizzed. "How so?"

"Did you load in a cocoon too?"

"Yes." Brit paused briefly. "I woke up hanging from the ceiling. Thank God Horn was here and had a Cosmic Knife, or I'd probably be reaper food by now."

She lied. Pik was almost certain. But she didn't know why. What benefit was there?

"Done." Horn handed Pik her plexiglass shield. She could truly call it that now, as straps had been attached so it was easier to hold. Upon inspection, a formal identification tag was triggered:

Shield of Lies, Level: unknown. This is a shield made of unknown materials. [Error] [Error]

"Isn't that a bit dramatic for a plexiglass jury-rigged shield?"

Horn shrugged. "It named itself. Where'd you find it?"

Brit reached out to touch it and gasped. "My system doesn't recognize its existence."

Things began to click for Pik. That was why the reapers didn't react to it. The shield was outside of the game architecture.

"It's an Exoreality Object." The statement sat between Horn and Pik. Brittany looked between the two, obviously unfamiliar with the term.

Pik's mind raced. Exoreality Objects was a term commonly used by Echoes. Mostly they were objects that folks like Horn would set up to load with the divers. Artifacts that came externally from the game and had limited application, either because the game didn't recognize they existed or because they were extradimensional to the game. The objects were tools like a Trace Tracker to find a missing teammate or a special weapon that discharged known projectiles or max damage ammo. Cheats. The fact that Pik found the shield had exciting implications. Who put it there? It certainly wasn't Horn.

It was curious that Brit couldn’t interact with the Exoreality Object. She’d loaded from the Metaverse just like the rest of them. However, the woman had spent a long time in a stasis attached to the game’s end boss. This shouldn't have mattered, though. She'd returned to their pod and reloaded like any other digital entity separate from the game. Brittany should have been able to interact with the object in the same ways Horn and Pik. Instead she had the same reaction as the juvenile reapers.

"We should get moving. There’s a whole second level to explore. You didn't happen to run into Junip, Timmic, or Trick, did you?" Pik left the mystery for another time. Brit’s sour expression told her she wouldn’t make any progress.

Horn was rifling through the pile of dumped weapons in the middle of the room. “You don’t meet many people hanging upside down in a reaper nest.”

"Right, let's move out. I think you've got most of my preferred settings set up. Give me a second to change my quick weapon react function." Pik frowned distractedly as she moved through her inventory again, setting up quick commands for half the available stuff. She touched Horn's arm.

Pik: We need to talk sooner rather than later.

Message sent, she moved on, brushing past Brit. "Let's go. We've got some more monsters to fry."

Horn waved a hand over the pile of violence-inducing implements that Brit hadn't wanted. They all disappeared in one fell swoop.

Brit's eyes were wide. "I wish I had that power while playing the game. I might have come close to winning if I had." Her tone was wistful.

Horn apologized, "Yeah, sorry Brittany. I can't seem to interface with your settings. Just like you can't interact with the Sheild of Lies, my interface errors out when I try to access yours." Pik gave them both a frown that invited further conversation. "Pik, I've never encountered this in a game. I can't edit her digital identity in any way. There is no back-end reprogramming to get a better map function loaded for her, but there's also no deeper stat data either. Her settings are hard coded."

"That's on purpose," Brit said softly. The two Echoes looked at her curiously before she explained, "The season before mine, two brothers loaded with what the game show declared 'cheat codes' that altered the environment to give them an advantage. They closed the customization and mods available for those loading."

Pik watched Horn. She'd never really cared to learn the details. Pik's job was to shoot things. Horn knew the ins and outs of modifying environments.

"That makes sense." Horn's tone was light, but Pik could see the illogic of it bothered her. "Closing the back end would allow the game developers to control all elements that would make a contestant successful or not." Pik and Horn knew that an artificial limitation like that was normally not enough to stop Horn. There was a deeper mystery here. Pik filed it away. She and Horn were overdue for some time alone to compare notes.

Chapter 10

Pik and Horn continued to level as the team confronted unending corridors of aliens. Brit wasn't able to progress. She was fierce as combat got heated, and she was detailed in her strategies and open to their plans and feedback. This was a boon as Brit had the most to lose, as squishy as she was with no levels. As Pik and Horn leveled in the alien death trap, it became more apparent that Brittany's character was different. Broken.

"I wish I could help more," Brit stated, her dark, blown-out curls plastered to her head in sweat. The truth was Pik wished it too. The Echoes were maxing out their damage output, and it was getting dicey. The game was scaling the difficulty level for three players, not two.

Horn's HUD flicked off. Her hazel eyes softened as she stepped forward and gave Brittany a quick hug for reassurance. Pik noticed these things, even if she didn't completely understand them.

"It's okay. We're alive." *Barely.* In her mind, Pik added the word that Horn left off. They were surviving, but it was close. She had a gash across her eye that was slow to heal and a bruise on her arm where a reaper had rammed her. As their health bars grew, it took longer for them to regenerate. Brit was the exception. She was approaching a one-hit kill. They'd have to hold her back or risk her dying.

"What do you think happens if we wipe?" Horn spoke again, trying to fill the uncomfortable silence. Forcing conversation wasn't Horn's style, and the awkwardness of it showed.

Pik had purposefully observed Horn's behavior for a week once. The woman had been so engrossed in a programming puzzle that she hadn't spoken for three days. Pik was pretty sure Horn hadn't even noticed. She wasn't a talker.

Pik watched as Brit made to speak but stopped herself.

"You know how it is in most games, Horn; we just reset. Here, though . . ." Pik left it unsaid. Here, it probably meant actual death. Or worse: something akin to Brit's enslavement. And no one was going to come for them. No Echoes would dig up this game after their explosive exit from humanity's Metaverse.

Brit cut through her musing with a quiet statement, "Death isn't the end here." She didn't elaborate. Pik wished she would.

"Did you guys die? Is that why you were strung up in the cocoons?"

Horn frowned. "I don't remember how I got there. I honestly thought I just loaded in upside down. How long had you been in the game until you found us?"

"Not long, I think. I'd been moving through the level fast and then passed out . . . ?" Pik still wasn't sure what to make of her fever dream with Trick and her near death. "I'm not positive how long I was unconscious."

"Gives me hope for Timmic and Junip. They could be wrapped up in a cocoon or trapped in a cargo bay, just waiting for us to find them. They've got to be alive," Horn voiced Pik's hope. A hope she was a little too pessimistic to believe wholly.

"Even if they're dead, they're still alive. This place is a bit like your Metaverse that way," said Brit. Again with her cryptic statements. Pik had given up on pushing her. Every time she asked a question, the woman clammed up. It would be at her own pace if she were to reveal her secrets. It was infuriating, and Pik was losing her temper.

Not losing one's cool was a core rule of the Echoes' operating manual. Pik held back, but it was getting harder. Losing one's temper was one of the truest threats to an Echo. Every rule was the result of something that had happened to a team. Trick had told her this story, and she'd vowed at the time that no team had the luxury of anger.

Edi was one of the early dive team captains. He was known for having a fiery temper. He'd been on a puzzle delve, and a particularly troubled logic puzzle had his team stymied. They replayed it five or six times. Failure just reset the puzzle. Trapped on the level, he kept them at it. Twenty retries, thirty. The feedback to the Command had started to lose apparent cohesion. It showed them reentering. At the subsequent failure, Edi would reload the game space, not allowing for a thought or question. The second in command he had tried to get him to hesitate. The words of caution cut out as he engaged in the game again. Four of them had loaded. The first load had been a brand new Echo, and they'd all been surprised when the kid had loaded in on his first try.

Logic games were particularly wearisome on the brain. They drilled away at one's intellect.

"I—I need a break, captain." Rising panic was evident in the kid's voice.

"Command copies—" the feed cut out as the game restarted. "Command copies, Captain Edi. We need a pause after this round."

Edi's voice was tight. "We'll take a break when I say we take a break." The game progressed, and they made a failed move seven steps in—their worst iteration yet.

Trick had paused at that point in the story. He'd looked into Pik's eyes and spoke directly to her, "You've got to be careful when you're in charge." She'd almost interrupted him to tell him he'd always be in charge, but he cut her off. "You'll load alone someday or be in charge. It doesn't matter. When you're in charge, you must keep your cool."

The argument in her dissolved, and Pik asked, "Why? What happened?"

His voice, thick with emotion, brought them back to

the very moment.

"Edi hit the restart button before I—before Command—could stop him. In that game, Command had limited opportunities to pull the players. It could only be done between iterations of the game."

Pik had made herself small at his slip. Trick never talked about his former teams. At the time, they'd had some older teammates, grizzled Echoes, who'd been diving longer than she'd been alive. Not the fresher-faced team she'd built with him today. He'd been the Echo that hadn't loaded.

"The kid panicked. He set off the kill condition in two moves. The captain let loose on the boy. Obscenities I won't repeat."

The first lesson Pik had learned as an Echo fell out of her mouth, "You can't panic as an Echo."

Trick nodded. "They entered a loop, and the game stuck."

A chill ran up Pik's spine. There's no walking away when a game gets stuck in a loop like that. Trick had lost his entire team.

In Infestation, Pik centered herself—deep artificial breaths. The metallic smell of the scrubbed air of the ship filled her senses. They had to slow it down and break down the problem ahead.

"Okay, Brit. If you're not willing to tell us what happens when you die in the game, fine, keep your secrets." Pik couldn't stop herself from the dig. Her two teammates winced. "But help me out. What do we have in front of us? *We're in this together.* We're on the same team. We're on level four now. I'm having trouble remembering it all."

Brit took a deep breath. "As you know, we've got ten total levels. Level four is more of the same. Acid spitters and reapers, a boss with four heads at the end. It's doable, but we must be careful on this difficulty level. Honestly, five is what I'm really worried about."

"Why five?" Horn asked.

"It's a water level." Pik now remembered this from her first playthrough. She had yet to catalog the levels on her first run-through with Trick. She'd never thought she'd be back, so what was the point? Five had been memorable, though. She had considered returning the game to the Metaverse because of that level.

Sneaking—what had been getting them through sticky situation after sticky situation—wouldn't be an option in the water. Players were time bound by a breath timer, and the Acari swimmers were impossible to fool. How the game developers justified flooding half the spaceship on the fifth level in an alien survival game was beyond her.

"If we're going to die, it's going to be there," Pik heard herself say, control slipping. "Brit, you're going to have to let us in on the secret of what happens if you die. It's highly likely, at this point, that Timmic and Junip are already there." Pik knew she shouldn't push, but it *wasn't* okay that Brit was keeping critical knowledge from them. She'd waited for her to come around, but it wasn't happening fast enough.

Brit's face transformed. It went from a mature adult to a hurt animal as a small whimper escaped. Horn put an arm around her, drawing her away while giving Pik a dirty look for pushing. Pik closed her eyes, trying to let go of her irritation. Whatever Brit was hiding would come out eventually, one way or another.

Pik flipped the switch on the improvised flamethrower they'd built at the end of the third level. She started torching the reaper webs that spun out before them. Sweat rolled off her face and into her eyes, stinging, as flames filled the corridor. Fire on a spaceship also didn't make sense. The game didn't have to, though.

Pik thought of Trick's previous team, stuck in a loop for eternity. She thought of her own team. Then she took a deep breath of the superheated air and stepped forward into the next knuckle filled with filaments. She could hear reapers screaming as the flames leaped up the webbing. Pik clicked the flamethrower off, watching the fire race up the webs in satisfaction.

Brittany wasn't willing to share what death meant in Infestation, but they'd find out the truth eventually. Flamethrowers didn't work on water levels. Death in this game was inevitable.

Pik had doomed everyone in the urgency to rescue Trick. This game wasn't winnable. The deck was stacked from the beginning. Brit knew it. Horn knew it. Pik knew it.

Chapter 11

Water levels were notoriously hard. Pik hated them with a passion. Game developers and creative AI game engineers couldn't resist embedding a random water level to throw off the game mechanics. Pik had yet to meet an Echo who liked them, even if they were popular with the general public.

First, it was wet. The three of them had stripped down into the bare minimum clothes needed for decency. Everything extraneous would create drag as they tried to swim through the crystal-clear water seeping from the walls. It was always clear on spaceships. Pik should have been grateful. She'd been on swamp water levels where the murk prevented her from seeing more than a few centimeters. Those levels also tended to incorporate leeches. She shuddered at the memory.

The second horrible thing about water levels was that standard weapons were useless. Guns fired underwater generally caused bullets to move so slowly that the water-adapted creatures could effortlessly slide off to the side. Plus, the concussion from the weapon firing usually stunned the shooter. Swords were better, but it was hard to swing one with enough force or velocity to do any actual damage. And the energy swords they had were useless. Electricity and water didn't mix well.

A nice spear would have been preferable, but in this game there weren't any primitive options in this "advanced" technology spaceship. They each had a small dagger—pretty much useless—and a flashlight. Horn had tried a Taser and almost electrocuted herself. Pik laughed heartily once she confirmed Horn was okay. The programmer's hair stuck straight out in all directions, as though she'd put a fork in a light socket. The levity was nice, Pik hadn't realized she needed the laugh until it happened.

The final reason Pik hated water environments was that the monsters were always worse. They were suction-cupped tentacle monsters or lithe, fast-swimming fish with razor-sharp teeth. No matter how you sliced it, you were at a disadvantage in speed, and stealth wasn't worth anything when the creatures sensed your movement through the water.

This game, thankfully, took care of another problem Pik had always had in most of these under-the-sea adventures. Oxygen masks with what seemed to be an unlimited amount of oxygen using fake regenerative technology were available. It was a small win, but Pik was thankful she wouldn't die suffocating in the dark.

"You ready?" Pik looked at her ragtag group: Horn, half fried, and Brit, a shadow of herself.

Brit looked bad. She was pale as a ghost and was noticeably shaking. Horn squeezed her shoulder. "You okay? Can you do this?"

Brit nodded with a wan smile. "I don't have a choice, do I?"

"What's got you so spooked? It's going to be hard, but not impossible. Trick and I managed. It is doable."

"You went through on an easier difficulty setting, didn't you?"

Pik nodded. Easy mode meant finishing quickly and efficiently.

Brit looked haunted as she spoke, "This is where I died on my run." Pik was surprised. It hadn't occurred to her that Brit had died anywhere but when she was facing the final boss. She'd assumed part of the glitch that kept Brit in the game was that she'd died in that creature's lair.

"Here?"

"Yes. I ran the game at this difficulty, and the boss was a beast from the deep. The Acari can be relentless, but the maw at the end . . ." Brit's voice trailed off in memory.

Horn muttered about the ridiculousness of a game that doesn't keep with its theme, "Aliens and deep-sea monsters shouldn't be in the same game."

"It's a leviathan and tentacles," Brit described the monster, "and a maw that gnashes at you. Crushes your bones." Pik hadn't encountered that boss during her run, but they'd played at a lower difficulty level.

For a second, Pik thought about asking for some advice on how they should handle the beast. But it was obvious from her initial outcome that Brit probably shouldn't be the source. When Trick and Pik had played through, there were blue-streaked biting fish called Acari, and the boss had been a swarm of the fish. The game held a lot back on the more manageable difficulty levels.

"The coldness—it slows you down. Then out of the dark, a tentacle grabs on and the maw rips you apart." Brit's voice was hollow as she relived her nightmare. "When you feel the drag as it pulls on your leg, it's too late."

Pik took a deep breath, feeling a well of panic burble in her chest. Trick wouldn't let a giant tentacle monster—essentially a Kraken—stop him. She was sure he'd fought one in a pirate sea adventure game three months ago and survived. What could an underwater spaceship Kraken bring?

"Are you sure we have to go this way? Some games have bypasses." Horn's voice was hopeful. She didn't want to fight the monster any more than Brit.

"No, Trick and I looked for a bypass. You know how he hates getting his hair wet." They shared a smile. The team relentlessly teased Trick about his vanity. It wasn't enough that he was one of the best Echoes in the Metaverse; he always had to look good doing it too. "We just had to go for it. I thought at the time that it was too easy. I guess I now know why."

They talked, mapping out a couple of possible strategies for the leviathan, mostly related to feeding it grenades or distracting it and then swimming past. Pik was done planning. They could assess further when they got to the boss. Time was being wasted.

She wouldn't have rushed if she'd realized how cold it would be as she took a bold step into the waterlogged hallway. The other two watched. She could feel their eyes, looking for a sign of weakness. She refused to flinch. "You two coming? These beasts are not going to kill themselves."

Pik watched as her compatriots took their first steps into the water. Horn outright squealed a bit at the sudden temperature change. Brit just looked like she might barf.

"Flashlights, rebreathers, and weapons?"

They nodded affirmatively, and Pik moved forward, staring at the shadowy pool. The light of her flashlight flickered in the water. Although she couldn't see the bottom of the passage, she took a deep breath and stepped into the abyss.

The artificial gravity drew her down slowly. She took a few calming breaths, knife out at the ready, as her body slowly sank into the shaft. Her eyes were prepared for any attack.

Pik's hair floated around her as the chill took hold. Air bubbles floated around the group as the rebreathers went to work. Pik was impressed that everyone was focused and calm. Brit's wide eyes scanned the water for threats.

One of the developers took mercy and eased the requirements for comm use in water. The function worked without touch, so the group could share a voice channel. Physical touch was still required to sent private text-based messages though. It was a small piece of luck. If they'd had to rely on hand gestures in the murky deep, it would have been all over from the start.

Horn: I hope we find Junip soon.

Pik had to smile. Horn was a woman of few words and passions. It'd taken Pik a long time to catch on. In her mind, there wasn't a least likely pair. But it became obvious eventually that the two cared for each other.

Pik: And Timmic.

Pik could almost hear Horn's awkward blush through the com channel.

Horn: Of course, Timmic too. Junip is less of a fighter than I am.

Pik decided to take pity on her anxiety.

Pik: I've seen Junip fend for themselves admirably. I'm sure they're okay.

Brit was silent. Pik had noticed that the two were also getting close. Horn tended to be protective, and Brit seemed as vulnerable as they came.

The ship was spooky underwater, light refracting in beams. Floating debris kept them alert. It had the effect of providing a low level of chaos to the environment. The unexciting gray and blue corridors they'd traversed faded further into a dull, monotone pallet.

Brit: Did you see that?

Pik should have been paying attention. Horn was a

nervous talker, and it was distracting. Brit's flashlight twisted in front of the group wildly. Pik peered into the dark. She hadn't seen anything. Brit was having trouble swimming and controlling the flashlight. It kept bouncing around in a way that was making Pik mildly sick.

Horn: I don't see anything. What was it?
Brit: A slice of light, like a reflection on scales.

Pik and Trick had speed run the water level. Trick and his vanity didn't allow for any research. Pik started to swim past yet another door when she paused. The room designation read "Aquatic Lab." This was a bad idea. It would likely unleash a mob.

She knew they were doomed without more knowledge. They couldn't afford to wipe. She pointed her flashlight at the door and nodded in its direction. Horn and Brit hadn't dived enough to know this decision was wrong.

Pik: Be on your guard. We're probably going to get attacked.

They each dog paddled in place, flashlight in one hand, knife in another. Pik swam forward first. Having the most armor, health, and experience, it only made sense. She tapped a red button with her knife, and the door slid open.

Inside was chaos. Floor-to-ceiling fish tanks sat, wholly enclosed, with blue lights dancing spectrally off plants and fish alike. The tanks held many fish she'd come across in the previous run and a few she hadn't. Quicksilver was a fish she hadn't encountered, and the lab was full of them. Swimming to one of the tanks, Pik read the tag: Name: Quicksilver, Batch 1-23, Aggression: High, Health: Low, Unsuitable for Alpha Prime. She scanned the immediate enclosures. They all had fully contained specimens with various batch numbers and ratings.

The fish, catching her movement, attacked the sides of their habitats with dull thuds, attempting to reach their prey. Surrounded by attacking but impotent fish, Pik was shocked to see blood drifting up from her arm. A deep crimson ribbon of blood swirled away from her body.

The cold numbed the pain—until it didn't. A gasp escaped her throat, causing a horde of bubbles to escape her breather.

The fish were attacking. So smooth and sharp, she didn't even feel the attack.

Pik went on guard and surveyed the area. It was hard to differentiate the caged fish from the threats.

Pik: Turn off your lights. They're going to swarm me since I'm bleeding.

She glanced back at her companions. Brit had a trail of blood coming off a leg. Horn looked panicked. They all flipped off their lights. The eerie blue glow of the aquariums filled the laboratory.

The fish were attracted to light. To blood. To noise.

Pik was on guard as she slowly tried to reach one of the room's corners. They had a chance if they could sit with two walls to their backs. Another slice. Her arm lit on fire as awareness of the injury grew.

The Quicksilver fish didn't bite you; they sliced with their fins. Pik caught one coming at her face. Bold. She acted like she hadn't seen it and, at the last moment, brought the case of her flashlight straight down on its nose. The hit stunned the creature. She knifed it, finishing its small health bar. These weren't the larger tuna-like Acari she was expecting. These were switchblades trying to sneak between a player's ribs.

Pik: They're susceptible to blunt damage.

A scream erupted on the coms as Horn was found. Pik quickly muted the feed, attempting to save her ears.

Another slice. This time, it bisected her ear. She watched it circle back toward her head. The greedy soul. Pik brought the hilt of her dagger down knocking it out. She sliced the stunned fish in half with a quick wrist flick. Peering upward, she finally saw what she'd expected—the swarm.

None of the slices caused much damage. But they compiled. And one of her party members wasn't very healthy.

Pik turned her back to the swarm and pushed Brit toward the corner of the room. At first the woman fought, but she relaxed as Pik pinned her, her own back laced in attacks. Horn had followed. Pik only had a brief moment to be thankful. When unmuted, she was still filling up the coms with hysterics.

Pik grabbed Horn's shoulder and twisted her around. They formed a human shield for Brit. Checking the party's health, Brit was already down to 30/50 HP.

Pik: HORN, SHUT UP. Brit, patch yourself before you bleed out.

They were all suffering from a bleeding condition—two more slices along Pik's legs.

Pik: Brit, blind them with my flashlight and yours. Horn, bash and slash.

Pik wasn't confident in Horn's ability, but at least she'd stopped screaming. Quickly she traded out the flashlight for a second knife, Pik whirled around. She spotted an attacker and reversed her grip to drop the heavy pommel of the knife on the fish. A slash of her other hand cut it in half. The motions repeated, threat after threat. The fish fell one by one. Brit pointed both flashlights at the oncoming horde.

Horn had dropped her knife and held a Quicksilver in her hand, examining it. Pik wanted to shake the woman. Now wasn't the time to do a code autopsy.

Pain radiated from dozens of cuts. Pik kept slicing but could only kill one fish at a time. She was only one person.

Before she could scold Horn into helping, the woman's voice cut through the numbing cold, settling into her mind.

Horn: Blink them. The code indicates they're susceptible to patterns.

Horn started flickering her flashlight. Then she jerked her dagger in a weird pattern. Pik wanted to kill her. Brit just followed along, blinking her lights. She was down to 11 HP.

Pik decided to ignore the motions and save them all. She swam forward to the swarm, ready to underwater ninja the mob . . . only to find them docile. She swam farther. They had stopped moving and just stared at Horn and Brit. Mesmerized.

Pik shook her head as she used her fish ninja skills to butcher each and every fish.

Chapter 12

Pik: You can stop now. Do you realize you both look like idiots?

Pik said it with a rare grin. Chunks of chum surrounded her. Every Quicksilver in the lab was dead. The weird theatrics of flashing and jerking their lights and knives had mesmerized the fish.

They were in bad shape. Brit was the worst. Her health bar was down to just a handful of points. The icy water stung the cuts Pik received, but everything was slowly healing. Each breath brought another regenerative health tick.

Brit: That was amazing. Will you teach me how to read the code like you?

Brit's voice held awe. Pik watched as Horn blushed. She didn't do well with compliments, but Pik didn't judge. She didn't either.

Horn: I can try, but it'll take some training. It's not a game skill; it's something I have studied for a long time. I'm just glad you listened to me when you did. If you hadn't, we'd all be goners.

Pik poked around the lab while the team recovered. Now that it was cleared, she didn't have to worry about getting ambushed—one advantage to stirring up a swarm like they did. The lab equipment still worked underwater. It was another impossibility the developers ignored. In no world would the electronics be sealed against water on a spacecraft. Pik swam over to a still-intact tank, bringing up the information graphic.

Quicksilver Fish

The genetic manipulation success rate is high. Alpha 2b is used to colonize a planet, swarming and killing off local hostile aquatic life to prepare the environment for more suitable Acari-based genetic life. Health is high. Edibility is low.

The visual gave information on the total mature length, width, strength, and breeding cycle of the Quicksilver fish. Based on the data, Pik guessed they'd have to fight a few more swarms before they were done.

The next aquarium had squid in it. The display gave basic information on the "base squid" genetic code, hinting that genetic alterations were made on other specimens. The other tanks contained the basic Acari and a variation that Trick and she had encountered. There was no new data beyond what was already in front of her, but the squid foreshadowed the boss fight that had killed Brit.

Horn: You find anything?

Pik: Just your standard mad scientist genetic lab. Nothing revolutionary.

Brit's rebreather released a throng of bubbles. At first, Pik thought she'd let go of a breath she'd been holding. The rebreathers typically let out a large mass of air every few minutes, but Brit's bubbles continued. Pik swam toward her teammates. Horn was grabbing Brit's arms, trying to get her to stop thrashing.

Horn: Calm down. Pik, get over here. Something's set Brit off. I can't get her to slow her breathing.

When Pik reached them, Brit's eyes were wild. She fought Horn almost instinctively. Pik checked Brit's stats on their team interface; she wasn't losing her health. This was just a freak-out.

Pik: Let her go, Horn. Brit, listen to me. You've got to slow down your breathing, one breath at a time. We're here together. We're a team. Slow down. You're okay. Can you see me? And Horn? Do you see my flashlight here?

Pik walked her through a grounding technique that Junip drilled into her. She'd always been worried about someone losing control on a dive, and Pik knew she wasn't prepared to handle that sort of emotional turmoil. She'd made Junip rehearse the steps with her over and over again. They practiced outside dives, especially when the team onboarded a new member. She'd never used the technique in an actual situation. She'd always been the one on edge whenever Horn loaded, as the woman was so high-strung.

Pik: You okay with Horn giving you a hug?

Consent was vital. Pik watched Brit get enough control to nod. Horn hugged her, and Pik knew they'd won when Brit leaned into it. It took a few more minutes, but Brit's breathing slowed, and the bubbles returned to their normal discharge. Pik didn't want to set her off again, but she had to know what had done it.

Pik: Are you feeling better? Good. Can you tell me what set you off?

Horn wasn't hugging Brit anymore, but she stood close. They had masks on, so reading facial expressions was challenging. Pik knew, though, that she'd asked for something from the woman that she didn't want to share. Brit stared out of her mask at the two of them, eyes darting from their faces. Pik waited. Pushing now wouldn't work. This was the moment the woman either had to trust them or not.

Brit took a deep breath and began.

Brit: I told you death wasn't the end here. It was supposed to be. I don't think anyone knew about the Doctor. When I died, I didn't just leave the world or fail my mother and daughter. I was sent to hell.

A slurry of bubbles was released. Brit's voice came through the coms strained.

Brit: The Doctor performed psychological experiments on me and other contestants who had lost the game. He did it for years. Manipulations of us, the environment, our abilities, and our digital physical bodies. He was ruthless. He . . . he seemed to like me a lot.

She stopped. Pik wasn’t sure she wanted to hear more. Horn stepped in, offering a comforting excuse.

Horn: It's okay. He's not here, we are. We'll keep you safe.

Brit: This game is his home. We're not safe.

Pik: Alright, then, let's get moving. We'll be safe when we can solve this game and get Trick back.

Pik began moving to the door calmly, but her mind was whirling. They now had a villain. She was positive Brit had more to tell them, but one thing Junip had drilled into her was that trauma took time to explore. Pik's heart constricted for a moment. She missed Junip. She hoped they were okay.

The three of them made their way deeper into the level. Several swarms of Quicksilver fish attacked, but they were dealt with efficiently as Horn and Brit did their dance, perfecting it as they went, and Pik slaughtered the mess. Pik was racking up the experience for the kills, leveling massively. She just wished she could share the experience points with Brit.

Acari were mixed in, but only in groups of two. The giant, tuna-like fish had intelligence. They would lurk behind debris to dart out, teeth first, and chew into the unsuspecting swimmer. The three had worked out a formation: Pik and Horn faced forward, sandwiching a backward-facing Brit between them. This kept Brit in the most protected spot while giving the team eyes in every direction.

Brit: We need to stop here.

Brit stood on the bottom of the hallway, tugging at the two Echoes' arms. Her brown locks floated around her head eerily, backlit by a red panel light in the wall. Her face was pale. For a brief moment, Pik's imagination got the better of her, imagining Brit's dead body floating on the deck. She shook her head, bringing her attention back to Brit's words.

Brit: —next room over.
Horn: Are you positive?
Brit: Yes. I remember because my wetsuit got hooked on that jagged piece right there.

She pointed at a support beam that'd broken in half, a nasty edge of metal protruding out into the hallway.

Horn: Wait, you had a wetsuit?

Pik had a tank top and shorts on, but Horn seemingly had loaded with "sexy sidekick" gear, which didn't have useful clothing options. Both of their outfits were worse for wear, stained with blood, sliced half to ribbons.

Brit: I had a bit of gear that we don't. Remember, I trained for this exact game, so I prepared more than we were able to do for this run. The point is, as soon as I crossed that part of the hallway, the monster attacked.

They still needed to set a plan for the boss. The three scoured the rooms and hallways leading up to the room, looking for an out. Nothing presented itself. Pik was racking her brain for a strategy when Pik remembered her plexiglass shield in her inventory. She pulled it out and faced her team.

The plan was simple but required the group to work together as a unit. Something she wouldn't have thought possible until they'd tackled the Quicksilver fish together. Pik was going to go first. She had the trickiest job but was also the most skilled in diving. Brit had too low of health and Horn's delve experience was nonexistent.

It was the sort of ruse that Trick would have done. Pik had to concentrate on her breathing. Her heart was accelerated with nerves.

The plexiglass was just long enough to cover an entire human body. The whole feat depended on its unique properties of providing complete cover to whoever was behind it. Horn tied rope around the shield and Pik's body.

Horn: You look ridiculous. I should take a picture for our team scrapbook.

Pik: I feel ridiculous.

Horn: This is going to work.

Pik nodded. It had to. She tested the build-out, trying to float with the shield on her back, propelled by her feet gently kicking, a long string of rope dangling behind her. They made a few adjustments as one of her hands briefly peeked out. The maneuver was dangerous, but it was their best chance. Pik could have had all the time in the world and still not felt truly ready. Junip, Timmic, and Trick were counting on them.

The team set themselves up. Pik had the plexiglass attached to her back, like a top-heavy turtle, arms by her side. She waited for the shove off.

Horn: You've got this.

Pik's teammates pushed her into the Kraken's lair. The velocity they gave her vanished almost instantly, the plexiglass providing significant drag. The Echo floated for a moment, then slowly began to kick. She held her breath, waiting for the attack. Putting her first had its risks. If the leviathan attacked, she was strapped so tight to the plastic sheet that she'd be useless in the fight. It was an all-or-nothing plan.

Nothing happened. Pik began to wonder if Brit had misremembered where the boss was. She kicked a little faster. The room was large, replete with hulking machinery. It could have been some sort of water pump or part of the engine. Pik wasn't up on fantasy ship design. The whole place was lit with a soft blue light from some panels in the ceiling.

A shadow passed overhead. By the size of it, Pik knew the beast had to be large, even if she couldn't see it. Her heart thumped in her chest, and she resisted the urge to kick faster. The top of the plexiglass tilted up from a rising current in the water from the monster's passage. Pik flexed her abs, trying to keep it in place. Keep her shell from rolling. Thankfully the pull didn't last long. She floated for a second, trying to unclench her body. Slowly she started kicking again to the far side of the room.

The final part of the maneuver was going to be difficult. She had to change the perspective of the plexiglass. As she neared the wall, she had to twist vertically to keep the shield between herself and the monster. There was a crevice she'd be tucked into while the rest of the team made the same maneuvers.

Pik eyed the wall as it approached. Carefully she pushed her hands out in front, fingertips barely over the shield's edge to cushion the impact. She used her hands to walk the contraption up on its end, then she shuffled to a space behind a bulkhead. Brit had told her that a team had once hidden behind the barrier for hours as they used a torch to cut through the wall and escape into the wall structure, finding an air duct up to the next level.

That would be their play once they got everyone into place. Pik quickly untied all the ropes and reattached them for the pullback. She tugged twice on the extended rope, signaling Horn to pull it back. So far, the plan was working. They'd made a lot of assumptions about the boss ignoring floating debris and ambient movement. Pik had to hand it to Horn. She'd been right about the boss's behavior so far.

Brit was going to be next. She would be easier, as Pik kept a trailing length of rope on her side. Pik would help pull Brit across instead of relying on her self-propulsion. Horn and Brit started tying Brit up. Pik was careful in watching, ensuring the bulkhead stayed between her and the predator. She didn't want to get attacked now that she was safe. Horn struggled to get Brit under the plexiglass completely. She was a bit taller than Pik.

All in all, two tugs signaled that they were ready to send Brit across. Pik gently pulled at the rope. It ground against the side of the bulkhead, but so far, the Kraken didn't seem to mind or care. Brit slowly sneaked between the tension that Horn put on the rope and Pik's pulling. She made good progress.

The Kraken left its hole about halfway through the journey, doing the same thing to Brit that it'd done to Pik. Pik watched in terrifying fascination as the long, tentacled legs flowed behind the giant cephalopod as it swam across its domain. The creature was surprisingly majestic.

What they hadn't accounted for in their planning was the mental challenge of having watched Pik cross the route and the anxiety-inducing fear that repeating her crossing would elicit. Brit held still, but a giant swarm of bubbles was released from her rapid breathing. Pik winced as they burbled right in front of the creature's path. The Kraken stopped, confused for a moment, and Pik's heart sank as the beast turned its eyes down to investigate the source of the bubbles.

In moments, its tentacles wrapped around the plexiglass, flipping the piece of debris over. Brit screamed, bubbles flying everywhere. The rope was yanked from Pik's grip.

Pik watched helplessly as the Kraken slapped an appendage onto Brit's leg and pried the woman off of the protective shield. Pik hesitated to join the fight. If she died here, Trick, Junip, and Timmic likely lost their chance at survival. She watched as Horn swam toward the monster, dagger extended. Pik considered figuring out how to break into the wall paneling. But the Kraken turned to Horn, reaching out to grab her as well. Pik watched in horror as a tentacle wrapped around her friend's waist.

She couldn't help it. Pik moved, joining the fight. She loaded two daggers and kept a Cosmic Sabre on standby. Pik might have been able to survive by herself, but some costs weren't worth it.

The Echo shot forward, all speed and grace. She hit

the back of the Kraken with both daggers, sinking into its soft skin. The boss whirled in a way that only those born of the sea could. Pik was grabbed and spun in a confusing twist of bubbles. She pulled the sabre out, her last real hope.

The weapon fizzled in the water, sending a shock through the water. The predator was unimpressed.

The beast undulated, bringing Pik closer to its maw. She felt her body being crushed. Pik pulled a pistol from her inventory, firing it ineffectually. She pulled a grenade but wasn't able to pull the pin before darkness took her.

Her last thought floated up with the bubbles from her party. *She had failed.*

PART 2

Chapter 13

Endings are painful. Ironically, Pik's parents prepared her for that—their parting gift. Trick had enough sorrow in his life, enough teammates he'd lost or left. He also had tried to impart the lesson. Pik knew she was stubborn. She still held a grudge against her parents. She'd worked through a dozen variations of what she'd say to them if she happened to stumble into a stranger and a glitch revealed her parents reincarnated.

Dozens of variations of anger, bitterness, and denial.

It wasn't possible. When people reincarnated, they weren't recognizable and carried no previous memories. Pik's fantasy always evaporated into an empty longing.

Getting ripped apart by the tentacles of a giant Kraken made it all seem pointless.

Pik woke up dead. A dull headache thudded in the back of her digital head. Her eyes squinted shut in pain. Wherever she was, it was bright. Too bright. The first real sense of self and a fragment of hope came from Brittany's panicked voice.

"No, not here. Not again," the words squeaked out between thick gasps of air. Brit was hyperventilating. It always surprised Pik that developers of the Metaverse, or these antique games, would include such flawed mechanics as hyperventilation. Even the idea of panic should have been cut on the editing floor. Both sensations were utterly useless.

Before she could speak, Horn's voice tried to soothe the woman. "Calm down. It's okay. I'm here too. We'll get out of this together."

Pik blinked rapidly, trying to clear her vision to make sense of the facility they were now being held in.

Internally she rolled her eyes at Horn. In the history of panic, no person had ever calmed down by being told to calm down. She'd learned early on that giving someone anxious something else to think about was the best course of action.

"Brit, can you hear me?" Pik took command of the situation, trying to imbue her voice with command.

"Yes." Her voice was shrill and tight.

"I can't see anything. It's too bright. Do you know where we are? Can you see anything? Can you tell me what this place is?"

"I—It's the test lab. Th—the Doctor lives here." Brit choked on the word "doctor." This person wasn't a helper or healer, wasn't a medic like Junip. Whomever the Doctor was, Brit was scared to death of them.

"Okay, well, we're alone now. At least, I assume we are since the Doctor hasn't said anything. So let's figure out how to get out of here before they return. I need your help with that." Calm, even-toned. She had to break through to Brit. Break through the panic.

Although a digital existence didn't require panic, anxiety, depression, and other negative emotions, the digital experience included them anyway. The world's programmers cursed the digital generation with the same frustrations of biological brains. The theory floating around the Metaverse was that it made it easier for biological humans to transfer into a digital existence. What is humanity if not a bundle of anxieties and unhelpful physical reactions?

"He might be here. He hides sometimes. We can't escape." Brit's voice moved from anxious to a dull, hollow monotone.

Pik's vision began to clear. The highlights were blown out of her sight, but she could make out the space they occupied. It was a fluorescent-lit laboratory. Similar to the underwater one they'd been exploring, but instead of fish tanks, they were in human holding tanks. She was surrounded by a glass-like circular barrier. The lab had two to three times the amount of lighting needed for the space, causing her eyes to water.

She, Horn, and Brit seemed to all be in floor-to-ceiling specimen tubes, each set with an exterior blue panel. As her sight returned further, Pik noticed her health stats displayed on the panel. They all wore basic, dull tan cotton scrubs. These were an upgrade for Brit, but they chafed at Pik's skin.

"Pik, can you see them? JUNIP! Over here!" Horn called.

No one answered. Pik wiped the tears out of her stressed-out eyes, finally making out additional filled tubes on the other side of the room. Junip and Timmic stood in their tubes. Both slumped against the glass. Neither appeared to be moving. A worm of concern wiggled in Pik's gut. She hadn't truly let herself believe that either of her teammates could be dead, just like she couldn't accept that Trick was lost.

"Timmic?"

Their hope rebounded as neither of their friends answered.

"Brit, now is the time to open up and tell us exactly what's happening."

Pik looked over at Brit's tube. Tears were streaking down her face, but her eyes were glazed over, like she'd given up hope long ago and checked out.

"When I died in Infestation, I woke up here. They were honest about the possibility of death, and I'd been okay with it." Brit's tone was low and her cadence slow with resignation. "If I died, I wouldn't have to watch my mother slowly waste away. By that point, my daughter had early signs of the wasting sickness as well. They interviewed us. They wanted a player profile and a good thirty-second clip to show everyone why we were willing to gamble our lives. It was supposed to generate sympathy and viewership."

"There were wild claims that if viewers fell in love with your story, they'd help you win. It'd be good for the game's publicity, even if they had to pay out the prize money. People did win. Don't get me wrong, it was possible. Which just made it all the more tempting. The truth and guilt I've had to live with is that I was okay if I lived and saved my family or died and didn't have to deal with it anymore. To be free at last, either way."

"The problem is, the Doctor doesn't let you die when you lose the game. You get deposited here. His lab. His experiments. Time is odd here. Has it been a month? Millennia? I know I sat here as my mom died. As my child was diagnosed. The Doctor would tell me time is eternal and laugh. All I know is I lived a few lifetimes under his thumb before he put me into that mindless shambler you found me in."

Pik had a good imagination, but it didn't extend to hundreds of years of torture. The horror of an endless experiment. She could understand why Brit was shutting down.

"Were you the only one here?" Horn always sought that next piece of the puzzle.

"Of course not. Others gambled their lives and lost. My daughter Jada was one of them. I'm sure the producers thought it was a fitting sequel to my fate. Probably worth a ton of good ratings."

Time passed as Pik and Horn digested Brit's story and poked at their jail cells. The whiteness of the room muted eventually, Pik's eyes adjusting. She could spot a faint surge of condensed air on the side of Timmic's and Junip's glass tubes. They were still alive.

Horn finally broke their thoughts, "Did you ever get close to getting out?"

At first, Pik thought Brit was hyperventilating

again. Her voice was rough and lurched. "No. He would allow me to think I was making progress. I even teamed up with other contestants, only to find out the 'escape' was a step in the experiment. I hadn't progressed at all. He'd allow me to see Jada, but I never got to talk to her. She was always a prize to fight for, a reason to try again. I think that's why he liked me so much. It took me a lot longer to give up." Pik realized the woman had started sobbing.

"Look, Brit. Please take a couple of deep breaths for me and listen. You are stuck in this game with the best Echo team. We've beaten hundreds of game traps. We can figure out a way to get ourselves out of this box. It's what we do. Horn here is the best programmer I've ever met. We will figure this out."

"This is what Pik does," Horn's voice backed her up. "I've watched Pik wiggle herself out of hairier situations. She's as much a genius as I am. Trust me, if there's a way out of here, Pik will find it. She and Trick are unstoppable."

"I thought you'd never bring me up," Trick's voice cut through Horn's narrative.

Pik blinked as Trick sauntered into the lab space. She watched him, looking for the doppelganger to give himself away. She was waiting for the mimic to reveal itself. The man moved like Trick, smooth and lithe, yet he had an edge to his smoothness like he was always ready to pounce. As far as appearances were concerned, the guy was Trick. Movement was one of the hardest things for games to emulate in a person.

"Is—is that really you?" Pik tapped at the glass—three taps.

Trick approached her tube and smiled. "In the digital flesh." He tapped back his "safe" code with two rapid taps. They'd worked out, over the years, a protocol to protect the group against infiltration. Pik's heart dared to warm—was it really Trick? Horn initiated the second phase of identity verification.

"Trick, this is like that dive against the Revenge of the Plants load, where we were trapped in those vines for hours. Please tell me you can release us from these traps." Codes could be broken, mimicked. But Horn initiated a test of memory, a partial truth.

Trick nodded as though they were passing a test he'd set up for them instead of them testing him. "You're misremembering; it was plants—it was sentient moss. The plants of that planet were downright friendly. It was the moss patches that held tight. How long were you stuck there?"

Trick had passed the knowledge test himself and instituted a counter-validation. In truth, they'd been stuck in the moss for ten hours on that gods-forsaken load. Each team member had an individual answer that had been pre-agreed upon so that no one could review the old video logs and come up with the same answer.

"You know I was the first one in. I held in place for twenty-five hours." Horn had given the correct answer for herself. Pik wanted Trick's counter-answer before giving hers.

"How about you Trick? How long was it for you?"

He gave her a nod of approval and flashed a grin. "You know I was only in there for 420 minutes."

Pik rolled her eyes, returning his grin. Four hundred and twenty was his answer if he thought they were safe and unmonitored. "Yeah, well I would have had you out sooner if you'd loaded me sooner. I was only in there for seven minutes, only as long as it took me to laser-cut my way out."

He'd given all the correct answers. A weight lifted off her shoulders. Trick had approached her tube and began punching numbers on the keypad.

"Now that that's done, I need to tell you, we aren't entirely alone. I've got a rider. I can hold out for a while, but the Doctor is here with me. Right now, I've got control, but it won't last forever, and I'm never positive when he will exert control. "

"Do you know who it is?"

He lowered his voice for only her ears. "It's the Doctor Brit's been talking about. I don't know who he is, but I have a theory."

It concerned Pik that Trick had been watching them interact without interfering. "Can he hear you while you're in control?"

"I don't think so, but the guy is clever. I am a silent observer when he's in control, but I don't think he's realized yet that I can take control. I don't think he can observe. He seemed very confused when I saved you in the nest." This solved Pik's suspicion about what'd happened to her. "I can't figure out what will trip my existence to the forefront. I keep waking up in his sleeping quarters, and when I'm not here, I exist as the end boss mob on the last level."

"Do you have any warning at all when he's reasserting? Why are your consciousnesses merged?"

"Just the beginning of a headache, and I caught my eyes beginning to glow in a reflection once. I think his body just rematerializes where he last remembered himself being. As for why, I don't know anything for sure. I think he needs me to keep his cohesion. He's old, very old."

The tube slid down, and Pik took a grateful gulp of fresh air. She hated tight, enclosed spaces, and Trick knew it.

"Thanks for freeing me first."

"Of course." He shot her an understanding look. They split their efforts, Trick focusing on Horn while Pik moved to Brit.

"You sure that's your friend? This Trick we came to find?" Brit's voice was hushed.

"Yes, I'm certain. Although it seems like your

Doctor guy is still around. Let's get everyone freed and then we can talk it over."

Brit was tense as the tube slid down. Her eyes were glued to Trick, waiting for the inevitable betrayal.

Chapter 14

Incorrect.
Incorrect.
Incorrect.

The red words of rejection blinked at Pik. "Damn it." She lost it for a moment, hammering the console. A dull, unimpressed beep of denial came from the command interface. They needed to get through.

Incorrect.

"Slow down, we'll get them out." Horn's voice was tight. She was frustrated, too, because her console hadn't given any more promising statements. "Trick, a little help here." It was terrible for Pik but worse for Horn as two inches of glass separated her from Junip.

Brit was no help. Pik had gotten her free of the tube, only to have her immediately collapse into a heap. She rocked back and forth, watching every move Trick made. He wasn't much help either as he hovered over the two of them. He'd given the proper codes but didn't feel like Trick. Games redefined an Echo. If you smelled a certain way or preferred your hair to be parted in a specific direction—all those minute choices that a person put into their hygiene and appearance helped cement them in the digital world. No one smelled. Body odor was nonexistent, but they all took showers after a long dive. Most folks put on some scent profile to keep them all more human-like, even if, ultimately, they were all ones and zeroes.

Trick didn't smell like himself, Pik realized. His face was too clean. He didn't act weird, but he was just a touch off. It could be the parameters of the game. Pik felt off herself. Non-Metaverse locations didn't always have all of the options, like scent profiles, or facial hair, of the Metaverse. Especially in older games, like this one, it was common for things to be a little off. It still put Pik on edge.

"I don't know how to free them either," Trick's low voice said mournfully. He stood towering over Pik's slight frame looking at Timmic through the glass.

Pik closed her eyes and breathed deeply. "Why don't you try? I need a moment to think."

Trick came over to the console, sweat beaded on his face. The room was hot, and the stress only made it hotter. Pik gave him a nod as he started typing in commands and codes into the console. They could do this. She squeezed his arm. They'd found him. He was real. He gave her a tight smile, eyes never leaving Timmic.

It'd taken a while, but Pik's eyes finally adjusted to the brightness of the lab. The place was all sterile, sharp edges. The countertops were white and metallic, with scientific equipment that she didn't recognize sitting on lab desks. The only biologicals within the laboratory were the trapped humans. White light damped down the red glow from the error notifications. Pik walked over to Brit.

She was a blubbery mess, a stark contrast to the over-engineered lab. Brit was distinctly human. The entire place gave Pik the creeps. She'd been in real labs and in-game representations of labs; nothing was this clean.

"Hey, hey, you okay?" Pik wasn't good at consoling. She tried to make her voice warm.

"This is a trap. It's a trap. None of this is real." Brit rocked back and forth. She was seemingly unaware of Pik.

Pik tried to access her inventory for the twentieth time to pull a rag out so Brit could wipe her nose. Nothing happened. She could almost hear the "Incorrect" in judgment. Time to try a different tact with Brit. "Why do you think it's a trap?"

Brit rapidly shook her head. She seemed unable to

reply, to form the words of explanation.

Pik turned and examined the room from Brit's perspective. Why would this look like a trap? Unease squirmed in her chest. Timmic and Junip *were* trapped, and without a reason, the commands Trick used to free Pik weren't working to free the other two. Trick continued to poke mechanically at the console. Determination furrowed his brow. He looked like Trick. He moved like Trick. He knew the passphrases to spot an infiltrator.

Digital environments were strange. Pik played a lot of games, good and bad. Sometimes the imbalance of an environment could throw an Echo off. This environment was the opposite. It was too balanced, too symmetrical. Down to Timmic and Junip, both slumped in their tubes in opposite directions, breathing in time with one another.

Pik stood up, walking as casually as she could muster over to Horn. Pik stepped close, closer than she would normally. Horn immediately picked up on it. Pik touched the back of Horn's shoulder.

"Any luck? Anything?" Horn shook her head, tears running down her face.

Pik lightly tapped in code on Horn’s back. "Brit is right. It's a trap."

One of the most challenging aspects of being an Echo was memorizing the different codes and communication techniques to share knowledge between teammates covertly. Infiltration games were common. These games would attempt to trick a party into thinking that an intruder was a legitimate teammate. Pik had never been good at them. She noticed things about people when she wanted to, but for the most part, she exercised action, not observance.

Unlike Horn.

Horn played her part perfectly. Without hesitation, she slammed her hands against the tube. "I can't take this. We have to get Junip out." The outburst may have been faked, but the emotion in her voice wasn't.

They both turned to Trick. "Trick, can you walk us through what you did to release us?" Horn's voice was level and serious.

Pik's fingers itched for some weapon. She tried to call her inventory again.

Trick sighed. "I had just typed in a release executable, like I told you."

"Yeah, but how did you know the correct executable?" Pik asked, scanning the lab for anything that could be used as a weapon. The equipment along the walls was nothing more than heavy scanners, and nothing came to mind outside of a couple of unwieldy microscopes. The generic clothing she wore had no pockets. None of her previous clothes or any of the weapons had come with her.

Trick frowned. "I don't know. Could I be drawing unknowingly from the Doc's knowledge?"

Brit grew louder, "It's a trap, a trap!"

The damn girl was going to give up their ruse. "Calm down, Brit. Stop overreacting. We're just going to need to free our friends and get out of here." Pik turned back to Trick and resumed their conversation. "If that's true, then close your eyes and try a couple of your old meditation techniques. Maybe you can float the information from your subconscious." She gave him a smile that wasn't faked; she never did believe in the glories of meditation.

His eyes twinkled as he closed them. Horn swung into action, stepping forward and swinging a flashlight she must have had on her person when they died. Trick's blue eyes snapped open as he grabbed her hand on the downswing, stopping it cold.

It hadn't taken any effort. His muscles weren't strained.

"So you've figured it out. It's been a long time since I had fresh meat." Trick's voice had changed completely, losing all of the warmth and qualities that made it his.

The flashlight spun out of Horn's hand as the man—Pik refused to think of him as Trick—wrenched her arm back. The Doctor stopped her other hand, too, as Horn tried to swing in with a punch. Pik went to help but found her feet couldn't move; they were glued to the floor. Looking down, red lights encircled her shoes, keeping her in place.

"What have you done to us? What is this place?" Pik didn't try to hide the alarm from her voice.

The Doctor held Horn's arms close to her body and marched her back into the tube she'd been trapped in. With a quick voice command, red lights glowed around her feet, and before anyone could object, the tube-holding cell whipped up around Horn.

Pik watched helplessly as some sort of gas was released into the tube. Horn met her eyes. Horror danced between them as Horn slowly slumped to the floor.

Pik eyes were daggers. "Why are you doing this to us?"

Brit answered, "He likes it."

The Doctor ignored Brit, his garish grin directed at Pik. "I would have thought it'd be obvious. I need to experiment on people. To save humanity." The man—if he even was a man—didn't have an ounce of remorse in his voice. "Now, if you'd kindly take two steps backward into your test tube, I'll reset the experiment."

Pik stood defiant, legs locked in place.

The Doctor sighed. "Digital command interface enabled." His eyes glittered as a command interface materialized within his vision. As he began to hit buttons, the red light holding her in place released, but Pik's body went rigid. She lost complete control over her muscles.

"No sweat off my back." The glitter of the interface left the Doctor's eyes—Trick's eyes. The man walked forward. Pik felt powerless watching him. He grabbed her collar and dragged her effortlessly back to her restraint tube. She couldn't turn her head to watch him or lift a finger to stop him. She was as helpless as an ant watching the descent of a shoe.

Pik couldn't even move her lips to scream. It was almost a relief when the tube spun up around her and the Doctor filled it with knockout gas. Pik's last conscious thought was of retribution.

Chapter 15

Pik woke up in a glass tube. She squinted, her eyes adjusting to the diffuse brightness of being awake. Horn was slumped in the tube right next to her. Pik's mind was fuzzy. She needed to figure out where they were. The last thing she remembered was the Kraken ripping her apart. She couldn't see more than a few feet from her enclosure, the space outside was shrouded in a thick fog.

"Horn! Wake up! Brit? Are you there?"

Pik thumped against the glass. It didn't budge. Her hands slapped uselessly against it. The contraption didn't show any weakness, no groan or chip. She tried pulling from her inventory a gun, a knife, or a sword. Her inventory didn't exist. This, more than anything, settled her bleak reality on her shoulders. Pik was helpless.

Pik couldn't remember the last time she existed without an inventory. She had a limitless one at home, but every game had the option. It might not be much, but most games had some starter gear. Something.

Oddly, Pik was still wearing the clothes she'd worn in the water level. She stood in her sports bra, with her button-up shirt tied around her waist. She had blue shorts that went mid-thigh and a black ring she'd picked up. The ugly thing had given her a +1 to energy storage for no apparent reason, but it was a good perk, even if the fashion choice was questionable.

Pik contemplated her options. Her memory was like the outside of the tube, an indistinct, incomplete landscape. The last thing she remembered was searing pain, yet she felt no pain now. There wasn't any blood on her clothes or scars on her arms. This place felt different, familiar, but separate from the ship. She shook her head. Step one: figure out how to get out of the tube. Step two was figuring everything else out.

There were few options to escape through the two-inch thick tube. Through the glass was likely not the way to go. It was thick and impenetrable. If it weren't digital, it'd be almost impossible to build. Sadly the world wasn't confined to simple rules of possible and impossible.

Games came in two main types: those that threw an approximation of the world at a virtual build that was good enough not to terrify participants and those that were tirelessly exacting to the physical universe. If one paid attention to the repeating graphics, the too-symmetrical rooms, and the lifelike-looking goo that felt like paint when touched, the first type could be beaten through cheats. It looked superficially like the laws of physics were followed, but an Echo could sneak into the game's cracks and break it. A slapped-together existence had faults that could be exploited, as it was just a cardboard cutout with foam rocks.

For its age, this game was well-crafted. They'd put more money into the art and design. A complete world made for prime-time entertainment. The architecture of this reality was realistic and called for real-world solutions.

She needed to breathe, so it followed that the tube likely had to have an air intake to "keep the human specimen alive." Even liquid removal capabilities to keep it clean were a possibility. The floor appeared seamless, the tube dropping into a skinny gap. Pik spent a couple of minutes trying to pick at it with a fingernail, to no avail. As many prisoners found, the floor was harder than their fingernails.

Pik shifted her focus to the ceiling and was instantly rewarded. A slotted air exchange panel circled the entire top of the tube. Her only problem with doing anything about it was that it was a meter above the highest point she could reach. The tube was tight. She couldn't even squinch down to sit on the floor.

The narrowness of the tube gave her other ideas. Pik wedged her body between the walls of the tube and pushed up, only to use pressure to hold steady as she pushed herself higher. Quickly, with effort, she used her feet and back to navigate to the top of the tube. Her skin ached at the pressure required to keep her body at the top of the tube, but she'd accomplished her immediate goal. Pik examined the intake vent, looking for a weakness in the structure.

Muscles shaking, her efforts were rewarded as she found four small flathead screws flush with the metal rim of the vent. Taking her longest fingernail, she reached and began twisting out the screws one by one.

They fell to the floor, metallic pings ringing out as they bounced. Pik hoped she wasn't going to need to replace them. It would be difficult to find the screws in the tight space.

A memory floated to her mind: Pik stood on a ladder, helping her dad replace light bulbs. Being short, she was on her tippy toes at the top of the ladder so she could reach. Her dad held her legs, steadying her as she wobbled. A wave of grief hit her unexpectedly. She'd give anything for her dad or Trick to help.

Pik's knees ached as they pressed against the tube, bringing her back to the last screw as she turned and reset her nail.

The plate fell as the last screw released, smacking Pik in the head. Momentarily stunned, she slid a couple of inches down the tube, swearing. The soft glow of a power conduit illuminated her face. She examined the contents behind the ceiling panel, locking them in her memory.

Pik slid down, the squeaking of skin on glass irritating in the confined space. She stood again at the bottom of the tube, thinking. Below the vented panel she'd painstakingly removed sat nothing but death, and it made no sense.

The video game design didn't need to make sense. Like the lightbulb in her childhood home, the reality was painted with a brush that was sometimes too accurate. Burnt-out light bulbs in a non-physical reality were stupid. Her dad's theory was that it was supposed to be a reminder of the movement of time. They were immortal beings, but even for them, time marched onward. Lightbulbs burned out, the sun rose every morning, and the planet rotated around the sun, even if the earth, the sun, and lightbulbs were relics from another reality.

Pik looked at the power cable. She'd used one just like it to electrocute a predator on the sixth floor during Trick's run. She'd pried off a panel and taunted the creature to attack. Trick had hidden in the shadows and shoved it into the gap in the wall. The beast had screamed as wild arcs of electricity jolted through its body. Pik had been close enough to get singed herself, and they had to wait a bit before moving on.

Pik looked up at the ceiling, her heart sinking. She couldn't reach through and manipulate the wires she needed to free herself without breaking the power cable. The game had designed them to be brittle—easy to use for a trap or a source of accidental environmental death if a player wasn't careful.

Pik stared at the cable. Was she even still in the game?

Horn picked that moment to regain consciousness with a snort that made Pik jump. "Where the hell am I?"

"In a tube standing next to me."

"You and your damn dry sense of humor." Horn stood straighter, glancing around. "Have you seen Brit?"

"No, but I can't see much. Any idea what this is?"

Pik heard a groan, but it didn't come from either of them.

"Brit? Is that you?" Pik pushed an ear to the tube wall, trying to make out where the sounds came from as she scanned the fog. Had it grown thicker?

"BRIT!" Horn's yell made Pik wince.

"I'm here, I'm here. You can stop shouting." Brit stumbled out of the fog. She stood before them, clothes ripped and dirty, face red with an imprint of whatever she'd been lying on. She slapped a hand against Horn's tube, leaning for support.

Pik said what the two had to be thinking, "You look like hell."

"You would, too, if you'd been stuck in the meat grinder." Brit began tapping at a panel, and within a few seconds, the display gave an approval beep, and Horn's tube loudly slid down. Horn stumbled as the support keeping her upright vanished. She didn't look much better than Brit.

Pik silently watched Brit move to her panel, tapping a sequence in. The "Incorrect" beep flashed, indicating a code failure. Pik frowned. The error message felt oddly familiar.

"Sorry, I typed the command in wrong. Give me a second." Brit's hand moved again over the controls. Typically Echoes spent months training together before they dived as a team. Humanity became obsessed with infiltration games for a while. A party member would get swapped out by a doppelganger or mimic. Teams set up complicated methods of verifying each other's identity long before they took one step into a virtual world.

That was one of the problems with Brit: they didn't know her very well. Pik wasn't so sure she hadn't been a plant from the beginning, infiltrating their virtual world. A green acceptance popped up on the command console, and Pik's tube started to glide down reassuringly. Her relief was rudely interrupted by a screech as the tube's descent ground to a halt.

Brit looked at the console, confused. "That should have worked."

Pik knew precisely what happened. Gazing down, she immediately noticed a screw wedged between the crevice of the floor and the tube.

"This one's on me. It can't retract anymore. It's a mechanical error, not a programming problem." Pik examined the gap open at the top. If she were careful, she might be able to wedge through the two-foot opening as long as she didn't brush the power cable.

"It's another trap. Another trap. There's never a way to escape." Brit began to melt down.

"Hey, I think I can get out of here. No need to lose it." Pik had caused the issue; she knew she could figure it out.

Horn went from surveying Pik's tube to trying to console Brittany. "What are you talking about? Whose trap would it be? We'll be okay. We can work through this."

"He wiped your memory, didn't he? It's the Doctor."

The way she said "doctor" made Pik shudder. She knew of the Doctor. He'd done things to them. The memory was fleeting. She suddenly felt drugged, altered. Like Brittany saying the truth made her remember. Some of the fog from the lab started to fill the tube she was in, glowing in the blue light set off by the exposed power conduit.

"I know the Doctor. But I don't. You said he screwed with our memory?" Pik asked, still examining her options.

Brit breathed. "We've had this conversation a dozen times. Sometimes he wipes your memory; sometimes he doesn't. I thought I'd tricked the system this time. That it was going to be different."

Pik tried to comprehend. *Did* he wipe their memory dozens of times? It just seemed too surreal. What purpose would that serve?

"He runs experiments, psychological experiments . . . physical experiments." Brit shook at a memory. "Most of the time it was here. I tried to escape so many times.

Eventually he gets bored, and you're a monster on the floor, stuck in a preprogrammed reaction even if your mind is active. Sometimes it's just a dream, and you don't think—can't think—but more often than not, you're free to think and watch, but you can't do anything about it."

Brit's voice broke. "I didn't tell you this. I'm sorry. I had hoped that when I escaped and found you, that I'd escaped him. I'd been stuck as one of the mummified zombies Iraxinus for so long that I'd almost forgotten the Doctor. I watched my daughter play the game when humanity still played. I watched her die. She's stuck in this experimental hell too."

Pik watched the woman admit her heartbreak, wondering why she was telling them now. Brit looked numb. How many iterations had they played some demented fate out? How many times had Horn and Brit watched Pik electrocute herself as she tried to climb out of her tube?

"Why weren't you in a tube, too?"

Brit shook her head, obviously trying to care enough to think, respond, and struggle. "Last iteration, we talked about it. He doesn't seem to be able to see me, like I'm a ghost. Horn had speculated—"

Horn interrupted her, "I probably thought that the same malfunction that prevented you from leveling in the game made him blind to your existence."

Brit nodded.

Horn continued slowly, thinking it through as she went, "Which means that you're the mechanism we can use to wrench ourselves out of whatever loop this doctor set up to trap us."

Brit gave them a sad smile. "It's funny how every version of you rebooted comes to the same conclusion. The unfortunate truth is that we haven't been able to figure it out. The Doctor doesn't recognize I exist. He's aware something's causing aberrations in his experiments, but he doesn't seem to be doing anything about me. It would be on brand for him to allow me to think I'm in an altered state to give us hope."

Pik shook her head. She didn't fully remember what they'd experienced, but she did have feelings—a strong position. It was as though all her opinions survived even if her memories hadn't. "I don't think so. I don't think he's aware of you," Pik said.

"Do you remember anything? We'd tried" —a pause. Pik could tell Brit was editing something out—"something different with the hopes the two of you would load with some memories."

"Something different?"

Brit nodded, not adding any explanation.

Pik let it go for the moment. She gestured to the power cable. "I imagine this is a trap. There's no reason a power cable should be that close behind a perceived air exchange."

Brit nodded. "Yeah, you're expected to try to get out of the tube and electrocute yourself."

"I should have enough space." Pik knew she could be optimistic in games on executing a physical feat, but this looked fairly reasonable as tight spaces went.

"Yeah, you're supposed to think that. You don't realize yet that this fog is mildly conductive, so as soon as you get anywhere close to that conduit, it will arc."

"What does the Doctor get from that? Just proving my arrogance will kill me?"

Brit pointed at Horn as she talked, nodding. "He probably gets to torture Horn emotionally as she gets to watch you fry."

"How did we think this load out would be different again?" Horn asked. "I have no desire to watch Pik barbeque herself."

Brit looked away, not wanting to meet either of them in the eye.

"Brit, cough it up. You're going to have to tell us eventually." Pik was losing patience with Brit dancing around what she thought would make them uncomfortable.

She sighed. "We enacted a looped brain net in our matrix."

"We did *what*?" Horn's voice was shrill. Matrixing their brains together was a crime and abomination in the Metaverse. Pik had kept silent. Horn's mouth was agog, and Pik didn't blame her.

Brain nets were a risky enterprise. They could backfire in spectacular ways. Theoretically an individual might link to another and share processing capacity and thoughts. They *might* live a successful hybrid existence. But they were outlawed for good reasons. The few that had been attempted in history had gone poorly, leading to a mutated singular existence, in which—in the best case—everyone involved slowly went insane. Pik didn't even want to think of the worst cases.

"A brain net? Are we insane? Thank the Network it didn't work." Pik could see the consternation in Horn's face. It had to be hard for her to even imagine attempting something so taboo, much less the two of them agreeing to it.

Pik felt Brit's wince. "How desperate were we? I can't imagine Horn and I melding together well. No offense, Horn."

"None taken." Horn looked as put off by the idea as Pik felt.

"It was actually across the three of us." Brit's voice was quiet as she watched them.

Pik couldn't believe it. Just couldn't believe she'd trust a stranger like Brittany to exist in a three-mind net. She couldn't even imagine a reality in which she and Horn agreed to it willingly.

"You wouldn't have done it in a sane reality. Last time, though, he loaded you with the memories of all your loads in this laboratory of horrors. All of them. Imagine the weight of all of the emotion and torture and death. You were willing to do anything. Horn had concluded I was the gristle in the Doctor's meal, that if you two could latch onto my existence, my ephemeral qualities, the two of you could escape. That his system would spit you out."

Pik met Horn's appalled countenance. Both of their minds raced, working through what those memories had to have been to get them to agree to a mind net.

Pik blinked, wiggled her nose twice, and tapped on the glass—a verification code to Horn. She wanted to confirm Horn was real.

She watched, shocked as Brit stepped forward, tapping a complex pattern on the glass, giving Horn's confirmation. Brit looked confused. "Was that the right code? I'm not sure why I did that. I was standing here, and it came to me."

Horn's face was dark, and her expression didn't match the optimism of her words. "I think it did work."

Chapter 16

Pik stood in the tube, surrounded by the fog cloaking the rest of the laboratory. She'd never agree to be linked, and neither would Horn. In the Metaverse, it was a good way to ensure permadeath for all involved. They were either being experimented on by the Doctor that Brit kept muttering about, or something truly horrible had been done to them for either to consider it a viable option.

"What about Junip? Timmic? Trick?" Pik knew Horn had to be worried about Junip. They weren't the most physically robust of the crew. Pik always thought Horn's protective instincts made her underestimate the team medic. Junip's ability to support the team psychologically made them seem softer because the non-binary medic used their sensitivity to connect with the entire team. Pik had observed Junip go hardcore on a few games that they loaded into together. The medic could kick ass in a game when required.

"I'm not sure. Some of the simulations the Doctor set up had Timmic and Junip, but they were not conscious. It may have been a simulation of them. Most of the time, Trick is present but is controlled by the Doctor. He seems to be able to fool you for a short period of time, but one of you always figures it out." Brit's words weren't reassuring.

The Doctor as Trick took a moment to sink in. The last thing Pik wanted was for the Doctor to have access to Trick's mind or digital identity.

"Why do you think the Doctor's using Trick?" Horn focused on the thing Pik was trying to avoid. Since she'd been freed, Horn had started pacing. She liked to pace while she picked at a problem.

Brit paused, mulling it over. "I would guess it's just a ploy to torture the two of you with the idea that Trick is part of your torture. However, the Doctor hasn't shown up with his original face once. It's possible his former avatar lost cohesion. I know I was put on a shelf for years. I was one of his . . . one of his favorite play-things." Pik saw anguish in the words on Brit's face. It had to be hard to admit to being anyone's plaything. The psychological stress she'd been under for centuries was impossible to comprehend.

"Any thoughts on how I can get out of here? I'm tempted to try climbing; the worst it could do is reload us into another scenario, right? It could trigger the Doctor to visit us." Pik was starting to feel the claustrophobia set in as the fog made her space feel even smaller.

"We could try closing the tube again. That would possibly pop the screw out of the channel where it's lodged. I really want to avoid another reboot if possible." Brit dreaded summoning the Doctor again.

Pik shook her head. While Brit was technically correct, the screw would just get stuck again. The fog was completely in the tube at this point, and Pik wouldn't be able to make sure the screws weren't going to get sucked into the floor. "I don't think that'll work. It'll just wedge again, or the tube will get stuck higher. I wish I'd never unscrewed the top. If I'd known Brit could just let us out, I wouldn't have messed with it."

They stood there in the cold murk, thinking. Pik shivered. The lab was frigid, and the grey mist was creepy. Faces swirled in its depths. She shuddered, trying to avert her eyes from the ghosts.

Her parents had floated behind Horn's shoulders. "Are there any drug properties to this fog? I swear I saw a face hovering behind you, Brit." Pik snapped her eyes shut, trying to banish the shapes in the haze.

Brit nodded. "Yes. The fact that it hasn't affected you until now is a sign that we are networked, that my immunity is leaching into you. It's pretty powerful stuff.

The last simulation like this, the two of you went crazy before I figured out how to lower the tubes."

Horn snapped her fingers. She'd been focusing on the control panel. "I've got it. Pik, you're a genius."

"Now I know you're hallucinating," Pik said dryly.

Horn rolled her eyes and started tapping out sequences in front of her. "Brit, when the Doctor resets the program, does he use a specific control panel, or will any of them work?"

"Give me a sec; let me think." The brunette stood, enshrouded by fog. Pik could hear the voices whisper to her. They were telling Brit what to say.

"Any conso—"

"You can't trust her," Pik blurted it out. She couldn't stop herself. This woman couldn't be trusted.

Brit touched Horn's arm. Pik immediately knew the truth as Horn began typing. They were conspiring together. This was a simulation; they were fake people, and Pik was the only one there. Now that she thought about it, she'd conveniently found them together, hanging in those cocoons. Then, only a few levels later, they ended up here. The two of them set her up. She could have saved Trick, Timmic, Junip, and the genuine Horn by now. They were the real enemy. They'd set this trap for the Doctor, and Pik had walked right into it.

"I found it!" Horn declared, glancing up at Pik's face. "It'll be okay. Just remember, don't remove the ceiling panel." Horn looked her right in the eyes. Horn's deep hazel eyes. They pierced through the fog, the haze in her brain. "Don't remove the panel."

Horn slammed her hand down on a control. The world went blank.

* * *

Pik woke up with a headache. She was slumped sideways in a giant glass tube. It was tight—too tight to sit down. She blinked, smelling only refreshed air and a hint of her body scent. This game was way too realistic. She squinted through the fog in the room and recognized an unconscious Horn, also slumped in her tube. Slamming her hand on the wall, Pik yelled "HORN!" as loudly as possible. The only reward for her efforts was a throbbing hand and a worsening headache.

Pik gazed down at the floor. It was smooth—no grates to leverage, which was probably good. She couldn't bend down to reach the floor with her hands, and her toe dexterity was pretty low. Looking up, the ceiling seemed a lot more promising. A grated air vent stood at the top. It sent in refreshed air and was the source of a low hum.

As Pik wedged her body in the tube to push herself higher, she couldn't shake the feeling that this was the wrong choice. Something about the grate. Her knee slipped. She fell to the floor, her skin making off-color squeaking sounds as it rubbed against the glass.

Two hands, sticky with sweat, slapped noisily against the outside of the glass. Brit peered in, huffing, "Oh, thank *god*. I caught you before you monkey climbed up the tube again. Give me a minute, and I'll have you free."

Pik was relieved; her knees were raw, and she wasn't excited about having to pry open the grate. The thought was interrupted as a green message flipped on the command console's screen and an affirmative beep sent the side of her tube sliding to the floor.

"Thanks, Brit. Let's get Horn out. Then you can tell me what you mean by 'again.'"

She jumped as Brit touched her arm. "Stay with me. It will be essential to stay within physical contact. The fog has hallucinogenic properties. Pik nodded and waved Brit over to the console. She hadn't imagined anything yet—and the quicker they could get Horn, the faster they could get out of here.

Horn groaned, which was good. Pik didn't want Horn to collapse from the friction of her skin leaning on the side of the tube as soon as the glass slid down. Pik shuddered at the mental image of Horn crumpled up, unconscious, skin peeled off on the lab floor.

Pik thumped on the side of the tube. "Wake up!"

Horn groaned again and leaned off the side of the tube, her eyes opening. "Pik, is that you?"

"Go ahead and hit it, Brit."

An affirmative beep and a squeeze on Pik's shoulder confirmed the success. Horn stumbled toward Pik's open arms in seconds and embraced. Then Brit came up behind them and wrapped her arms around the two of them. Pik hadn't been involved in a sandwich hug in a long time. That's what her dad would have called it. He'd wrap her and her mom up together in a group hug and squeeze them tight.

Brit loosened up the hug quickly but kept her body in contact. She spoke rapidly, preventing Horn or Pik from interrupting, "This is the fifth time we've restarted this instance of this load. You're going to have to trust me on this. I will explain it all; listen and don't interrupt." The brunette from another century accented that last word by squeezing Pik's shoulder. The woman continued, "This will be hard for you to understand, but we're trapped in the Doctor's lab."

Brit went on to explain incredible things: They were linked, and Brit had immunity and stood outside the Doctor's plans. They'd loaded repeatedly, and Pik was annoyingly quick at unscrewing grates. The longer they stood, and Brit talked, the more Pik's sense of comfort grew. She realized she did trust this woman. It might have been the fog's mind-altering properties, but she felt connected to Brit and Horn—a thread between their skin.

"And finally, our link seems strongest when we're in physical contact. For now, at least, we need to stay close, or else you will start losing your minds." Brit was out of breath. Pik didn't have anything to say. As Brit talked, some foggy memories started reappearing.

"So, if I've got this right, we must vent the fog. See if Timmic and Junip are in the lab and potentially free them. And reload our memories?" Horn methodically tried to map out their next steps.

"I'm not sure I'd advise reloading your memories. These traps"—Brit shook a bit—"the traps are meant to test the psychological limitations of human consciousness. I wish I could forget what he did to me. I'm not sure I have all my memories, but I definitely have more than I want."

"I want my memories back," Horn said firmly. Pik shrugged. She was more grounded in the present these days. A thousand rounds of torture sounded like something she didn't need.

They shuffled over to a control console, Brit keeping a hold of both their arms. Even without the link, the fog had grown thick enough that it was probably worth staying in physical contact to mitigate its psychological properties. Horn began muttering to herself, typing into the command console.

Pik contemplated their situation, confident that if it was a programming problem, Horn could figure it out. A brain net or link was a dangerous thing. In the best-case scenario, they'd still have mental bleed-over. Pik's mind bounced around to a few horror stories. The idiots she'd heard about linking had been exclusively young reboots who felt like they'd "found their soulmate." They'd overrode the Command's boundary limits on personhood. A quiver of anxiety churned. Those teenagers never made it out of the link in one piece. It was one of the few forms of actual death granted in the Metaverse.

"Stop it." Horn's voice was tight. "I can't

concentrate with your anxiety nipping at my mind."

Pik looked at Brit, who was looking at her. Pik grimaced guiltily. "Yeah, sorry. This linked minds business is going to take some getting used to."

Pik tried one of Trick's meditation techniques. She imagined sitting by a babbling brook, letting each thought cascade away like a drifting leaf. She wasn't sure how much time had passed, but a distant clank and a soft whooshing sound eventually announced that Horn had managed to vent the toxic atmosphere.

Chapter 17

Meditating on the gurgling of a tree-encrusted brook hadn't done much for Pik's mental state beyond making her want to pee—another useless mechanism in a digital world.

"Junip!" Horn broke their circle, running over to a tube that contained an unconscious medic. Horn began tapping on the console to bring up the status of the occupants.

Horn's next words broke Pik's heart: "They're dead."

Horn numbly proceeded to a tube containing Timmic and tapped in similar commands. Brit took over Junip's console, putting in the release command. Junip's dead body slumped out of the container.

Pik felt a wave of hopeless despair. She'd lost teammates before, but not like this. Not under her command. She knelt, fixing Junip's limbs as they bent unnaturally. Their face was pale. All the intelligence and warmth of Junip's soul was removed. Pik had never seen a real dead body. Video game gore, sure. But actual death in the Metaverse came with a disbursement of digital code, a moment of static, not a flesh-and-blood body.

"They're not dead," Brit's voice broke through Horn's trance and Pik's sorrow. "It's just another scenario. If you managed to figure out the initial trap puzzle, he was going to torture you with the dead bodies of your loved ones. I've found my daughter hundreds of times. I have faith that she's still in here. You can only really die once. If we can figure out how to restore your memories—if that's what you want—you'll see you've found Timmic and Junip dead dozens of times."

Pik couldn't shake the fear. It was not an emotion she was used to. She'd been brought back from the precipice, but it still haunted her thoughts. It was an ever-present specter taunting her to decide on what they were going to do next. She then realized it wasn't her at all. It was Horn. The bundle of fear in the back of her head was Horn's emotions bleeding through their link.

"Hey, Horn. It's going to be okay. We're going to find them. That's what we're going to do next."

If the fear was Horn, then the bundle of despair, hopelessness, and entrapment, the claustrophobia that had Pik on edge was Brit. Brit stood, back straight, face schooled. None of the turmoil that she was experiencing was apparent. The black hole that consumed her thoughts wasn't obvious as Brit appeared to be calmly focused on the next task. Pik didn't bother trying to comfort her. Doing so would be like throwing a blanket on a tornado; it would get sucked away without the tornado realizing its intention. Brit put on a good face, but she had to be barely functional.

"It's going to be up to you, Horn. We've got to break through the programming of this place. Can you do it?" Pik pushed, trying to keep them focused on action.

Horn took a deep breath, then two more. She didn't have to say anything. Pik could feel her resolve taking hold.

"Okay, I've got to break through the initial build of this place and get at the underlying infrastructure. If I had to guess based on Brit's assessment, the experiment iterates on a loop mechanism. Try a hundred different scenarios, generate data on our responses, generate a hundred new scenarios."

The cool analysis, usually what Horn was known for, felt good. They were getting back on the footing that made their Echo team, Trickshot, great. Pik watched as Horn started breaking down the problem through logic. The knot of anguish in her head unwound as she tackled a problem she knew she could solve.

Pik touched Horn on the shoulder, their connection flaring for a moment. Pik put all of her confidence in

Horn's programming skills into their link. "What can we do to assist?"

"Just give me a moment with the command console. The two of you can explore, do whatever, but try not to trigger the environment to reset."

Pik nodded, stepping away. She pivoted, examining the lab, trying to distract Brit, waving a hand at the scientific machines surrounding them. "What does this equipment do?"

Brit's face tensed. This was the wrong question. Pik backpedaled. "It's okay. I can poke around without the insider knowledge."

"Is it me or is our connection getting stronger?" Brit whispered to Pik, trying not to distract Horn.

"It's not you. We will need to figure something out once Horn breaks this trap. I'm guessing the idea of networking brains together wasn't yours? Did you even have this concept in your . . ." Pik hesitated. What word to use? Timeline? Reality? "In your technological era?" She chose the professional language.

"We did not. You were both pretty freaked out about attempting it. But also, since you'd had memories from your previous loads, you were getting desperate. I'm not sure what makes me immune to all of this." Brit waved at the lab. Her gaze turned down as though she couldn't even look at the whole of it. Pik could see the truth; Brit wasn't immune to any of it. She was numb—perhaps a bit disassociated—but not immune. "I spent a lot of time here. I tried so hard once I realized my daughter was also caught in the game. Eventually, though, you give up. You don't have a choice."

Pik didn't have to be bonded with the woman to see the shame she felt. Pik had spent fifteen minutes in this place; Brit had spent millennia. Pik's heartache was a drop in the ocean compared to the other woman's torment. Once they freed Junip, they'd have their work cut out for them trying to help Brit.

The equipment in the lab was old and unrecognizable. Pik had seen a lot of graphic representations of labs, some futuristic, some realistic, but none matched these hulking monstrosities. She looked at a giant white clamshell of a machine that appeared to be a full-body scanner. She picked a heavy oblong wand that seemed to be a localized brainwave detector. Fumbling with the controls, she pointed it at Brit and hit what she thought was the "scan" button.

"Don't!" Brit's voice was abruptly cut off as she momentarily faded from reality, then reappeared. "Oh, it didn't work this time. Pik, if you ever point anything at me like that again, I swear to God."

Abashed, Pik put the scanner back on the table full of implements. The toolset was a diverse set of plastic-coated devices, all of which looked relatively harmless until she felt Brit's disgust. "Sorry, I didn't realize."

"That dematerializes a matrix so he can put you into that machine over there." Brit pointed to the clamshell. Looking closer at the scanner, Pik could see scalpels attached to robotic arms.

"What is the god you keep referring to? Do you ascribe to a specific god? Or is that just a thing that you say?" Pik was genuinely curious. Humanity had left the idea of a real "God" when they'd uploaded into the Metaverse. Their gods were the whims of the technological infrastructure keeping the Metaverse afloat. Horn was muttering in the corner, a ball of determination in the back of her head.

"I'm not sure I believe in God anymore, not really. Not since being stuck here." Brit's voice trailed off as she thought about it.

"But you did at one time?" Pik wondered.

"Don't you have the concept of God? Or gods?"

Pik paused before she replied, not wanting to offend

someone so much older than her. "In our Metaverse, gods are concepts we interact with through entertainment. You play a game, and your crew is holed up in a church defending itself against a zombie horde. Or the local tribe's deity is grateful you saved her village, and she grants you a boon. But we don't go to church, a temple, or a synagogue. Nothing like that."

"I should probably find that sad, but it makes sense. In my world, God was an idea. You could find history books—ancient ones—claiming the direct influence of a god, but it'd been thousands of years since a god knowingly walked the earth. I-I used to . . ." Brit paused, having trouble saying something she didn't believe. "Hell, that's a lie. Part of me still believes. What is the closest thing to a god that your people even have?"

Pik had never contemplated the nature of existence in this way. "The closest thing we have might be the creators of the Metaverse . . . ? The Architects that developed the infrastructure and technology that allow the Metaverse to exist. We curse the Architects sometimes for making it the way it is. Horn's ability with the system is revered like one might venerate clergy. She has the deepest understanding of the code behind it all than anyone I've ever met. Trick had to pursue her for months to get her to join our team."

They both looked over at Horn, who rapidly tapped at a homegrown interface she'd developed in the last ten minutes.

"She's *that* good? What was she doing before you guys landed her on the team?" Brit leaned against a lab table. The conversation helped her forget the nature of their surroundings.

Pik smiled, remembering. "She was a professor of technology at the University. Youngest reborn to ever hold the title. She was so young that they accused her of manipulating the rebirth protocol. That her previous iteration cheated and retained innate knowledge of a prior life."

"Did folks know who they thought Horn was in a previous . . . iteration? Am I using that word, right?"

Pik relaxed, warming to the conversation. She leaned next to Brit, watching Horn work. "Rumors abound. The great Phyllis Neerfam created the tunnels that allow us to explore the greater Metaverse as Echoes. Or Thom Erdras. He was the last Administrator from the original upload of humanity. There were a dozen possibilities of her previous iteration thrown around—one of the Architects themselves. I've worked with Horn for a couple of years at this point. She is brilliant. I think she is the most brilliant programmer of this iteration, but now that she's not in the University spotlight, she doesn't get all the accolades. I've worked with her, and if she has some hidden ageless personality, she's a master at more than technology. If you haven't picked up on it, she's hopelessly fallen for Junip. Their relationship is new, so who knows if it'll last. The lovesick look, though, that doesn't sound like some ageless demigod of technology. You'll understand when you see them together."

Brit nodded along as they both watched Horn work. The woman's eyes and fingers flew across a projected keyboard as she navigated problems only she could see. Brit went to ask another question, this time of Horn, but Pik reached out and stopped her. "Don't interrupt her when she's like this. That's a flow state—it's best not to disrupt. Especially since it's our butts on the line."

Pik felt an almost impossible-to-resist curiosity at the touch of their arms. She let go quickly.

"I felt your caution," Brit commented on their connection. "We've got to figure out how to set boundaries between each other. I'm sure you also have things you'd prefer to keep to yourself."

Pik nodded, thinking of half a dozen emotions she

wished she could bottle up already. "Any ideas?"

"I'm hoping Horn has some formal possibilities for us with code, but I have some thoughts. There was this one prisoner—that's how I came to think of myself: a prisoner. The guy's name was Andy. He was this giant of a man. A gentle giant though. He lasted longer than me. I never did find out what drove him forward. He'd been here before I was deposited and still resisted after I was sent into the game to marinate."

"Andy?" Pik tried to get her back on track. "What did he do?"

"Ah, yes, well, for a few iterations, we were trapped together, and he had this method of putting mental barriers between himself and the traps he inhabited. He could interact and participate but saved a bit of himself by cordoning his mind. That way, when they reset, he'd remember a bit, even if a mind wipe was part of the protocol."

Horn snapped her fingers. "A partition!"

Pik watched as Horn delved back into her program. "How did he he do it? Was he a whiz like Horn?"

Brit shook her head. "No, I think he thought he was a self-stylized genius. I expect you've got a right to if you figure out how to beat this place, even minimally. He used a technique that you seem to be moderately familiar with."

A sinking realization hit Pik. "You're not—please tell me you're not talking about meditation?"

With a rueful grin, Brit nodded. "Yeah. He believed that here, this place's mind and infrastructure were connected. By meditation on the visualization of a physical partition, you could actualize it within your mind. He had this whole theory that this was the Doctor's philosophy as well. That these experiments were trying to change our brain patterns to match something the Doctor was looking for."

"And you think he was successful?" Pik found it

hard to believe someone could use meditation to alter their brain pattern to that extent.

"I was confident he was. He knew things that no one else I encountered seemed to have the faintest clue about." Brit was serious, she had a reverence for the guy.

Pik laced her fingers, stretching them until they cracked. Resignedly, "I think this place is set up to torture me one way or another. Let's get started."

When Horn finally looked up from her work, her two compatriots sat cross-legged facing each other. "What are you doing? I'm over here toiling and you're sitting on the floor holding hands?" Brit and Pik had sat with their legs crossed and hands out. They held hands to connect, trying to build walls between their minds.

Pik opened an eye, face red. "We're meditating. You finished?"

"Yes, and I'm going to need your help. The Doctor is coming."

Chapter 18

Pik snapped her eyes open, looking directly at Brit. She'd spent the last twenty minutes trying to contemplate the universe and her connection to it, following Brit's calm meditation. The link between them provided a focus that Pik had never had in a meditation. There was nothing calm about Brit's expression as Horn declared the Doctor's imminent arrival.

"How do you know he's coming, Horn?" Pik stood, her body protesting moving. She offered Brit a hand up, trying to purposefully share some calmness.

"I can see the code warp around his presence. This entire place is built to serve him, so the systems respond as he moves through it."

"Could you tell where he was before he headed this way?" Pik was curious.

"I'm sure I could, but that's not important now. I've cracked what I need to, but it's not all-encompassing. Pik, I need you to get back in your tube and act trapped. We're going to play out a failed attempt at escape, but when we reload, we should both retain our memories and a few other things that will be helpful."

"What should I do?" Brit's voice was high-pitched and tight.

"You get to continue to be a ghost and keep doing that meditation. I could see some effect in the environment of your connection, even if Pik is a lost cause. The Doctor can't see you, and we're going to leverage that across the entire group."

Pik grumbled as she stood in place, waiting for one of the others to activate the enclosure. Horn walked over and keyed in the command code. The tube swished into place when Pik realized their error. She was standing in the space that Horn had initially loaded in. Before she could voice their mistake, the door to the lab slid open. Trick, in a lab coat, sauntered into his experiment.

Horn played up frantically tapping at the command console, "trying" to get Pik out before the Doctor got close.

"This is an unusual situation I haven't encountered before. How did you get in there?" Trick's voice lilted out of the Doctor. It was horrific.

"Who are you? Where's Trick?" Pik yelled, thumping on the glass ineffectually.

"Ah, this tired old dialog. I should replay the feed for this scenario when I have time. This could prove entertaining."

"Go to hell!" Horn went at the man, throwing a data pad that she'd been using. She used the distraction to swing an old-school microscope at his face. The man laughed at her as both passed right through his form.

"Do you see how useless it is to fight me? I completely control this environment, your friends, and your lives."

"But why? What's the point?" Pik shouted through the thick glass. This was the sticking point for her. She could write the guy off as a sadistic maniac, but why go through all this trouble? The gladiatorial game had pulled in all sorts of people. Why do it? Why not just have a small, curated group to torture for eternity? Why use real people at all?

The man swept his hand around, making a grandiose statement that said nothing. "It's for the science, of course!" Pik rolled her eyes as he tapped a few commands on his personal data pad, and the world became static.

This time, Pik kept conscious as everything greyed out. The feeling was much like transferring to a new game. Instead of the Metaverse speeding past at the speed of light, she stood stationary, watching the ones and zeros embrace her existence. The lab loaded, with the same tube set up—although this time it was utterly dark instead of full of toxic fog. Only small pools of blue and red light reflected from different terminals. Instead of just the team's tubes being occupied, the lab was full of dozens of humans.

Pik could see Horn, Junip, Timmic, and twenty other captives. She spotted Brit, a dull shadow crouched in the corner. The Doctor was still in the lab, moving from tube to tube, unaware that Pik was still conscious. She moved as minutely as possible, trying not to draw his attention. Instead she shifted her eyes to peek at Horn, who was also cautiously looking around.

Their eyes met briefly, but it was enough to convey all of Horn's triumph. She'd done it. This holding tank contained the base representations of the Doctor's victims over the years. This was where he was hiding out while experimenting with others. Pik vowed to use the opportunity wisely and cataloged the similarities and differences between the two environments.

The other environment was more themed with the game. It'd been a biological lab meant to contain, restrain, and study ecological samples. Pik watched as the Doctor returned to what looked like a command center interface. He observed a half dozen experiments play out on different monitors. She immediately wondered what she, Horn, and Brit had appeared to be doing in the last load out. Had he been paying attention? Could he look at a playback? Would Brit show up on one of those monitors?

For Horn's part, she had managed to smuggle in her customized interface. Pik could tell as the glazed-over look—only worn by dead fish and wholly zoned-out humans doing work in their HUD—came across her face. Horn began to work. Unfortunately for Pik, she was the muscle. There was nothing for the muscle to do while locked in a cage. Neither she nor Horn dared move in fear that the Doctor would notice. A defiant itch began to grow between Pik's shoulder blades. She resisted the instinct to scratch. To distract herself she focused on the Doctor, kept an eye on Horn, and tried her best to catalog everything.

The Doctor stood at a bench. It was organized, clean, and contained no personal effects. He mostly ignored the monitors that were showing video feeds of experimentation rooms and instead focused on a monitor with graphics and data. Pik imagined the video feeds were only used to review unexpected results. This may have been how they floated under the radar. She was okay with that.

Unable to glean any more details from the Doctor, Pik shifted her attention to the tube to her right. Inside stood a very old man. He had to be in his nineties. He looked like a standing skeleton with skin stretched across bare bones. His eyes were open just like hers, but there was no consciousness behind them. Grey wisps of hair stuck out in all directions on the man's head, and his grizzled jawline was covered in stubble. He, and most of the other people Pik could see without turning her head, had the same sort of outfit: some red or blue cotton derivative with yellow lettering denoting their name. A woman in a blue jumpsuit was slumped inelegantly against the side of the tube beside the elderly man. She had the plainest features, with long brown hair and too-short bangs covering her forehead as her nose and face pressed into the glass.

All of the people looked more real than Pik had ever seen. They had pimples and unfashionable glasses and weird haircuts. Her Metaverse was exciting, but it didn't have mundane-looking people. In her world, a person just changed appearances to suit the latest fashion trends. Nobody had to live with a bad haircut or poor eyesight. Pik felt something unexpected. She wanted to free Brit, her team, and herself from the Doctor; however, none of these people deserved to be held captive either. The Doctor had to be stopped. Not simply bypassed or escaped, but stopped. Every person in a holding tank needed to be freed.

For the first time in her life, Pik contemplated murder.

Pik forced herself to focus on the Doctor and to take this opportunity to watch him seriously. Find out something she could use against him. He wasn't wearing his Trick skinsuit this time, which was odd. As far as Pik could tell from her view of the room, she didn't spot Trick anywhere. The ever-demanding itch had grown. It distracted her with its persistence. She used her considerable willpower to ignore it, trying to connect to the details of the Doctor.

Instead the man looked plain, boring even. In many ways he was disappointing. The mastermind of an evil laboratory should have some abnormal-looking trait, some snappy attire or physical features pushing him higher or lower than the average human. Rather, he was remarkable in his normalcy. He had light brown skin, brown hair, and brown eyes. His hair was sprinkled with grey, and his face was covered in scruff. It looked mildly unkempt. Otherwise, his clothes didn't differentiate anything. He was in a lab coat, even though that was a farce. A digital lab didn't have to be sanitary. The whole thing felt performative.

The man wore tennis shoes, assuming his physicality played by the same rules as theirs, which meant he prized comfort over matching the lab coat's clean room aesthetic. He had old-school pens hanging out of the pocket of his jacket. That told Pik that he may have well been from Brit's century. No one in the Metaverse but Echoes even knew the purpose of a pen. The man hummed a tune to himself. It was disjointed, mildly off-key, but catchy—some fragment of a long-forgotten song.

She watched him watch Junip on a screen. They were pleading for Timmic's life. The Doctor's version of Trick stood in the simulation unmoved by their begging. Pik watched him observe the facsimile of Trick calmly activate a death protocol to melt Timmic in an acid bath. Junip crumbled into a heap. Pik could hear the muted sobs through the Doctor's earpiece. He was utterly engrossed in the scene, and Pik used this as her moment. She moved her right hand quickly, silently, to bend and scratch over her shoulder.

The Doctor froze in his observation. He turned, dull eyes scanning the tubes. Pik froze in fear. She repressed a grin, though, as the itch had been scratched. The man's eyes were flat. He stalked through the lab, examining each tube. As he examined her, it took everything she had not to look back into his eyes. To search for an element of humanity. He tapped a few keys on her tube. She tried to be calm, but her heart thundered in her chest. If he checked her interface, he'd see she had an elevated heartbeat.

He scanned her readouts, grunted, and moved away, returning to his awkward humming. When his back was turned, Pik glanced at Horn, who dared to wink. Horn was using her brain to get control of the environment. Pik hoped for Junip's sake that she left the "restore all your memories" protocol off.

The man eventually reached his monitors. Pik guessed that he reveled in the harsh moments of the tests. He was drawn to them, but his face held no real emotion. No positive or negative reaction. He'd type down a note or data point in his interface at random intervals and move on. It was like he was a machine. He was recording data detached, with no connection to the dramatic scenes playing out before him. He'd either lost his humanity or he didn't view any of them as human. They were, perhaps, a few steps below lab monkeys.

The last sequence ran its course on Timmic and Junip's experiment. Their tubes glowed green as Pik guessed their consciousnesses were reuploaded into this primary lab. The Doctor came over to their tubes and did a cursory check on their "health." Pik examined her friend's bodies. They looked more tired than they had before they were rejoined with their physical avatars. She took a moment to wonder how she looked.

The Doctor had returned to his main screens. This time, he was typing up a new load scenario. Pik wondered who was going to be next. Before she knew it, she had her answer as time and space became meaningless in the static of the transfer. A message from Horn flashed in her vision before she even inhabited her new body.

Horn: Do not move. I need five minutes to build a feed.

This time, Pik had loaded on a flat metallic table with an ugly-looking surgical robot equipped with knives over her prone form. She held still as Horn had directed, even though one of the scalpels was pointed right at her face.

Pik closed her eyes, trusting Horn. It helped that she knew exactly what Horn was doing. She was building a loop. The same thing she'd done for Command Central back in their home, trying to save them from the quarantine. Pik wasn't as confident that this would work on the Doctor. Home Command wasn't terribly on top of their game. The Doctor didn't have anything but his experiments. Nevertheless, she began a count.

When Pik was a child, her parents would play hide and seek with her, a novelty brought from another age. There was no hiding in the Metaverse. Everyone was tagged with a locator. One could find a friend, a parent, or a child in moments. But her mom had seen it in a family holonovel an Echo had pulled from another time. They'd switch off their locators and HUDs and her parents would hide around the house. Pik would have to sit there and manually count, as their internal clocks were turned off with the HUD. One, two, three. She'd count to sixty if they weren't given much time to hide, or, if she wanted a challenging round, she'd count to three hundred. Give them five minutes.

If she felt generous, she would count slowly, stretching out her minutes. Pik counted slow for Horn. Typically when the woman said she needed five minutes, she actually needed ten. Pik imagined her favorite variation of the game; her dad would count, and she'd hide. She'd be waiting, holed up behind a curtain or crouched under a pile of blankets, waiting for the game to start. Waiting to be needed, to be found.

"Pik, you there? Pik? Pik!" She was shaken out of her daydream.

"I'm here, I'm here. No need to lose it." The relief on Horn's face was gratifying.

"Good. I thought I'd fried your brain on this load trying to send you that message."

"Do you really think a loop will work? The Doctor seems more sophisticated than that."

Brit entered the conversation from the shadows with a smile. For once, she seemed better, as though the environment wasn't having such a detrimental effect on her mental health. "He probably would be, except that most experiments take hours and hours to load. In that last trial, you two were unconscious zombies for twelve hours before it even started."

"Yeah, it takes a long time to partition out what we should and shouldn't remember. So I just went with the last load, while he thinks we got wiped again. Anyway, it doesn't matter. Suffice it to say, when we want all of our memories, we will be a bit incapacitated."

Pik thought of watching Junip begging for Timmic's life. "I'm not sure I want all my memories of this place."

"Don't be silly, of course you do. First, though, we've got to figure out how to escape, and for that, we've got Trickshot back together." Horn disengaged the restraints. Pik carefully moved her head away from the scalpel's target area and quickly bounced out of that horror story. The cold edge of the bare gurney bit into her legs as she slid off.

To her surprise, a groggy Timmic and Junip sat on gurneys lined up for their turn at the robotic surgical array. A burble of hope rose in Pik's chest as she looked around for Trick. To her disappointment, there was no sign of him.

"We'll find him," Brit murmured, catching Pik's disappointment. This only made it more awkward. Pik turned back to her crew, hiding the disappointment.

"We've got the team back together. This is great!" Pik said, turning around, trying to save face. She was genuinely happy to see her teammates.

A disoriented Timmic sat up. "Where are we? I was looking for an armory and got hit by acid and woke up here. Are we in a hospital?" Pik knew Timmic was a bad first-person player, but she had no idea he'd be knocked out in the first level. Pathetic, even for a historian. Pik grinned anyway. It was good to see his golden beard and overzealous eyebrows. His looks had always baffled her. He played the distinguished older gentleman look well.

Junip came to with a gasp. They were worse for wear, green eyes jumping around like a wild animal. Horn was immediately by their side, trying to calm them. Junip looked worse for wear, their normally carefully manicured hair was greasy and stuck out in weird angles. This iteration, they leaned toward the feminine scale of their gender fluidity, sporting thin eyebrows and lacking the often-present short auburn beard.

Pik squeezed Timmic's arm, reassuring him, murmuring assurances as she undid the buckles strapping his legs to the gurney. They'd all survived, one way or another—assuming none of their party was an intruder. Pik tapped her verification code on Timmic's ankle once he was conscious enough to understand the signal. He returned with his verification. Horn was testing Junip. Brit hung back, an outsider, not wanting to ruin the family reunion.

"Brit, join us," Pik called to her. She wasn't sure when Brit had joined the team, but as far as she was concerned, the woman was now one of them. She may not have ever been a part of Trick's Echo crew, but she was a part of Pik's.

A grateful look and Brit was among them, catching up on their adventures, short as Timmic's was. Horn walked everyone through the lab, experiments, and introduced the concept of the Doctor.

Junip cut to the chase, "We have to understand why he's doing it."

"I don't need to know why. He's evil, and he needs to be dealt with." Pik's voice was cold. They didn't remember what he'd done to them, but Pik had seen enough. The image of Timmic melting in a vat of acid wouldn't leave her memory. She studied his face, the wrinkles he allowed, the minuscule receding hairline. She never understood his aesthetics, but she was so grateful he was still alive.

"I disagree; it's not enough. Suppose we knew why. We'd know how to hit him where it hurts. He's still got Trick. Until we can unravel him enough to get Trick back, killing him is a risk we can't take." Junip gave the one-two punch to Pik's heart; she wouldn't risk Trick, and they knew it.

Brit chimed in, "I've been thinking about the why for years. I kept most of my memories iteration to iteration. He's evil, but—and I hate to admit this—there's purpose to it."

"Sadism?" Pik couldn't resist.

"No, he's after some key element of the human psyche. Something for his program, his game." Pik felt Brit's rebuke in their link. The woman was serious.

Pik couldn't escape the feeling that if Trick were

here, he would know. He would have figured it out already. She almost vocalized her wish for her mentor, but Trick needed them to solve this puzzle. It was their job now.

"We need to figure this out. Brit is the person who knows the Doctor and this game the most." Three sets of eyes joined Pik's, who swiveled to study Brit. She looked fragile, her skin pale and eyes nervous. Brit didn't look like a fighter. Pik waited for her to decide what to do.

She stood before them, a ghost. A fragment of a long-forgotten version of humanity. Pik felt the resolve build in their bond. She was the ghost with the key. For the first time on the journey, Pik saw her own it. Own the moment.

"Yeah, okay. How much time do we have, Horn?"

Horn's eyes got the faraway look as she examined her HUD, hand entwined with Junip's. They'd never been that physically open about their relationship in front of the team. The openness suited them.

"I found a function to time dilate us. Since the Doctor is waiting for us to load, we'll have hours."

"That's precise." Timmic did not do well with unknowns. Horn just stuck her tongue out at him.

For Brit's part, she just nodded. "That'll have to be enough."

Chapter 19

"Horn, Pik, you both experienced his lab. He had what, thirty, forty people in there total? I saw my daughter. I saw the four of you."

Pik agreed. The lab had been almost full, with eight to ten rows of five tubes each.

"Do you remember anything about the people? Did anything about them stand out?"

Horn's reply was a non-answer. "I wasn't paying attention to them. I spent most of my time trying to code us out of that trap, allowing us to keep our memories."

The entire team turned to Pik, and she suddenly grew self-conscious. What could she say about the people? There wasn't anything special about them. "They were ordinary. Like in ways that you don't see in the Metaverse. Each person was ugly."

Timmic snorted. He considered himself the ugliest in the group and kept it as a point of pride.

"No, Timmic, not ugly like you." Pik realized that sounded bad but quickly continued, "Like, you're a great comparison. You consider yourself an academic. There is no need to worry about appearances and the rest. But strip away the absentminded professor look, you're still handsome—gorgeous even. Even your receding hairline isn't too much; it's just enough to make you look distinguished."

Timmic blushed.

"But these people had pimples, smudged faces, and noses too big." Pik thought hard about the people she'd seen. At the time, she couldn't rip her eyes away. "They had grey hair, not the sexy salt-and-pepper look that's in style right now, but literal patchy grey hair, and one guy was completely bald."

Brit nodded. For the first time in a while, Pik thought she might have contributed something truly valuable to the conversation, even if she didn't really know what.

"Yeah, this has been bothering me about the four of you. You're too perfect. You're like game avatars. When we loaded in here, you all retained your base look from the command pod, so I know it's not the skin of the game. I think you're the simulation. You're part of his game."

The statement was idiotic. Pik had been waiting for the big reveal and was astonished that she'd come up with this.

Horn was the first to reply. "Absolute rubbish. I can interface with the game and see the code and how it interacts with us. We're not a part of this simulation. This code is very different than what makes up the Metaverse."

"Why are we wasting time on this lunatic? I was suspicious of her when she swapped out with Trick, and now she's trying to convince us that we're some illusion and she's the real thing? This is ridiculous." Timmic wasn't having any of it either; he was the least flexible of the four of them, right up there with Horn.

Pik waited to speak. She wanted to see Junip's response. They were the most flexible in mind and a good study of humanity. Or, according to Brit, good studies in the simulation of humanity.

"I want to hear her out. It doesn't make sense to me, but our entire existence in the Metaverse is also an illusion. I exist in the dream I created with the three of you. This isn't that much of a stretch. I know Horn, Timmic, that you'd like to think that our lives are what we make of them. It fits your personality profile, but at the same time we are all just reflections of what we think we are. Nothing in the Metaverse is 'real.' She's right in saying that we are simulations of humanity. We've all, Brit included, left our physical selves behind."

Timmic rolled his eyes. He'd never gotten along well with Junip. "Well, what do you think, Pik?"

"I want to hear more." Pik idly tapped a code into the workstation she was leaning against. It was a call to confirm. She watched her peers as they checked in, one by one. Horn rubbed at her nose, mimicking an itch. Timmic stood stoically and reached up to tug at the lower edge of his golden beard. Junip put a hand in their left pocket. They always wore oversized pants with large pockets. The team confirmed. Pik did it for two reasons: She wanted to ensure they were who they said they were. But she also wanted to remind everyone that they were part of the team. Whether reality was fake or real, they all had each other.

Pik continued slowly as she watched her team, putting an easier-than-expected smile on her face, feeling better after everyone checked in. "I want to hear more, but I also want to say this. After observing all those people in the lab, I want to free them all. This isn't just about our consciousness. This is about everyone's. They deserve to be free too. Even if they are ugly." She said the last line with a smile, letting the group in on the joke. Pik could feel the knot that was Brit in her mind ease a bit.

Pik looked from person to person. Each gave her a nod. It wasn't forced. They were all good souls. She wouldn't have had them on her team if they weren't. Pik gave them one last smile, then turned to Brit.

The link between them pulsed with gratitude before Brit continued, "Well, at least on that, we can agree. Look, I kept thinking about the Doctor. Why is he doing it? I used to exist fully in the real world. I had a family, and I walked the Earth. Why would a person set up a death game and then not follow through on the death part? I'm sure my family thought I was dead, but instead, I get pulled into this tortured reality. But why? What's the point?"

She glanced at Pik and Horn. "I mean, he could just be sadistic, sure, but did he look like he was just an unhinged torturer? Would that be enough to sustain him for hundreds of years?"

Pik noticed Horn shifting uncomfortably. Pik waited, wanting Horn to come to her own conclusion. She felt Horn begin to pull together her own threads of possibilities.

Horn spoke slowly, thinking as she did. "No. I mean, I was busy, but his lab screamed that he was a scientific professional. A twisted monster, sure. But someone with a purpose."

"Yes, exactly. He's unwinding something about life. Something he needs. And the only thing I can think of is that he's been working on the upload problem." Brit revealed her conclusion.

"What's the 'upload problem?' Does it have a century of origination?" Timmic's engagement was a good sign he was coming around. He was deeply familiar with humanity's history. It was uncommon for him not to recognize a term from the last three hundred years.

Brit blew a renegade curl of hair out of her face as she explained, "I'm not surprised that wasn't one of the things ported into the Metaverse, because, for the Metaverse to exist, the problem had to be solved. The upload problem comes down to this: Humanity has pursued immortality for most of its existence. The fountain of youth, ambrosia, and even the quest for the holy grail. All these historical examples eventually escaped humanity. The best a person could have hoped for is to create something so glorious that they'd be remembered."

Brit rushed forward getting her thoughts out, "But with the technology of my world, they'd dabbled with a proper solution to the immortality quest. They'd started to figure out how to upload consciousness at a basic level. What they'd managed the last time I interacted with the natural world was a partial upload. One would be connected to a headset that read and could influence one's brain waves. It tricked one's brain into thinking a game like Infestation was real, sure, but it was reliant on a physical body."

Pik wanted her to speed it up; this was somewhat elementary in understanding the Metaverse.

Brit cleared her throat. "Yeah, so what if the Doctor was working on having people step outside of their physical bodies and fully into a remote existence? We had problems with uploading. The few who tried were fine for a while, but the lack of complete sensory data eventually made people lose their minds. We'd have this semiconscious artificial intelligence that just went wild. It almost caused another world war."

Brit breathed heavily. "I think the Doctor's been torturing people to figure out the formula for success. Technically, once I died in 'game,' he uploaded me and the other contestants. We were probably the first semi-successful uploads. I say semi-successful because I'm not sure we're all sane or even sentient at this point. Could the Metaverse just be another holding tank for his uploads?"

Pik felt sorry for Brit as she watched the faces of her team. They mulled over her story, but they didn't believe it. Even if it was true, they weren't going to believe it. To believe Brit was to unwind their existence. No human consciousness, digital or not, would willingly make that leap. Brit's interpretation of reality was that she was the only legitimate entity in the room, which was convenient.

"I think you're right," Timmic said. Pik typically held an excellent poker face. Not much had surprised her over the years. Timmic's declaration was at the top of the list, right below her parent's decision to transition into their next life.

"You do?" Even Junip was shocked.

"Yes. Some of what you're saying makes sense. There is a significant gap in our technology advancement history that's been noted over the years. When and how humanity made the leap from the physical to the digital. We have our Architects of the Metaverse, but there's shockingly little on the upload problem, as Brit states. The Doctor's research *is* centered on keeping uploaded consciousness—likely the first of its kind—viable. What if the Doctor solved the upload problem and the rest of humanity leveraged that solution? I don't think she's completely right; I feel like a distinct individual. However, it makes sense to me that the Doctor may have been working on some of the fundamental problems in the creation of the Metaverse."

Pik wasn't following Timmic's logic. She watched him talk, searching for a sign that he was lying. He never even glanced at her. He was focused on Brit the entire time. Pik shook herself, trying to recover from the shock. Brit was radiating confidence. She looked like she'd won a million bucks. The rest of the team just stared at Timmic. It was so out of character for him to agree with anyone.

Junip nodded along, but they were usually pretty agreeable. Horn—who, up until this point, Pik would have considered Brit's biggest ally—was all storm clouds.

"You guys, don't you get it?" Pik just waited for Timmic to burst out laughing like he was pulling a joke on them. His tone was dead serious. "This—this twisted existence is the cradle."

"That's a myth." Pik found her mouth moving without thought. "It's a myth. You can't believe any of it."

"The cradle that's an adept meta—"

The floor shook. Pik was knocked from her feet. A gurney skittered across the room and tipped over on her.

"He's coming. Give me a moment," Horn said, tensely tapping commands into her interface. A long crack appeared through the middle of the room. Dust choked the air. White ceiling tiles fell from overhead, knocked out of the flimsy frames they'd occupied. Pik didn't like being dependent on Horn to save everyone. She liked being in control of her fate.

Pik reached for her inventory and felt her mind take a twist. She reached through her connection with Brit, and a small pistol began to shimmer into existence.

Horn stared at her with wide eyes. "What are you doing? How are you doing that?"

The room shook again. This time, a crosswise crack ran down a wall. Equipment scattered everywhere. Timmic fell into one of the surgical droids and had been sliced by an errant scalpel. Pik shook her head as she watched Junip run and tend to him. Timmic was all preparation and no action. He was useless in a crisis. Pik gave another tug at her inventory, and the gun solidified. She unclipped the magazine, checking to make sure it was loaded. It was. Slapping the clip back in, she put it up and faced the door—the only entrance to the lab.

"Pik, I need you to pull something else from your inventory. You created a connection back to the game. I need that to make this work." Horn's voice was tense but excited.

"How long do you need?"

"As much time as you can give me."

It was a good thing Pik picked up everything. She looked at the team and handed her pistol off to Brit. She didn't wholly trust her, but she did believe that at the end of the day, Brit would point the gun at the Doctor if he came barreling into the room.

Pik pulled at her inventory through the link again. The feeling was odd, like pulling something out of a vat of molasses—a thickness. Typically an inventory pull was instantaneous. Pik had always had an excellent meld with the games. They measured her in the top 1% of Echoes for interfacing with a system. This one, however, was a strain.

The audible pop announced the arrival of a spoon. For the first time, Pik's penchant to pick up anything not nailed down was going to pay off. Spoon after spoon popped onto the floor. The resistance she'd encountered started to diminish. Each successive spoon and then fork came through the barrier more easily. She moved on, pulling at her Cosmic Sabre.

The sword took more force, but it popped into the lab in a reality-bending manner, all fierce electric fire, ready to shred the Doctor into bits.

"That was it!" As the world elongated, Horn's triumphant voice was the only warning Pik had. She saw Trick's face as the Doctor slammed through the lab door. For a brief moment, before she lost consciousness, Pik was sad that she hadn't been holding on to the gun. She may have been able to kill him if she'd held it. The sabre would have worked, too, if she'd had time to swing it.

All of them loaded into the "beach," the level of Infestation right after the waterlogged trek through the center of the ship. The beach was nothing of the sort. It was a tunnel that led up to the mess hall, one of the few "safe" areas Pik had found in the game. It was the launch pad for the home stretch. Pik awoke groggy, as though the load had pulled her through a filter. The ceiling in the mess hall was distinctive, with several crystal chandeliers dangling, surrounded by multi-tiered moulding. Her sabre was gone. Pik sat up, taking stock of herself and doing a head count.

Her head ached. She could see Junip and Timmic. Junip was already tying a strip of cloth around the cut on Timmic's arm. Brit sat in a ball to her left, her arms wrapped around her legs, holding herself tight. Pik grabbed a table to leverage herself into a standing position. Her body felt like it'd been through a gauntlet. Every muscle held some bit of soreness. As she stood, she turned around to find Horn standing next to Trick.

Immediately Pik was on guard, pulling a bolt machine gun from her inventory. She leveled it at Trick.

"Horn, step away from the Doctor."

Horn was experiencing the same transfer sickness

as everyone else. Her fuzzy eyes glanced to her right, and she quickly scrambled away. The Doctor just sat, not making any move, and looked at Pik.

"I'm not sure who the Doctor is, but you best not be pointing that gun at me unless you intend to use it."

It couldn't be Trick. He couldn't be Trick. Pik kept her gun up. The man stood slowly and used a shoe to scratch absently at his shin. It was Trick's sign, his signal, but Pik didn't trust it. And they already knew he had access to details about their signs.

Trick looked at her. Pik looked back at him. "Stay there." She took a step back, trying to increase the distance between the two of them. He was still wearing the Doctor's lab coat.

Horn had edged her way around the room, away from the Doctor, and brought up her analysis tools. Trick stood, hands out to the sides, showing he meant no harm. He took a step toward Pik. She held her gun pointed at his chest. Guns were so easy. With the pull of the trigger, she could end him. A spray of bullets at this close would rip his body apart and send him back to respawn.

"Pik, it's me. You don't want to do that. This isn't Alpha Centauri." The reference was a purposeful one. Alpha Centauri had been a hidden traitor game, and in the end, a Trick doppelganger had gotten the best of her. It had been her first failed mission, and it had hurt. Only Trick knew how the game had ended because when they got back to Command, he'd told everyone that it'd been his fault they didn't get a payday. "I need you to stay back," Pik's voice wavered. Before she could think about it, he'd stepped forward again with his outstretched hand, grabbing the barrel of the gun. She still hadn't fired. Trick pulled it from her limp fingers. She couldn't bring herself to pull the trigger, not on Trick.

Three rapid shots rang out, and Pik was splattered in blood.

Trick reached for her, his eyes starting to glaze over with death in the too-realistic game mechanics. Pik turned to see Brit holding out the pistol, her hands shaking.

"I had to kill him. It was the Doctor."

PART 3

Chapter 20

"He's both."

Pik pulled her second Cosmic Sabre out of her inventory, changed her mind, and pulled one of the smart, cheap daggers. They were everywhere, much more replaceable than the sword. She kept a stack of them in her inventory. The blade's edge was sharp. She picked at her fingernails, listening to Horn explain.

"Here, join my interface." A Horn-original interface request popped up on Pik's screen, and she absentmindedly connected. A reverb of static hit her feed.

"What the hell, Horn?"

"Don't leave. That's part of the discovery. Just tone down the interference. Apply these settings." She dumped settings reconfigurations on her screen, and Pik couldn't hit yes fast enough. The static instantly faded out. It was still visible but didn't have the earsplitting screech with it.

"Warn a girl next time."

"Sorry, I'd forgotten how bad it was before I reset everything."

"Horn, tell them what we discovered." Junip was being pushy, and they were never pushy. That, more than anything else, got Pik to focus.

Horn cleared her throat. "Well, Junip and I were examining Trick's digital corpse." Pik reflexively looked down at the floor. Trick's body lay covered in blood, glazed eyes gazing back at her. She shivered, returning to the conversation. "Looking for anything. Mostly I wanted a trace back to the Doctor. Some proof that Trick was actually the mad scientist. I didn't find anything."

"So Brit did kill Trick—the real Trick?"

Junip jumped in, waving off Pik. "No, don't you see? He was a generated clone. Independent. He doesn't have Trick's signature. I know Trick's digital identity. I've performed more decontaminations and reconstitutions on him than anyone else. Whatever that was"—they pointed to the clone's corpse—"it wasn't Trick."

The knot in Pik's chest loosened.

Horn took the conversation back over, "That's the crazy part. He's an independent snapshot clone. Superficially close enough to Trick—he might fool us for at least a little while. But he had to have some of the Doctor's agenda imprinted within him. Right? There should be some trace."

"But there isn't?" Pik didn't know why this mystery was so important, and her tone let them know she was losing her patience.

"Exactly. There isn't, so we debated what that meant."

Timmic butted in this time, "It means he didn't have any way to report back. The Doctor doesn't know we killed him."

"Yes, he does. Look around. I've been able to set up a visual interface to highlight the Doctor's influence." The overlay that Horn had set up was still full of static, but Pik could make out a red glow associated with different pieces of the environment. Trick's body was cast in blue, a dead blue. Their bodies were a brighter version of the same blue, and to her relief, even Brit's was a vibrant blue with no red overtones. The walls of the place held trace filaments of red. They pooled over an arrow pointing out the exit from the beach safe zone.

Pik noticed blue lines connecting her, Horn, and Brit as well. No one had asked about the significance of it.

"I told you! The arrows mean something." Junip poked Timmic, settling an argument they'd been having.

"They might, but I can't search for a script variation like that in the archives that easily," Timmic grumbled.

Pik looked at the knife in her hand. Her throwing

skill was pretty high in the game. She took it by the point, pivoted onto her back foot, and threw it unerringly. In Horn's filter, the doorway lit up in an explosion of filament. Everything with the "red" influence that was connected to the node snaked back away as though it were alive.

"Well, that was rash." Horn was never one for physical action. "But we learned a lot. It's a virus. It's technologically alive. Did you see it react? That was a pain reaction."

"Which means we can hurt it. Horn, why didn't you see this before?" Pik surmised that they probably had been surrounded by the Doctor's influence the entire time they'd been in Infestation.

"We can hurt him." Brit's voice was fierce.

Horn cheeks flushed. "I didn't know what I was looking at. I saw it when we were playing through, but without observing the Doctor directly, I just thought it was part of the game build."

"Horn, can you refine this filter and get us all a little more muted but have targeting on the nodes? We need to exterminate some contamination." Pik pivoted away from Horn to Timmic and Junip. "How far did you get in the game? What does your inventory look like?"

Pik, Horn, and Brit had gotten decently far in the game. Junip had died on their first encounter. Timmic had made it a bit further, playing an evasion-based game. But on hard mode, evasion only got him to the end of the first level. Eventually a player had to face a boss, and that's where he'd fallen.

As an Echo team, they hadn't managed to load as a group too often, but Trick had made them train for the day. Trickshot logged many first-person shooter simulator hours, and Pik was confident she could get them moving as a unit. Junip was a top-notch sharpshooter, and Timmic played a tank. Pik was great at just getting in the way and absorbing damage.

Horn was a generalist, better at strategy than actual combat. When pressed, she could put up decent damage numbers. Horn was good at seeing moments where they could, as a group, maximize advantages. She'd set up choke points and elaborate traps and spot sniper positions. She was also going to make an attempt at being what Trick excelled in, the team's wildcard.

Pik had dumped her backup armor kit, several upgrade units, and medkits for Timmic. For Junip, she still had the uncharged energy rail gun and a low-grade sniper rifle. Sniping was not Pik's strong suit. She looked at Horn, leaning in on the trust factor. She handed over her arsenal of grenades, energy traps, and a lot of her miscellaneous items.

"Why didn't you give me all of this before?"

"I was solo running it at that point. You were just tagging along with Brit. Now, though, the team's back together. We've got to work as a unit. And, well, for that, you need to explode things."

Horn was good at holding grudges, but Pik relaxed as she gave her a big grin. "I am pretty good at blowing things up. Okay, so Junip, I think we should have you aim for the nodes. Just knock them out before we get there. I suspect this will have an impact on the monsters we're facing. They might get extra agitated, or hopefully weaker."

The game was already in hard mode. Pik didn't know how the team was going to hold up in real combat, but she loaded them out as best as her inventory would allow. Pik wished she'd been able to keep her plexiglass shield, but it'd been lost in the battle with the Kraken.

Brit still didn't have an inventory. She seemed to be a broken character, sitting outside the game yet still affected by it. Horn had analyzed her a dozen times and couldn't find the flaw in her build. She wasn't connected to the Doctor but wasn't fully connected to the game either.

They were as set as they could be. Pik took point,

with Timmic right behind her. She'd duck back behind him if they were jumped immediately. As Pik touched the door, a pop-up appeared in her HUD.

Do you wish to break the seal? This will initiate the BEACH protocol, and the safe room will be disabled. [Y/N]

She slammed the “No” option in her head and pushed everyone back.

"We've got to get a defensible position set up. As soon as I open this door, waves of aliens will come at us."

"Waves? How bad is it going to get?" Timmic looked rightfully worried.

"Bad enough that I wish we had a trick or two up our sleeves. Let's get some ideas going and figure out where we’ll hold out."

The only real place with any defensive properties was behind the food gallery. The island, where diners would pick up their food, had a solid structure. Pik initially rejected the idea since the kitchen doors behind them were a likely spawn spot.

However, Brit was put on door duty. Since she couldn't fully operate within the game's parameters, her job was to act as a doorstop, keeping the kitchen beasts trapped until they'd cleared the rest of the wave and could turn their attention inward. They tested her ability to hold the doors closed, which was almost effortless. Brit couldn't fight in the traditional sense, but this was almost more useful as it cordoned off a good quarter of the monsters they'd have to fight.

In these scenarios, it wasn't so much about sheer firepower. The team would lose in an all-out firefight. The strategy was about segmenting down the waves to something more manageable. Brit blocking the door was a jackpot of solutions.

"Are we ready?" For the first time since they dropped into the Doctor's lab, Pik felt like she was doing something she knew how to do. It wasn't confidence, exactly. She was still worried they'd be overrun in the first wave. However, they were starting to click. The training was coming to the forefront, and their planning was less chaotic. They had a plan and were prepared.

She got a chorus of mumbled “Ready.”

"I said, are you ready?" Pik added grit to her voice, demanding an answer.

"Affirmative." This time, they were all paying attention. They were locked and loaded. It was go time.

Pik raised her gun and shot at the handle of the door, causing it to pop open. Red flashing script dropped in front of their view, announcing they were about to encounter a wave environment with five distinct waves. They acknowledged the warning—except for Brit, who wasn't favored with any notification—and the game began. The first wave was a horde of miniature acid spitters. They entered the space, not through the main door but through ventilation shafts, causing mayhem.

Three dropped down on top of the counter that Pik was taking cover behind. She repressed a scream, switched weapons, and sliced across the counter with her Cosmic Sabre. The three chunked apart, green blood spraying everywhere.

"Preserve your ammo. They're low health."

Pik stepped forward, careful not to trigger any of Horn's traps. She took a stance before the countertops, offering the acid spitters a target. This proved unwise. Although physically unintimidating at their size, they still spit acid. Pik watched as a dozen spitters got within range and leaned back, aiming for her torso. She kept her eye on them, timing her actions. As soon as they opened their mouths, she dropped to the floor. They all spit, unable to adjust their trajectory. Twelve acid splats went sailing through the place she'd just been standing.

With her sabre, Pik lashed out at several within reach, one-hit killing them. Junip had yet to take her advice. Instead, they took potshots from her vantage point. Eight and nine of the spitters exploded. Timmic didn't pause. He came rolling through, his armor protecting from errant acid splatter as he took care of the remaining creatures in front of Pik. They all regrouped behind cover. First-wave acid spitters were still walking between their traps when the front and side doors of the mess hall opened. Larger, medium-sized acid spitters entered through the doors, surrounded by an entourage of smaller ones.

"Those big ones have nodes on them!" Horn splashed her visual filter across their HUDs, and sure enough, each of the big aliens, when they opened their mouths, exuded the sickly red glow of the Doctor's influence. Junip popped the closest with three rapid shots straight in the mouth. Red influence snaked away from the creature, retreating, although the alien remained on its feet. Pik had swapped guns again, this time a well-aimed pistol. She lined up, sending four pops of her own and hitting it in all four eyes. The creature was down in an instant. It was much quicker than the ones earlier in her playthrough would have been.

"Once you knock out the influence, they're weaker." Pik wasn't positive it was true, but it felt right.

The mini acid spitters, once their leader was killed, were thrown into a frenzy. They charged the base the team had built, crawling through the gaps in the stacked-up furniture. Pik had been worried about getting trapped. Junip, who lay above the ceiling tiles, gun peeking through, began hitting the second beast. Pik had swapped to her sabre again, stabbing through the rubble before the spitters could line up with a shot. Horn threw her knives, then picked up a bit of debris, waving it around like a hockey stick. She smacked mini spitters away from her in imitation of the players she loved.

"A little help?"

Pik whipped her head around to see Brit holding the back door closed while kicking at a mini spitter that had gotten past Timmic. The creature had walked up to Brit and started gnawing on her leg. Even she probably could have handled it if she hadn't been using every muscle to keep the door shut.

"I've got you." Pik moved quickly. She wound up and kicked. The spitter flew across the cafeteria, barely missing Horn as it splatted against the wall.

"Second mama's down," cried Junip. The pops of the sniper rifle fell silent as they reloaded.

Pik slashed with the Cosmic Sabre, taking note as the creatures continued wriggling through the chairs, tables, and equipment they'd stacked around them. The team had to get mobile or they were sitting targets.

"Junip, aim for the third mama. Brit break to the left on my mark." The team had to get moving now. There were too many little spidery spitters and too few of the crew.

"Mark." Pik dived to the right as Brit dived to the left. With the kitchen door no longer being held, it burst open. Angry buzzing spitters boiled out, aiming acid globs at their charging frenzied spitters. Already loaded, they spit at each other, causing more chaos and giving Brit and Pik a chance to escape. Timmic moved to cover Brit. Pik took four steps and vaulted over the barricade, squishing a handful of aliens as she came down.

Junip hadn't opened fire yet. "Junip, any time now."

Pik looked up, seeing the problem. Junip's sniper position, which they'd deemed so clever when they'd set up, was aimed outward toward the far doors, not inward to the kitchen. Junip couldn't twist their body enough to aim backward. Pik put the sword back in her inventory.

"Timmic, cover me." Pik pulled out a light machine

gun. The weight of the weapon fell against her hip, a long strip of ammo draping away from her body. An acid splat stung hard as it hit her back. She pulled the trigger on the mama acid spitter's head bobbing just above the countertop she'd vacated. The slugs tore into the counter and peppered the mama spitter in the face. Within seconds, the chaos evaporated.

Pik stood panting as all the mini spitters in the room dropped dead at once. They'd been linked to the mamas. Pik swapped the gun out for the sabre. The sulfurous metallic smell of gunpowder infiltrated her senses.

"Good job, Pik. Nice thinking." Horn patted her on the back, their link flaring with appreciation.

A countdown until the next wave appeared on Pik's HUD. They had twenty minutes. She shook her head. "No, we're only one wave in, and I've already destroyed our cover."

"I don't think it's going to matter. We're going to have to move around. You saw how quickly they made it through our barrier. We barely killed a tenth of the monsters before they were through."

Horn picked up a bullet-riddled chair to uncover a pile of mini spitter bodies before continuing, "It's sheer luck that they were linked to the bigger spitters. If they hadn't been, we'd be playing chase for the next hour, trying to avoid and destroy the critters." Horn's assessment was correct.

Pik's face flushed in embarrassment. Her tactics weren't good enough for the scenario they'd encountered.

"We still need Brit on the door," Pik found herself saying. Without the barricade it would be hard to defend Brit.

"Yes, but did you see—the creatures that weren't influenced by the Doctor completely ignored her. It was like they didn't see her at all." Horn's logic was impeccable. As long as they could keep the Doctor's monsters off Brit, she'd be fine.

"That's it! We've said it's like Brit's outside the game. No inventory, no armor, no levels, no aggro." Brit could hold the door indefinitely, as long as she didn't accidentally get hit. Pik replayed the spitter gnawing on Brit ineffectually in her head. It's probably just had a moment of luck and happened to stumbled upon her.

Junip called from above, "I picked up three levels in that fight!"

Pik hadn't leveled at all. She gave her best fake smile to Junip's enthusiasm. Junip had leveled so much because they were at a very low level to begin with—much too low for as deep in the game as they were. Pik hoped the medic earned more rapid levels so they could catch up. This first wave consisted of low-level monsters that they were serving criticals on. It wasn't going to stay that easy.

"The only thing in this place that's interested in Brit is the Doctor. None of the aliens can see her without his influence." Pik made sure everyone understood.

"I can't impact them either," Brit commented.

"Not true. You were able to segment them off by blocking the door. You can interface with the environment." Timmic was ever the pragmatist.

"This still doesn't solve our problem. How do we dance around while still leaving Brit vulnerable? They may not be able to see her without the Doctor's influence, but the mobs will start with his influence." Pik put the question to the group.

Pik watched as the timer on her interface went from fifteen minutes to fourteen.

The whole team stood, looking at their problem, Brit. Junip was also vulnerable, being in a static location. But they had a bonus to stealth and hide skills. Brit had no unique attributes.

"I've got it!" Horn stepped forward, swiping a hand through some goo stuck to Brit's shirt. "Look at this spot with the filter."

Pik did. The goo looked green, just like the alien bug parts lying around, and then she realized what that meant. "You're a genius, Horn!"

"Tell me something I don't already know!" Horn trotted around the place, grabbing alien guts. She smeared a large portion on herself but kept the juiciest bits for Brit. Pik followed suit, and so did Timmic . . . once he figured out what they were doing.

Brit hadn't caught on until they returned to her, fistfuls of dripping, seeping carcasses in hand. She'd been watching their insanity with distaste as she leaned against the doors.

"What's going on, folks?" Brit finally asked, not having followed their plan.

"We've got to douse you. There's no other way." Horn gave her an impish grin as she held out a pile of entrails.

"You've got to be kidding." Brit backed away.

"It hides your digital scent. Blocks out your signature. You look like just a pile of bug meat. As long as you don't move too much, you should be fine," Pik tried to reassure Brit.

Five minutes. They had to move quickly. Pik wanted to close her ears to the squelching sounds as they rubbed, draped, and covered Brit in bits and pieces of acid spitter guts. When they were done, she looked just as much like a lab experiment as she probably felt after centuries of the Doctor's probing.

"Two minutes left, everyone healed up?" Pik's voice cut into the fun they'd been having "helping" Brit. Heads nodded. "You all have enough ammo?"

Brit returned to her outpost by the kitchen door, firmly in place as a door stop. Timmic stood in the center of the room, ready to take abuse from all angles. Horn and Pik stood far from Brit but flanked both sides. They'd kicked over their barricade as best as they could. It would only be in the way of their current strategy.

The time ticked down to zero. Pik held her breath. The level was already different than on her and Trick's playthrough. She didn't know what to expect—whether it was the Doctor's influence or a higher-set difficulty level.

The lights in the room dimmed. Chairs, tables, and various serving plates and bins were scattered across the room haphazardly. Pik's team braced themselves as the doors swung open. They stood for a second, looking, peering into the dark corridor, waiting to glimpse the subsequent terror thrown their way. The doors swung shut. Pik waited. A faint smell of ash floated in the air. Junip fired once, twice.

Using their intercoms, Pik asked the question they were all wondering, "What are you firing at?"

"Turn on your filter! They're lit up in red." Junip's message was interrupted by their gunfire and static on the line. It was the static that convinced Pik, even before she switched over.

Glowing on both sides of Timmic were two assassins. They had long, sharp-looking mandibles. One was in the process of swinging for Timmic's head.

"Timmic, move!" To his credit, he ducked, even as he was still fumbling with his filter settings. The mandible impacted the wall where his head had been. Timmic moved, trying to escape the death that stalked him. He charged right into the belly of the invisible assassin in front of him. The Timmic and the assassin fell in a heap.

Pik opened fire, this time with an energy rifle. The sparkling blue flames lit the assassin in a way everyone would recognize. Horn copied her, trying to concentrate her fire on the other bug. The crackling blue outlined their frames, allowing Pik to see beyond the Doctor's influence. Her fire was hitting the body in general. Assassins with that high a stealth skill weren't usually too hard to kill, yet these proved incredibly resistant.

The crackle of her flames did almost nothing to bring the assassin's health bar down. The only one doing any real damage was Junip.

"I got it!" The health of the assassin on the left—the one Timmic hadn't knocked down—dropped significantly.

"Back of the head!" Junip called.

Pik's target was facing the wrong direction to knock out the node. She just kept her rifle firing, slowing ticking down its health. The alien had reoriented itself to take another crack at Timmic. He was prone on the floor, still tangled in his first target. Pik used a skill—Dash.

She sped forward, lowering her shoulder.

Boom!

The crack resonated through her body. The harder-than-expected carapace stunned her as she hit. Pik's small frame bounced off the bug and landed on her ass.

Instead of knocking it flying as intended, the assassin slowly turned to face her. If nothing else, she'd grabbed its attention from the vulnerable Timmic. Desperate, watching it raise a mandible to end her, Pik swapped weapons.

The thrust cut through the belly of the creature. A splatter of guts and fluid sprayed Pik's face, and the assassin dropped on top of her, dead.

Pik didn't know how the rest of the battle went. Instead, she wrestled with the dead assassin, its carapace extremely heavy and now visible. The mandibles had locked in place, keeping her trapped beneath its weight.

Blasts and shouting danced around Pik as she struggled. Eventually the battleground silenced. She couldn't tell which side was victorious, and she feared the absolute worst. Pik tensed, waiting for death to find her.

Instead, Horn was there. The stout woman used her powerful legs to leverage the assassin off of Pik.

"That was gross." Pik was finally able to stand. Pik

cringed as she tried to wipe slimy ichor out of her hair. “Thanks for the rescue, Horn.”

Brit's strained voice cut through Pik's complaint. "You have no room to complain." She struggled to hold the kitchen door closed. Her clothes were saturated in goo to the extent that it’d started to crust into her clothes as it dried. "Anyone got an idea for this last assassin?"

Horn grinned. "I do.” She began setting up one last trap.

“You ready for this?” Brit’s voice was tense. The woman had been holding the last assassin back for ten minutes as Horn had set up her trap. The team took one last look at each other and gave a wave of assent.

Brit rolled away from the entrance, plastering herself against the wall. The door swung open, tipping Horn’s dangling bucket. The container of slime emptied right on top of the assassin, covering it in wet goo. The effect was immediate. Its stealth became nonexistent, and the three Echoes on the cafeteria floor opened fire.

Within moments, the red glow of the Doctor’s influence evaporated. From then on, it was child's play. The assassin relied on its stealth abilities, and without them it was a huge target.

The team regrouped.

Brit stood, legs spread and arms hanging away from her body, as she couldn’t stand her gooey appendages touching anything. Horn wore a self-satisfied smirk, looking at the effectiveness of all of her planning. Timmic was grumpy; he’d had to be rescued by Horn as well after the assassin he’d tousled with had trapped him. The game chimed, bringing up a new notification. They had thirty minutes to prepare for the next wave.

Chapter 21

"I can't believe how easy that was." Junip's excitement cut over everyone's side discussions.

"You level?" Pik asked.

Junip shook their head. "Unfortunately, no. I barely got credit for that first kill. The game doesn't seem to recognize hitting a node as worthy of experience."

It made sense to Pik. The Doctor's influence was technically outside the game. It was an invader and an add-on. Granted the "add-on" almost doubled a monster's strength. Horn's filter was an invaluable asset. It gave them a real advantage.

"Alright, let's get to planning. I don't want to be caught by surprise again. Everyone, make sure your filter is locked on. The auto reset settings need to be turned off. If you're having trouble with it, speak to Horn." Pik took the lead, setting a serious tone.

She gave them a second to adjust their headsets.

"I want to talk about the next wave. I think I know what it's going to be." Pik waited until everyone's eyes focused on her. She examined the crew. Junip was all rosy-cheeked. They had the least in-game experience fighting. They rarely got their hands dirty, and they seemed to be enjoying it. Timmic looked a little pale. It'd been a close call with the assassin. His armor was still in good shape. He'd been close—an assassin's blow to the head could have been a one-hit kill, and he knew it. He was shaken. Horn was covered in gore. She'd been most impressive pivoting her strategy in battle. None of the three had much experience in a real game, but Horn had gotten over the shock of the blood, guts, and pain the quickest.

"First, I just want to tell you all that I'm proud of you. Whatever happens next, you're doing myself and Trick proud." They all puffed up at Pik's compliment, and it was time to hit them with the bad news. "The next battle's going to be hard. This game has a pattern when dealing with waves. It is generally a large mass, then a stealth-based, and then a speed mob. I'm thinking wall racers with the level we're seeing here."

"What are those? I don't remember seeing any in the game walkthrough." Horn frowned. She'd closely studied their fights and footage.

"You probably didn't know what you were looking at, though. Trick and I ran into wall racers on that pit drop-down on the seventh level in the original playthrough." Pik was all business.

"Oh." Horn frowned.

"Yeah. That level we almost wiped, except for one of Trick's timed traps. We'd stepped into a bay, expecting a boss. Instead we were cut down by these robotic wall racers that sent rotating laser beams across the room. I was sliced in six places, removing two-thirds of my health in seconds. Trick was cut down completely, but he set a death trap beforehand. Two auto-triggered grenades went flying from his body. One killed a racer on impact, and the other racer was deeply wounded. I finished it off." Pik paced as she talked. She turned to them, cracking her knuckles nervously, waiting for questions.

"Well, we've got twenty minutes. Let's set up some traps." Horn was ready.

Pik nodded, approving of her team. All business.

Five minutes later, they collectively concluded they didn't have the skills Trick did to set even mildly sophisticated traps. Pik had done an inventory of the types of grenades and quantities the team had. There were several different damage types—frag, cryo, fire, void, and flash. All had the throw-and-explode triggers. She could set them off in two to five seconds after pulling the pin. Trick had constantly refined his trap skills with timed, triggered, and remote-detonation capabilities. The team wasn't going to be able to develop any of that capability within the next fifteen minutes. To make matters worse, the aliens with the Doctor's enhancements weren't likely to take much damage from an area of effect attack. They were going to have to remove the nodes first before any grenade would make a dent in their health.

"We could try to slow them down, use some of this goo on the walls?" Junip's idea was shot down almost immediately; these monsters were a higher level and likely would be unaffected any of the goo properties.

"How strong do you think their laser attack is?" This question, surprisingly, came from Brit.

"You have an idea? The lasers are not too strong by themselves, but they build up the damage rapidly when multiple are continually focused on you. Like an immediate drain," Pik explained as she returned to pacing. She walked back and forth, her head down.

"Okay, hear me out. If it's not a strong laser in one blast, it can probably be reflected." Brit pointed to the cafeteria tables littering the ground around them. They all sparkled with a metallic gloss. "If we can curve these and hold them out inside, then they can fire on us, and it'll reflect their beam back at them."

Pik considered the tables. It was a risk, but it could work. It was also possible—due to the Doctor's influence—that the lasers would cut through the tables and kill them all.

"I have points. I can spend them on a Trap skill," Timmic interjected.

The timer ticked down to ten minutes.

Pik nodded at Timmic. "Let's do it. Unless anyone's got a better idea . . . ?" None of them spoke up, so moments later, Pik was helping Timmic set up some rudimentary grenade traps on the wall. Brit, Horn, and Junip dragged tables to the center of the room. They'd decided Brit would be off door duty. The more racers that flew around the room, the more likely they'd get hit by their own reflected damage. The preparations were frantic, and Pik was feeling less confident about the plan. With four minutes left, however, they were out of alternatives.

They huddled together, cramped in a tight hole with six tables encircling them and two held up by Timmic and Horn above. Junip was going to try shooting out between the cracks. Junip had used some of their leveling points to buy a skill that would slow down enemies when scoped through a sniper rifle. Brit sat in the middle, protected the most, because she had the lowest health.

"Some beams will likely make it through the tables and still strike us. But if this reflects as we expect, they will only feel like bee stings. Just make sure you don't break apart our defense in surprise," Pik instructed. The last thing they needed was someone dropping their table because they took a minor hit.

As the timer ticked to one minute, Brit voiced the fear Pik had tried to avoid thinking about, "And what happens if it's not wall racers?"

Pik tried not to cringe as she answered, "If it's not wall racers, then fight. Fight as hard as you can."

The doors flew open as the timer hit zero. Pik peeked out through a gap in the tables, and she immediately wished she hadn't. A laser beam flew straight through, striking her in the eye. She gasped, ducking down in pain, only to have the same beam hit Brittany in the chest. What little remained of Brit’s health bar dropped by half. If Junip was weak, Brit was a hundred times weaker. She hadn't leveled once, completely unable to gain experience.

"Drop down!" Pik yanked Brit to the ground. It was the spot the least likely to have lasers bleed through their defense.

So far, the plan was working. A majority of the beams were getting reflected back out into the room, hitting the very wall racers emitting them. The Echoes sweated, taking minor hits as some of the beams found seams in their cover.

Pik could see the writing on the wall, though. They were going to have to do something. As far as she could see, two racers had entered the mess hall from each door.

They were deflecting damage from the metallic tables, but what they were getting hit with between the gaps in defense was decreasing their health faster than the droids. It would be a slow death, but death nonetheless. Pik unpinned a grenade.

"Hole!" Timmic moved one of the overhead tables, and Pik let it fly. She got struck by a laser and 6% of her health evaporated, leaving her with 88% overall.

Waiting for the grenade to detonate, Pik tried to keep her eyes open, searching for the telltale red trails on their bodies. The droids spun around the outside of the room too rapidly to get a read on. The lasers were red, too, which confused the situation further. *Everything* glowed red. Pik ducked back down.

"Cover!" Pik commanded the team. The turtle shell condensed further. A grenade blast, even in this large room, would no doubt impact their defense. Pik counted the heartbeats, and an explosion of white rocked the formation. They blew apart.

"Form up, form up. To me! To me!" Pik yelled, desperate to bring the team back into their defensive alignment. The tables facing the blast warped where they took the brunt of the damage, yet the team returned to their shell. Their position had shifted closer to the back wall.

Relatively safe in their huddle, Pik took inventory of the damage. Her ears rang alarmingly, eardrums obviously damaged. The Deaf debuff icon blinked in her HUD-assisted view. She activated a medkit; she'd been using them sparingly since they didn't have many, but hearing was a requirement right now.

The nearest droid roared past. Brit was holding a table now, the one closest to the wall. The force of the racer's attack on Brit's shiny table jerked her back an inch. Then the wall racer blew up. The group lurched. The explosion was less severe than the grenade. Brit looked stunned.

"What happened?" Horn asked, loudly. She was obviously having a hard time with her own hearing.

Brit's teeth gritted as she shoved her table back into place. "It took the full force of the reflection."

Two droids remained, and Pik could tell they were intelligent. Instead of spinning along the outside of the walls like their doomed counterparts, they crisscrossed on the far side of the room. More laser strikes snuck through the group's damaged shell.

Pik opened her mouth, but Brit beat her to it. "Alright, we've got to charge. Keep the tables pointed right at them. We can't let the racers get behind us."

Timmic looked at Pik. He whispered, but it was loud enough for everyone to hear, "Are we listening to her, boss?"

Pik glanced at Brit. Her knuckles were white as she held the table legs up. Her arms shook. "Of course we are. She's got the strategy down."

That was enough for them.

Pik took a breath. "Pivot on three."

They sat for a moment, mentally preparing themselves. A laser tagged Pik in the chest. The burning sensation lasted only a second, but she was hurting and tired. It was time to finish the fight.

"Three . . . PIVOT!" They broke apart, and the back of the formation split. Two sets of tables pivoted—one straight up and down and the other ready to push up or jump to either side.

"Charge!" The second half of the maneuver sent them sprinting toward the droids, trying to concentrate on the reflection. Brit's team nailed it. Horn pushed, and they made a concave mirror, forcing the continuous fire right back at the droid. It blew up almost immediately. Timmic and Junip, however, needed to be in sync. Timmic took three steps and tripped, falling face-first on the floor. Junip persisted forward, but their table waved around wildly, not centering in on the droid.

Pik had been the reserve. She dropped her heavy table, realizing she had to move much faster than she was. Using an aggro skill to draw fire, she then hit her Dash skill. Pik darted forward and was struck by a laser immediately. Pulling a “sticky” glove from her inventory, she slid across the floor, high-fiving a silver platter.

Skidding to the right of Junip’s droid, Pik brought the reflective surface up and in line with the laser burning a hole through her chest. The droid hit it full blast. For a second, Pik used all her strength to hold it in place, reflecting the damage back. As her hand gave in to the pressure, both Pik and the plate went flying. The superheated platter hit the ceiling as a molten chunk. Pik blew backward, losing half her remaining health. She was, thankfully, in much better shape than the slagged droid.

A timer popped up in the corner of their HUD, congratulating them on their victory by giving the team forty-five minutes before the next round.

"Let's give it five and regroup." Pik laid her back flat on the floor, surrounded by debris. Her health began to tick up now that they weren't in battle. Pik closed her eyes as the despair set in. They weren’t going to survive two more rounds.

Chapter 22

"Pik, you okay? It's been ten minutes." Pik opened her eyes to Junip's worried face. Had she passed out? It'd been a long time since she'd taken a simulated nap. Digitally, she'd turned off the need to sleep decades ago, but she was tired. Bone tired. She'd been on it since Trick pulled his dumb trick. She missed him. She missed his mentorship and his stupid plans. She wanted him to magic them out of the nightmare.

"We're screwed." Leave it to Timmic to say what Pik was thinking. He walked off, poking at some debris in the kitchen, trying to scavenge anything useful.

She sat up on an elbow, looking at Junip. It was like them to check in, always with that extra bit of care. "Hey Junip, I'm fine. Just tired."

Junip squeezed her shoulder. "At least it isn't that marathon of puzzles. What was it? Ultimate LOLO? I wasn't even loaded in with you, but if I had to hear that music again . . ." They left the threat unsaid.

Pik smiled. That had been a marathon, a disaster. Every time they lost their three lives in that demonic puzzle game, they had to start back at the beginning. She'd dreamed of the game whenever she was in a simulated nap for months afterward.

"I can hear it now." The G major notes floated in Pik's psyche for a second. "What's getting me about this game is that it isn't a game. If we lose, we're back in that torture chamber with the Doctor. If we lose, we've lost Trick and maybe our lives forever. Every decision I think about has that weight to it."

"That's a lot of weight to be carrying around." Sympathetic, Junip wrapped an arm around Pik in a hug.

Pik nodded, leaning into the embrace. She felt better

just admitting it. Nothing was going to change the outcome of the next round. They were doomed.

"What did you just say?" Horn butted into their conversation.

"If we lose, we're back in that torture chamber?"

"No, before that, uh . . . it's not a game. What did you mean by that?"

Pik took a big breath in and released it, trying to let her stress flow out. She caught the vanilla scent of Junip. "It's just, the game's stacked against us. The Doctor's influence makes it way too hard. I'd never set the difficulty to this level. I'd never put the stakes this high. The game isn't playing by its own rules."

Horn was deep in thought. "We just need to figure out how to break the rules on our side to even things up."

"We already are with the Brit strategy," chimed in Junip. "It just isn't enough."

"What's our next step if we survive these last couple of waves?" Horn queried.

Pik had that part all planned out. "Easy, we go through and wipe the Doctor's influence from the ship. We go back through the game, the early levels first, and remove his corruption. Every time we destroy one of the nodes, the game gets easier. If we could freely roam the ship, we could do it. I think that's one reason why he popped us back in here. He knew we wouldn't be able to survive the waves."

Horn began to pace as an idea formed. "You think he intentionally planted us here?"

"I'm positive."

Timmic rejoined their conversation. "What's the next round likely to be?"

Pik sighed. "The spider crawlies, then a boss for the last round. When I played this through the first time, they didn't pause between the two battles. So this is the grand finale."

Twenty-five minutes.

"What happens if we leave the chamber and don't stick around for the last two waves?" Horn's feet squished in the alien body parts as she continued to pace.

Shaking her head, Pik said, "We can't. The cafeteria doors only swing inward, and the corridor is full of creepy crawlies at that point."

"We can't?" Brit's voice cut in. The team looked over to her as she pushed the main door to the cafeteria open.

"Well, our little infiltrator is useful after all." Horn whistled her appreciation. Brit-the doorstop-Montgomery could only effectively interact with the environment. That's why their door-stopping strategy had worked, but she could also break the game.

"She's our wedge, our game breaker." Horn's voice was introspective. Her HUD was already up, and she was running through code.

Twenty minutes.

Pik stood up with Junip's help. "Let's get out of there before the spider creatures start spawning in the hallway." The group moved with that motivation, and Pik patted Brit on the back. "You did well."

Brit ducked her head in pleased embarrassment.

In the hallway, they could see a couple of nodes hovering in the air, waiting to attach to the mobs. Junip raised her rifle and took them out with a couple of shots. The hallway lost its menace. The lights glowed brighter. The timer in the corner of their HUD vanished. They were free of the countdown of doom.

"Where to first, Pik?" Timmic asked, his voice gruff. Neither of them had thought they were getting out of that room alive.

"First we drown some fish, assuming Brit is willing to get wet?"

“Do I want to know?”

Pik smirked. “Probably not.”

The group went down a few levels, passing several nests by climbing down a lift tube. The descent got notably colder.

Timmic started to complain, "These stupid water levels make no sense. A starship like this would never hold this much water, and it would never flood just one level like this. Plus, the stupid attack fish just suck."

Junip teased him, "A starship wouldn't hold water? Timmic, how would you even know? It’s not like starships are real. You're angry about fictional semantics, the logic of the imagination?"

"Ah, my dear Junip, but starships were real." Pik recognized Timmic’s “teaching” voice when she heard it. The man loved to lecture.

Junip rolled her eyes. “Not something like this.

"No, but we did send that ship to Alpha Centauri. Humanity had figured out interstellar travel by the time it uploaded itself. Who knows, perhaps we're passengers on that ship, and this is just how they stored our consciousness during transit."

"You wish. If we were interstellar passengers, we'd have the memory of that," Junip spoke confidently.

"Sure, maybe. I'll tell you what, though, if I wake up on an interstellar passenger ship, I'm not going to expect to be underwater, getting chased by a bunch of glowing piranhas.” Timmic grinned. The two Echoes loved to banter with each other.

Junip responded by sticking out her tongue.

"Here we are. If you two are done bickering about the legitimacy of what we're about to do . . . I want to go ahead and do it," said Pik, drawing them away from their daydream. The Metaverse as starship transit was one of the common conspiracy theories that floated around the Metaverse.

They clammed up while Pik spun an airlock door. It

was shaped like a submersible door, with a giant spin wheel that kept the door-locking mechanism in place. She felt the lock disengage and turned to warn them.

"It's going to be moist in here, and loud. Brit, since you can interact with the environment unexpectedly, the goal is to stop the angry waterfall from filling up the lower deck. There's a manual control mechanism beside the door above us, but it was frozen when Trick and I tried the first time through."

"And you're hoping I can close the hatch?"

"Yes, the supposition here is that the water tank for the ship was being used to douse a fire on this deck, but the overflow mechanism was triggered. There was originally a lab, not too different than the Doctor's setup, which is where the fish came from." Pik looked at Timmic, waiting for him to argue. She continued when he shut his mouth, "If we close the overflow mechanism, we can vent the water out an airlock, and we'll have this level completely clear of beasts. Junip can double-tap some nodes, and we'll have the level cleared."

"When we swam through, I thought that the labs looked familiar. I wonder if we can leverage them to study the Doctor. Give ourselves a moment to trigger a complete memory regression," Horn pondered.

"Sounds like a plan that doesn't suck," agreed Junip.

Timmic broke in, "You know something's going to go wrong. It's not just me that can spot this?"

Pik glanced at the pessimist. Unease welled up in her stomach. "Nevertheless, Timmic, we're going to proceed. Be on guard for the unexpected, folks. Timmic's normally right, even if we don't like to admit it." She used her commander voice, much more confident and flippant than she felt.

Pik looked at the door latch a touch longer than was necessary. Muscles tense, she leveraged it down, prepared to jump back in case a pressure differential was going to violently swing the door. She was ready to start swimming if the water levels had already filled up to the hatch. As if mocking her worst-case scenario prepping, the hatch swung open without any issue. The only immediate impact on the team was the sound. The distant roar of a waterfall filled their ears. Pik peeked in, on the lookout for trouble. Instead, she found a moist, clammy, calm environment. Water condensed on the bulkhead. It was a cold humidity.

The corridor was dark. Red emergency lights flickered ominously. Emergency lights were always red in every single game that Pik played. They gave a certain ambiance. The team dropped into formation. Pik led with Timmic close behind, followed by Brit, Junip, and trailing Horn—again, the most vulnerable in the middle.

"Node," Junip's voice snapped Pik into focus.

"Where? I don't see it."

Junip took their rifle off of their back, pressing the eyepiece against their face while bracing the rifle's butt against their shoulder. "The Doctor's getting sneaky. He's hiding them under other stuff."

They fired, and a corner panel blew apart in fragments. Pik could see now an angry glow of a node, red tentacles snaking out into the passageway. Junip fired again, interrupting the nightmare. The mesmerizing tendrils vaporized.

"Nice shots. How'd you spot it? I didn't see the node at all in my vision. Especially with all the red in here." Pik was worried she was losing her touch.

Junip swung their rifle around, returning it into position against their back. They didn't load much in games, but they impressed Pik, a true pro. "It's a different red. It leaks between the panels with no outside source. You're looking for the macro threats; I'm looking for the micro ones." Junip felt a pulse of pride through her connection to Horn—pride, and . . . attraction? She tried to shake away the link.

"The Doctor's boosts are not what I'd call micro," Horn said, patting Junip on the back. They might have blushed; Pik couldn't tell in the red light.

Pik focused on her job, the macro threats. Gun extended, she stalked the hallway, waiting for a bogeyman to jump out. The roaring of liquid evacuating into the water level kept getting louder. The temperature dropped a few more degrees. Each step was sodden. An odd smell mixed in with the water. It was out of place. It smelled mechanical.

"I see another node!" The group paused as Junip swung their rifle forward and aimed in one smooth motion.

"STOP!" This time Timmic's voice rebounded down the hallway. Junip took their finger off the trigger and pointed it at the ground.

Timmic stepped forward, sniffing. He looked like a hound on a mission, leading with his nose. "That's a fuel derivative we're smelling. It's mixed with the water, so it's not as strong."

Pik took another sniff. She could place it vaguely. It smelled fishy. She'd associated it with the fish in the water level. When they'd been underwater, they'd smelled nothing, so she'd just subconsciously filed it under unimportant. Timmic's face glowed momentarily. He was checking some data in his downloaded Home Command files.

"It's unsymmetrical dimethylhydrazine. They used it in rocket fuel in Brit's era."

Brit frowned. "That may be from my era. I mean, I don't know. It's not like I hung around rocket fuel. But this ship design certainly wasn't from my era."

"An uninspired insertion," Timmic commented.

"I think that's what she said." Junip grinned.

Pik didn't need their commentary. "So we've got jet fuel, who cares?"

Timmic looked up, using his inventory to swap out

his rifle for a dagger. "We probably shouldn't use guns or grenades. Nothing that's energy or gunpowder-based. That includes your Cosmic Sabre." Timmic read Pik's thoughts as she'd almost replaced her gun with the sword. "Normally, in these games, rocket fuel is explosive. Highly combustible."

Pik thought through her inventory options, which were limited on damage output. She went for a dagger and crowbar combo. "Are you sure it's not safe?"

Timmic shrugged. "It depends on how the video game designers interpret aerosolized jet fuel. I'd guess they made it smell so that we'd pick up on it being present. The only reason we'd need to know it was in the air is to adjust behavior. I told you there'd be a catch."

Horn took out a hammer and gave it some experimental swings. "How do you know us hitting something manually and throwing an errant spark won't trigger something?"

"I don't. But we've got to defend ourselves somehow."

"Where's the node?"Pik asked, all business.

The corridor extended before them, turning sharply right. Pik peered forward, her filter on, sensitivity turned up. She couldn't spot it.

Junip pointed a panel halfway to the bend. Pik moved forward with her crowbar. "Dang, I don't know how you spot these."

"I've just got an eagle eye." Junip winked.

Pik squinted at them for a second as Horn and Junip shared an inside joke. She returned to the panel. Up close, she could see the faint glow. She wedged her pry bar into the gap and leveraged the panel open before anyone could stop her. The plastic popped off, spark-free. The red virus infiltrating the game reached for Pik's hand, and before she pulled away, it gripped her.

Her vision went white with a wave of nausea.

Suddenly she wasn't in the hydrazine-infested hallway with her teammates. Instead she was in a dappled forest. One of Trick's simulations he used for meditation. She usually didn't disturb him while he meditated. She'd only seen this particular forest once. Digitally enhanced memory was a bitch sometimes.

"Trick, you in here?"

The memory replayed. She'd been innocently looking for her mentor. She wanted to go over the simulation results one more time. Trick didn't respond, so she followed the path. It meandered between giant basswoods with encroaching brush. Eventually it opened to a small clearing at the base of a spring feeding a small river. The spring cascaded majestically from a cliffside. Despite the beauty, Pik didn't want to repeat this memory.

"Trick? You there?" The words were Pik's even though she didn't want to say them.

Pik stepped onto a rock in the stream, leaning into the water to look for Trick. Her efforts were rewarded. He sat mid-river, tucked behind some boulders. In front of him was a seam into the Metaverse—a cascade of ones and zeroes making up the foundation of their reality. Every inhabitant of the Metaverse knew that to touch the Architecture was to forfeit one's life. One of the three ways to accomplish a final death. Trick sat surrounded by trees, the gorgeous spring, and the river, and death a handspan away.

"Trick, what's going on?" Pik had had nightmares about the expression on his face when he turned toward her. The hollowness in his eyes, the hopelessness. She didn't understand why, but she knew that he'd been contemplating reaching out when she'd walked up.

He'd closed the panel quickly, taken a second to adjust his appearance, and returned to the team habitat with her. That was the day she took up meditation.

This time, when he turned, his eyes weren't hollow.

They were filled with angry flares of red.

"He sees you. I see you," Trick's puppet mask hissed low and threateningly.

Pik blinked. She was back in the corridor, cold, wet, and lying on the floor, Brit under her.

"What happened?" She looked up. The node was splattered all over the wall.

"Brit pried you away from that thing, and I ended it." Junip slapped the hammer against a hand as though they'd been swinging hammers their whole life.

Timmic added dryly, "And thankfully, sparks don't seem enough in this virtual simulation, or we'd have been blown to bits."

"I would have saved you too, Timmic, if you had been stuck in the node. No reason to be jealous." Junip grinned at them both.

Pik couldn't help but return the smile. She hadn't expected Junip to be the rash one, but, like Horn, they were highly protective of all the crew members.

"Let's go." Pik took Horn's hand, standing up. She tried to sound more ready than she felt. Pik wasn't sure any of them bought it. There was a tremble in her voice, the shake in her hand as she held her pry bar, the small puddle of puke she expelled once she got to her feet.

"We don't have to rush. We could take a moment," Junip said, concerned.

"Not with the hydrazine. That nauseous feeling we've all got will only get worse." Timmic had created his own pile of digital regurgitation.

"I'm good. Let's go," Pik repeated. She took a few steps forward. "Junip, why don't you come to the front? You can spot the nodes better."

Junip acquiesced, hammer in hand. They proceeded down the corridor. Two turns later, the group could see the chamber at the end of the tunnel. The roaring was overwhelmingly loud, so they resorted to hand signals.

The team crept forward, bodies tense, waiting to see if their goal was attainable. Pik was granted the first look into the chamber. The room was a three-story engineering bay. On the third balcony stood massive windows into the ship's water supply tanks. Water was spilling in a torrent from an open hatch.

It was a stupid design. No one needed a hatch into a water tank for the express reason they were all witnessing. The water flowed down three stories, hitting the lower deck with a crash. The pressure from the water seemed to have deformed the hallway. The water ran straight down the curve of the corridor, creating a river before it dumped down the deck into an access tube leading to one of the lower decks.

The stench of fuel was heavy, and Pik's stomach roiled. "First thing, we need to fix the fuel leak, then worry about the water." Her eyes burned as she looked around.

"According to schematics, it should be down there." Timmic pointed to the waterfall's base. Pik had initially assumed the pool that had formed was due to pressure from the torrent of water, but she was beginning to get the whole picture. The pool was a sink down into the engine. The fuel injectors lived down there. The engines were flooded.

"Now what?"

"Give me a moment. I'm examining the schematics." Timmic was thorough, but he wasn't fast.

Pik studied the room, looking for nodes. "See anything, Junip?"

"Not really, which is weird, right? This is where the Doctor should have concentrated his power." They combed the walls, looking in every crevice to find nothing worthwhile.

"Pik, I think you need to see this." Horn was looking down into the pool. Pik hadn't noticed it before, but a deep red glow came from the depths. She'd assumed it was an emergency light.

"What is it?"

Before Horn could answer her question, the question answered itself. With a splash of water, a creature came jumping out. A beast, a deadly mermaid of the sea, floated on a geyser of up-churned water. Its malevolent red eyes glared straight at Pik.

"You are mine," came an undulating, deep voice. Pik couldn't look away. She watched as the creature's hand lunged forward, wrapping around her throat. It lifted her feet off of the ground, choking off air. Pik's eyes were glued to its face, even as her windpipe closed. The scales along its hands dug into her skin. Pik's vision tunneled down to the malevolent eyes. Her hands flailed; she couldn't think. The rest of her team was shouting, but every word was unintelligible.

Pik started hallucinating, her consciousness swept up in its eyes. Her brain was shutting down. The only bit of consciousness holding on was her link to Horn and Brit. She imagined the creature burrowing into her soul. Becoming a puppet like Trick.

She let go of consciousness as her world ended.

Chapter 23

Pik rushed back to her body in a snap. Whatever influence the Doctor had over her mind evaporated in a cataclysmic explosion.

Pik wished she'd blacked out. Usually Echoes had straightforward control over things like pain and consciousness. There'd been a historical period where torture was a critical element to a subset of games, and no one would be an Echo if they had to endure it. The last-ditch option to avoid that pain would be for an Echo to exit the instance. Just dematerialize and end up back at Home Command. Pik had none of these options. When they had all loaded, they committed, and their pain controls had been removed.

This is why unconsciousness would have been far better than her current state.

Her lips cracked and her voice harsh, she said, "Medkit? Does anyone have one?" Pik was having trouble thinking. Did she still have a medkit in her inventory? She tried to bring one out but couldn't feel her hands. Did something appear? She tried to sit up but couldn't move.

"Help!" Pik's voice was barely above a whisper. Her health was at 5% and dropping due to several debuffs. She had Deaf, Bleeding, Tunnel Vision, and Broken—she hadn't seen that one in this game before. Pik couldn't move her neck. She couldn't move anything.

You have earned a skill: Death Below, Death Above

Surviving a loss of 95% health has granted you the skill Death Below, Death Above. This skill will trigger only in future situations in which you lose 80%

or more health in one hit resulting in death. In such a situation, your health will reset to 5%.

While the skill was undoubtedly useful, Pik wished it would do something for her now. Her health indicator was ticking down rapidly. If she didn't survive this moment, having the skill wasn't going to do anything.

A form appeared in front of her: Junip. Pik would have smiled, but her lips refused. Junip was saying something, unintelligible words mouthed in a rush.

Pik screamed in her head as Junip injected her with a health kit and began performing the First Aid skills. She went from broken numbness with a throbbing body pain to nerves on fire as her body slowly started knitting itself back together. The Deaf debuff was the first one removed.

"Can you hear me now, Pik?"

Pik managed to gasp out, "Yes." She had to grit her teeth to not cry out.

"Good, I hate to tell you this, but you already know. This is going to hurt. You were as close to death as I've ever seen a player. Timmic took the blast for the rest of the team, but you were right in the middle of it all."

Pik closed her eyes. Pain radiated down her limbs. She guessed she should be grateful she even still had them all.

"Keep going." Pik closed her eyes in resolve, knowing she didn't have a choice. She had to heal. The faster Junip took care of it, the quicker it would be over. A tiny part of her brain wondered how Timmic was doing. A medkit could only be used every five to ten minutes, having progressively longer wait times the more you tried to use it in a row. The First Aid was used independently of medkits and could be continuously applied, so Junip continued. Oddly, the medic craft was similar across games. Junip's training as the team medic crossed over into different game environments.

Pik counted heartbeats. Each one fired her nervous system, bringing wave after wave of pain. She focused on controlling her breathing. Keeping calm was critical. Flailing about as Junip put salve on her burns or straightened out broken body parts would only make it worse. Her health had ticked up to 15% with the initial application of the medkit. As she began to bleed from the damage, her health bar ticked down again. The debuffs continued.

She gritted her teeth as bones crunched. Junip pulled her leg straight. She felt relief as another medkit was applied and a couple more debuffs fell off. Her regeneration wasn't quite keeping up with the decreasing health, but it was becoming increasingly likely that she'd survive.

Pik couldn't make herself talk. If she opened her mouth, she was afraid she'd just whimper. It was too much.

Junip sensed the need for a distraction. "It was such a dumb idea to trigger the explosion, but it worked. You are still alive. Barely, but alive. The monster is dead. It, being a sea-based creature, had an intolerance to fire and explosive damage. At least that's what Horn said. Timmic," Junip paused, gathering themself, "Timmic didn't make it. Horn's using one of our resurrects on him now. I'm honestly glad he didn't survive after looking at you. I just hope the resurrect works."

Pik heard the worry in their voice. They only had two of the resurrection keys. A third one was available on the final floor before the boss, but it was tricky to locate. On her run-through with Trick, she'd died getting it.

"I've never seen Horn so steely-eyed than when she took the shot," Junip said. "She didn't ask anyone; she just went for it. It was pretty obvious that the monster was going to kill you. I couldn't have made that call. Not in that instant. Not with the possible consequences. It could have blown the ship up. For a moment, I thought we had all been eliminated. For a second, I knew it was true. Those red eyes just got in me."

Pik's pain levels were improving. The more Junip talked, the less she thought. The medic's androgynous, even voice continued, "I don't know why it affected me that way. I was just watching it kill you and did nothing."

Pik winced but answered the mystery for her friend, "I think it had a Doom debuff."

Junip nodded. They didn't look at Pik's face. She must look pretty bad. "That makes sense. Being in games is a lot different than watching from the Command Center. I always used to feel angry at myself for being unable to load out more often. After today, I think I'm just grateful."

"Do I look that bad?"

"Am I that obvious? You'll be fine once we get you healed up. Right now, the lack of ears is throwing me off." Junip was embarrassed, but Pik understood. In the Metaverse, one didn't have to cope with the damage warfare did to bodies.

"I must look like I've been through a meat grinder." She winced at the thought. No ears. Pik took a moment to be grateful she hadn't lost her eyes.

"Yeah, well, today isn't your best day. Thankfully, nothing's permanent. Thank goodness for magical in-game healing and that you have a firm self-visualization."

"You've got to if you're in this game too long." Even in the Metaverse, people's mental image of themselves influenced their appearance. Pik didn't want to see herself right now. She didn't want to get that image stuck in her head.

"I never thought of it that way," Junip confided. "I thought those warnings we went through in training were fake. I mean, we have to self-actualize in the Metaverse too. It's just a lot easier. I feel like I'm being constantly pressured to conform to the game's parameters. Even with this First Aid skill, I'm using it and leveraging my digital knitting knowledge, and the game keeps resisting.

With another injection, the pain spiked for a moment. Pik waited to respond, trying to chase the tail of her breath. "Damn, that one hurt. Yes, that's the trick of loading as an Echo that you, Timmic, and Horn must master. You have to allow your mind to be moldable enough to load, but then you've got to hold strong once you're here. Constantly negotiating when to push the boundaries and when to acquiesce. To be honest, Junip," Pik swallowed, her throat as dry as sandpaper. "I just want to turn into the puddle of goo my stats say I should be." Everything hurt too much.

Junip set another bone, and Pik groaned.

"Junip, you done over there? We need your help with Timmic," Horn's pained voice cut through the haze. Pik tried to keep her agony from the link, but bleed-through had to be permeating.

Pik opened her eyes. Her vision was a lot clearer. Junip waited, leaving the decision to Pik. She was still in a lot of pain, and her health was still ticking down, but she could move. She felt a knot of panic from Brit.

"Go." Her own voice came out as a rasp. Pik had never uttered a word so selfless. She concentrated on her breathing and even tried to give Junip a small smile.

Junip squeezed her arm. "I'll be right back." It was a lie. They both knew it. A botched resurrection was going to take some time to unwind. Lying was part of the medical profession.

"Save him. I'll be fine." Lying was also something a team leader needed to do once in a while.

Junip was gone. Pik started to sit up, cringing as some of her skin stuck to a grate. Gradually she propped herself up. She took a full account. Health sat at 25%, the total ticking down very slowly. She had a Broken debuff still. She commanded the additional info box to appear and was rewarded with the criteria to remove the condition.

Broken - Debuff granted when a player has multiple crushed or broken bones. This condition can be removed by fixing the player's body by setting bones, using concentrated healing over time, and using First Aid and Self-Mend skills.

That was it. No hidden text, no out. It's just plain healing. She looked at her skill tree, having little choice. All Echoes knew the rule: always hold back a choice in case you need it for that next boss, for that next moment, for that level you can't squeak through with your skills, inventory, or load. Pik had done it, such an old habit. She looked at her list, Dual Hand, Explosives, Assassin's Strike, so many good options. Instead she chose Self-Mend. She couldn't even pick First Aid, as the skill wasn't usable on herself.

The glow of a level-up surrounded her. The effect was immediate. Her health stopped decreasing and inched upward. It gave regeneration immediately, and with concentrated effort, she could heal specific types of damage, make herself resistant, and get more out of medkits. This skill was leveled by being damaged. The only saving grace of the whole experience was that she *was* significantly damaged. She was going to level the crap out of it.

Ten minutes later, Pik had healed enough to move her arms. They had both been snapped, she assumed, when she hit the wall after the explosion. With arms, she could apply the two last medkits in her inventory. Pik debated doing the intelligent thing, just letting her regeneration tick up. She lay there a minute or two but couldn't resist. She knew when to push and when to let go. This was a let-go moment.

Taking a medkit, she activated it. With the skill used, the kit glowed a deep, warm yellow hue and enveloped her. Relief flooded Pik's body for the first time since the nerves healed. Her legs straightened, her back healed, and her brain became less fuzzy. She looked at her subskills. She'd gotten two levels in regeneration and base levels in explosive resistance, fire resistance, Greater Medkit use, and bone knitting.

Self-Mend was much better than Pik expected. That was the problem with being an Echo. They had no walk-through like the public. Echoes had to figure out each game from scratch.

This skill, superficially, needed more utility. In practice, it could turn her into a tank with more concentrated leveling. She groaned as she stood up. It still felt like she'd been hit by a truck. She wasn't sure she wanted to ascribe to the concentrated leveling program to level up. Although theoretically, each time she took damage, it would improve her self-healing ability. Now that the skill tree was visible, Pik could see that the ultimate power unlocked was a Phoenix ability. Self-resurrection. Not bad at all.

Pik could barely stand, so she held the side of the hallway and staggered down to the group. She could feel her ears knitting into existence. The health regeneration was intense.

"Hey, how's Timmic doing?" They were all huddled around him. Junip gave Pik a sharp glance, astonished that she could walk.

"We have a failed resurrection." Brit's voice was dull.

"I want to use the last rez key." Junip sounded angry.

"We need to save it for later, for when we get to the boss." Horn was just as angry.

"And leave Timmic here dead?"

"You know he's not dead." The two went back and forth.

Brit chimed in dully, "He's with the Doctor. He probably wishes he were dead."

Junip and Horn faced off. Junip wanted to use the key. Horn just shook her head.

"Junip, I know you want to do everything you can, but you know the chances of success go down every time you try to resurrect the same corpse. If it didn't work the first time, it probably isn't going to work the second." Horn said it coolly, ever logical.

Horn's reasoning was sound. It probably wouldn't work. They needed healing and resurrection capabilities for the later levels. Junip was right too. Leaving Timmic in the hands of the Doctor was a fate worse than death. This moment was tearing Junip and Horn apart. Neither seemed to be able to see the other's point of view.

Pik would have to be the deciding vote. She just didn't know what the right decision was. The choice was taken from them when Brit grabbed the key and slammed it into Timmic's chest. "I'm activating it right now unless someone has the skill to increase our odds. Get out of the way."

Pik thought fast. "Wait, I've got an idea. Brit, I'm going to need you to remove the key. I need to use Horn's programming skills to edit some of Timmic's abilities before you apply the resurrection." She brought Horn close. "Look, I need you to break into his skill tree and have him use his reserve slot for Self-Mend. It's got a natural bonus to resurrection. That should increase our probability dramatically."

"I don't trust Horn to do what's right." Brit was on edge, her voice shaky. "She nearly killed us all. She almost killed me." Pik could tell she wasn't telling the whole truth. She was just scared.

Pik put her scarred arms out to show she was unarmed. Her regeneration bumped her to 75%, and it was still climbing. With a placating voice, she tried to talk Brit down. "Look, we're all trying to do what's best. I firmly believe this Self-Mend skill is the only thing that will bring Timmic back to us. We won't let any of us, including you, sit with the Doctor a moment longer than necessary. Let Horn do what she does best, even the odds for us. Then you can return to being mad. She's the only reason I'm here."

Brit didn't activate the key. She looked, eyes wild, between Horn and Pik.

"I'll follow Pik's orders. There's no use wasting the key," Horn said dejectedly. Pik knew Brit could feel it in their link that Horn had given up.

The resurrection key came off of Timmic's chest. Horn stepped forward, her HUD lighting up her face. She worked, lost in the code, evident by the wary expression Brit was giving her and Junip's step back as she got close. This was why Pik and Trick highly discouraged relationships on the team. It was stressful enough just being Echoes. Putting emotion into what should be logical choices could make the job impossible. The last thing Pik needed was some sort of flare-up between them.

"Found the unlock. It's a lot easier when you're dead. I've turned it on. Not sure the implications will hit before the resurrection logic." Horn's voice was monotone despite her success.

Pik put a hand on Horn's shoulder. "Any increase in chance is welcome. I'm just surprised he'd listened to Trick's training and had a reserve skill. You did good." Pik gave the shoulder a squeeze.

"He has three. I think he got full credit for killing that demon mermaid who had you by the throat. He was fairly low-level compared to the rest of us since he rarely makes the kill shot."

Junip reengaged with the conversation. "Make him pick First Aid, too, if he's got the points. It also has a minor bonus to heals used on a person." Junip's tone was consolatory. They already felt bad for overriding Horn so harshly. Pik admired Junip's resolve to stand by their morals. She gave the red-haired medic a slight smile of thanks.

Pik needed to learn about the perks of First Aid. It may have been a waste of a skill choice. They already had a medic, and Pik wasn't going to need much external healing, but at this point, she'd take any incremental possibility that they could get Timmic back. They would be in trouble if they didn't have their primary tank.

"Done."

"Okay, Brit, can you hand the resurrection key to Junip? They get a bonus for success for having First Aid. Also, with your game status, I'm not sure it would even work for you. We need to keep our heads, folks." Pik took a moment and looked at the team. Letting it sink in how much their rash decisions almost cost the team. "Thank you for saving my life, but we've got to think through our actions. Especially now without any resurrection keys. That move saved me but may have cost us Timmic and several skill-ups. Brit, you could have just wasted a rez completely. The Doctor wants us off balance. That's his whole game plan. He's the master of the psychological trick. We've got to be better than that. See a step or two ahead and plan for it."

Brit had the presence of mind to look ashamed. Horn did too. Junip nodded. Pik had them back on track, back on the same team.

"Alright, let's do this. Junip, you're up."

Sweat beaded on Junip's forehead. It wasn't easy to use the First Aid skill to influence a resurrection's success. They had to micromanage the knitting together of Timmic's body, prioritizing the healing that would create a body capable of being alive. Considering the depth of his injuries, this wasn't going to be easy. He'd taken just as much damage as Pik, perhaps less crushed and broken bones, but he had a couple of metal shards almost straight through his body.

Junip examined Timmic, pulling out the worst of the shrapnel. Pik was shocked to see that one of the things sticking out of her friend was her own knife. It must have flown out of her hand while the mermaid was choking her.

Junip took their time as a professional. They took out a medkit and opened it up. Part of their First Aid skillset allowed them to use specific elements of an actual medical kit to target specific healing. They found some needles and thread and began stitching up the worst injuries.

"Yes, he's a corpse, but the player comes alive instantly during the resurrection, and the game assesses the body's viability. It's likely the first resurrection failed because his body was too chewed up. This stitching doesn't do a thing for his life now, but hopefully, during that appraisal, it'll tip the scales in our favor." Junip continued to narrate as they cleaned the wounds, applied preemptive salve to the burns, and made two tourniquets, one for his arm and another for the leg. They were the essence of a medic.

"Okay, he's as ready as he's ever going to be. If we wait too long, we'll get penalized for the body being too old. Brit, hand it over."

Brit handed over the metallic resurrection key, its bronze casing glowing with life. This was it. Pik held her breath. Junip reverently placed the key on Timmic's chest and activated the resurrection cycle. A warm glow permeated the space, and Timmic's body rose off the floor. Junip reached out and touched his chest. They closed their eyes, obviously able to see a view of Timmic's body that the rest couldn't. Pik just waited.

A minute passed. Two. Horn looked at Pik, asking with her eyes how long it would take. Pik shrugged. It would take however long it took. After ten minutes, the moment's wonder had passed, and Brit, Horn, and Pik sat down. They didn't talk, not wanting to break Junip's concentration, but neither were they going to stare at the two unmoving pair.

Pik started taking inventory of what she had left. The hydrazine smell had returned. The explosion hadn't rid them of the leak, so she was limited on what would be available if she didn't want a repeat disaster performance. They needed a way to deal with the nodes without an explosive round or an energy weapon.

She had almost an unlimited supply of the combat daggers. She looked around at the torn-up corridor for inspiration. The explosion had ripped through the structure of the ship. The insides of the walls were exposed, displaying wires, bulkheads, and pipes. Pik looked at a section of piping. The whole place would have blown if this had occurred on a real ship. In video game land, the coders had only made the environment able to take moderate damage. Something to keep the realism, but nothing significant. No gaping holes into the next floor or the vacuum of space. But exposed wires and pipes, sure.

Pik wandered over and ripped out some long wire. Thankfully it wasn't carrying a current. She then found a section where a bundle of pipes had been sheared at one end. Carefully she bent them out and, before the hydrazine could build up to dangerous levels again, took a torch and started cutting through the base of the pipes. The work was quick, which was fortunate as Horn looked like she would kill Pik when she'd brought out the torch.

With the five pipes, Pik began arts and crafts time for warriors. Using the wiring as twine, she wrapped her standard-issue dagger at the end of the pipe, giving her an effective spear. The first was moderately impaired, but the third was solid. After getting the knack, she rewrapped the first two spears, making them tighter and less likely to break off in a fight. She handed one to Brit and Horn. It wasn't a perfect solution, but it would give them a good two to three feet of poking so they wouldn't have to get too close to a node or an enemy.

Thirty minutes had passed at this point. Junip was pale and sweaty. Their eyes were closed in concentration, the dull glow of their HUD display still lighting up their face. Pik just sat on the floor, anxiety spent, and watched Junip. She studied the medic's face, realizing she hadn't looked at Junip in a long time. The medic looked worn out. Their short, auburn hair was ragged and greasy. They hunched, scrapes and scars running up their arms. Their uniform was an old marine-issued green vest with a long-sleeved undershirt that they'd ripped the sleeves off to make tourniquets. Junip usually had an ephemeral quality. They floated above the crisis of the rest of the team. The medic was too precise in their appearance to be considered masculine. Their eyebrows were perfectly manicured and clean. Somedays they'd come in with a programmed beard, but lately, they'd been entirely baby-faced. What disturbed Pik now, was the dirt smudges across their face, the scratches up their arms, and the disheveled state of their hair. Pik had never used the word unkempt to describe her friend, but Junip looked like they'd been to hell and back. They needed to rest.

"That's all I could do. Now we have to wait for the calculation to decide if it's enough," Junip said, stepping back from Timmic's body. Their voice was as exhausted as they looked. Timmic's body floated in the air, still lifeless.

"Calculation? What do you mean?" Horn hadn't paid much attention to the minutia of the gameplay.

Brit answered her query as Junip sagged against the wall. "The game takes a moment to calculate all the factors. If we hit the five-minute mark, chances are it failed."

"Why would a failure take longer?"

Pik knew the answer to this question. "Because the game environment is hoping the party will get attacked within the time, disrupting the resurrection naturally." Pik stood up, handing Junip their spear. "So if the Doctor's paying attention, now is the time he'd likely attack us?"

The whole party went on guard immediately. They weren't in the most defensible position, but the corridor only had two options for an attacker coming at them. They split into two, Pik and Brit going up the hallway toward the source of the water overflow and Horn and Junip facing down the corridor from where they came.

The splashing was loud, so loud that they had to nearly shout at each other as Brit and Pik stood near the bay entrance.

"I hope he survives," Brit shouted.

"Me too."

"What do you want me to do about that?" Brit waved her spear toward the sight of water from the hydration tanks spilling onto the floor.

Pik shrugged. She was out of ideas. Timmic and the hydrazine had sapped her resolve. She also wasn't entirely sure her brain wasn't wholly fried from her own near-death experience. She scanned the water, searching for any telltale red edges that would suggest the Doctor's incursion.

"Do you think we can beat him?" Pik couldn't resist asking. The Doctor was Brit's arch-nemesis. The woman had spent hundreds of years ineffectively fighting the man. It seemed like an impossible task.

It was Brit's turn to shrug. "I don't know, but we've got to try. The alternative isn't really an option."

Pik didn't expect anything else from her, stoic as she was.

A cold, clammy hand reached out, touching Pik on the shoulder. She yelped, jumping several feet into the air.

Timmic stood behind her, ashen face smiling. The whole crew had snuck up behind them, footsteps covered by the rushing water.

"Miss me?" came his gruff voice, thick with emotion. Pik teared up as she brought him into a hug.

"Absolutely. I’m so glad you're back in the land of the living."

Brit stood aside, looking him up and down. Pik put two and two together, realizing she was scanning him, looking for signs of the Doctor.

"All clear," came her affirmation, and she stepped forward and hugged him too. "Thank you for saving us all. That took bravery." The admission seemed heartfelt.

Timmic blushed with the compliment. "Nothing to thank me for. I was only doing my job."

Chapter 24

At Pik's insistence, the group backed off from their next goal and took a break. Creatures hadn't attacked, and the hallway was clear. It was time for a break. The team was in good spirits with a mostly healed Timmic back in their midst. The usually grumpy man was even in a good mood, cracking jokes and poking at Horn. He needled the programmer for letting him take all the credit for saving the crew. Pik smiled as she watched them. She'd opted to sit a bit apart. Told them she wanted to take a nap. She sat, her back against a metal bulkhead, closed her eyes, and listened to their banter. It warmed her soul.

Nothing made Pik happier than having her team, her family, back together. They were just missing one last person. She allowed her thoughts to drift to Trick. She imagined him, the curly hair swept back out of his face. The twinkle in his eyes as his whole face lit up with a new idea. The wide shit-eating grin he'd give her when he'd pulled off another one of his stupidly risky plans. His nod of approval when she managed to accomplish a feat in a game. For a second she felt the warmth of his praise. She missed her mentor. She kept the team together by a thread, but every step in this forsaken place seemed like a misstep. The Doctor had the upper hand at every turn, they were trapped.

Pik's vision of Trick took shape. She imagined him giving her an encouraging smile. She lived for those moments when he had the answer, but he stepped aside so she could try her plan. Her attempts didn't always pan out, but he'd be there to catch her. This time, though, there was no safety net. No one was going to save the team but themselves. The thought was terrifying.

It was a challenge he'd been preparing her for. To

fly solo. Resolve built, she would fight and scrape to get them over the finish line. They would find Trick and escape. The other prisoners would flee with them. The Doctor's reign of terror would end. Pik leaned into the optimism.

Pik opened her eyes. There was always a trick to sidestep a trap, and this whole game was one giant trap, courtesy of the Doctor. There was always a trick, a cheat, a . . . the thought trailed off.

"Hey, you guys, do you know where that hydrazine comes from? Is that something we can locate?" Pik's mind began focusing on the threads.

"Sure, boss. But I hope you're not thinking of using it. I'd prefer not to get barbecued twice in one run," Timmic said with humor.

Pik smiled. The Doctor wanted them too afraid to find a way out. The fact that he'd invested so much energy into the mermaid meant he was worried about this spot in the game. Pik's mind raced. It meant that something here in Infestation could hurt him. The environment, perhaps?

"I'm starting to have a plan." Pik glanced at Timmic and his singed beard. "And unfortunately, yes, it does involve explosions."

"I was afraid of that," murmured Junip, almost too low to hear. "She's got that look. That one that Trick gets when he has a terrible idea."

Pik's grin doubled in size.

The first phase of the plan was simple but the most controversial. They had to link the rest of the team into their net. So far, the triad had held successfully, but the entire team needed Brit's resistance to the Doctor's environment. The problem was convincing the rest of the team to do it. The taboo nature of linking with other consciousnesses in the Metaverse wasn't easy to overcome.

"Absolutely not, I don't want"—Junip paused, self-editing—"everyone knowing what I'm thinking."

Pik had expected a fight from Timmic. He was an exceedingly private man. Junip, though, surprised her.

"Junip, it's not that bad. It's not like how they talk about the links back home. This is lighter. I can vaguely feel Brit and Horn, but it's not like I can read their minds. I am just aware of their general emotional state. Right, Horn? And we need this. We need to level the playing ground with the Doctor as a team."

Pik could tell Horn was uneasy, but Pik wasn't lying. "Yes, so far that's true. I have a general feeling of them both. Pik was obviously able to leverage the link to use Brit's unique status in the Doctor's lab. You have to admit, her being able to pull from her inventory was a game changer."

This was the key Pik needed the entire team to be able to leverage. They all needed that separateness from the environment that Brit had. It gave them power in the Doctor's home. They'd be stronger together.

"There is a cost. You just haven't paid it yet. As a medic, I've taken the training. The mental entanglement. Folks don't just die. They don't end. They turn into nightmares." Junip's face was serious.

"I'll do it." Timmic's calm statement surprised everyone. Junip's betrayed expression demanded an explanation. "I died. If you hadn't resurrected me. I was there in the lab. Just for a few minutes, but I was helpless again."

Brit chimed in, "Any cost is worth it." Her voice carried the weight of centuries of torture.

Pik wanted to pressure Junip more. The plan wouldn't work if they weren't all committed. Pik knew when to hold back, though. Junip's red hair wasn't just stylish, but a warning of how suborn they could be. Pik watched Junip look into the eyes of their friends.

"I made the link as light as possible. It'll be easier, honestly, with two more in it. The load is shared, no one has priority, and no one is subservient," Horn explained.

"Can you add in a failsafe? A way to personally exit the link if needed?"

Pik watched as Junip's mind slowly changed. Their trust in Horn overriding the taboo of the Metaverse. The solidity of Brit's insistence that the Doctor's fate was worse. The inkling of doubt from not witnessing a link gone wrong before. None of them had actually seen or known a person succumb to a bad link. It was the monster under the bed that young Metaverse citizens were warned of but no one witnessed.

"Yes. I didn't originally. The programming was a bit on the fly. But if we've got time now . . . ?"

"Of course." If this is what it took to get Junip on board, Pik was willing to spend the time.

"Then yes, I can work on it."

Junip nodded solemnly. They were in agreement. Pik was on her way to getting her team agency in the Doctor's very lair. It seemed an eventuality that they'd have to confront him in the heart of his web. The helplessness of that environment had bothered her. No inventory, skills, or abilities. No control. She felt Brit's resolve and Horn's confidence, and they felt her relief. The team was going to face the future as a unit, a more capable, fully armed team.

Horn might have been a terrible game player, but she was a magnificent programmer. She worked out the new link parameters quicker than anyone expected. Before Pik knew it, she had two more bundles of emotions in the back of her head. An eject button had also been added to her HUD to cancel their link. She could tell Junip wasn't happy, but their unease slowly disappeared as they experienced what it was to be linked.

The triad had turned into a pentad. Timmic had provided the word. Echo teams were always groups of five. It was considered a lucky number, a strong number. Pik drew from the strength of their connected minds. She felt like the team was whole.

The next part of the plan involved acquiring as much explosive matter as possible. Pik intended to follow one of Trick's axioms: explosives, in sufficient quantity, can solve any in-game problem.

The team pivoted. Instead of clearing the whole ship of the Doctor's influence, they were going for the end game. The nodes were a trap. The Doctor could influence where they were and lay ambushes. The mermaid incident proved it. They needed to change the rules of the game.

Pik had spent most of her Echo career following Trick around, trying to learn the rules of engagement. What the answer was for any scenario. She was the perfect warrior. The lesson she'd never appreciated until now was that rules were meant to be broken. Exploits were meant to be used. If the game was unfair, *she* had to change the game.

Trick would have laughed. He'd been too kind a teacher. It'd taken Timmic's near-death experience and her personally getting crushed for the lesson to sink in.

Chapter 25

"I'm not sure I can go in there," Brit's voice shook. The team stood at the ominous glow of the red bay doors to the final boss, Iraxinus. The monster who had turned Brit into a tormented, walking zombie. The original fight that had set off the chain of events that led them here. Weary, bedraggled, Pik's crew didn't look great, but they were here.

"You just have to walk in. We'll do the rest." Pik tried to reassure her.

"It's not that, it's . . . this is it. This is the end game. I either save my daughter, or I don't. I either survive, or I won't. The Doctor wins, or he doesn't." The finality of Brit's statements hung in the air.

"Isn't that what you've worked toward for your whole in-game existence?" Pik didn't understand. She craved the fight. The end.

Brit didn't say anything for a moment. Her lips pulled together, tight. Tension creased in every line of her face. Pik practiced patience. The woman was worth listening to, so she waited.

"I've been working toward freedom for hundreds of years, but I never went all in. With every step I took, there was always some hope left. I never tried something this dramatic, this final. In the end, I gave up. Death by a thousand cuts. We're about to risk death by"—Brit looked at Pik—"getting blown up. It's so final."

They all felt Brit's anxiety in the back of their heads. The fear that she'd lose her daughter for good. It pressed on them all, urged them to do something less rash. The concern ran away from them all. Pik's muscles clenched.

Timmic slapped Brit on the back, breaking the spell.

"And that's why none of it worked. You've spent hundreds of years trying to slice him down. This problem requires something different." Pik's muscles eased as Brit calmed. The woman wasn't exactly happy, but Timmic's words and resolve had eased the panic.

“Everyone, let's do a final equipment check.” Pik grabbed Brit's elbow, pulling her away from the group as they performed a standard pre-action check. She whispered, “Brit, you've been living in limbo for a long time. Trapped. Even if we lose, won't it be nice to get some closure? You've tried your best. Your daughter knows. It's time to end it.”

"You think so?" Fear and trust battled inside Brit's mind. Brit's high cheekbones were smudged with dirt, her clothes were riddled with tears, and she was bleeding from a couple of shrapnel cuts. Bags under her eyes framed worry furrows on her face. Brit needed closure more than any of them.

Pik acted on an instinct she didn't know she had. Awkwardly, she wrapped the woman in a hug. "I know so. It's going to be okay. One way or another we're going to finish it." Pik was shocked when Brit leaned in. The woman let out a gasp of breath and let go. Ugly sobs escaped, gasping and cathartic.

Pik held on, waiting for the Brit to finish. Pik wasn't much of a hugger, but even she could tell Brit needed it. When Brit finally leaned back, she had composed herself. The warrior mother from another time had built her resolve. She looked at Pik, steely-eyed, ready for battle.

Pik moved back to the group, giving Brit a bit of space. She checked on Junip and Horn. Junip sat against a wall, intently watching Horn work as though it was the last chance they'd get. They looked like they were memorizing every line of the programmer's face. Horn was completely oblivious, wrapped up in code.

Pik whispered, "You two have come a long way." The two had always shared a connection but had always hidden it from the team. Relationships on Echo teams were frowned upon. More than one had resulted in the dissolution of a group. At first Pik hadn't understood their need for a relationship. She thought it was juvenile. But in the dive she'd begun to appreciate how their love made them stronger. Gave them both a purpose to fight longer and harder. Pik astonishingly had found herself rooting for the two of them.

"It's this place." Junip looked over as Pik knelt down by them. "Everything here is so real. No, I know. Not the aliens, or the ship, or the mechanics of the game. Nothing like that. It's the decisions we're making. I don't believe, in this iteration or the ones I don't remember, that I've ever been a part of making a decision that could end my or anyone else's existence. It makes you want to live."

It makes you want to live. The words struck Pik, and the link unraveled something frozen in her. The medic's eyebrows knitted together in concern, reacting to the twang of nerves in Pik's connection.

As many moments go, this one was ill-timed. The epiphany. The realization that she, too, wanted to live. To find out what it was to live. The concern of Brit for her daughter. Of Junip for Horn. Trick had been working on melting the coldness of the void Pik's parents had left. She cared for her team, but she found she wanted to *connect* with them.

"Pik, are you okay?"

Pik didn't know what to say. She'd been convinced that she was okay with not surviving. That she might as well throw her life away if she wasn't able to rescue Trick. He'd given her life purpose, but not meaning. She felt the connection between herself and the team thrum with life. It'd been there, this background noise she'd ignored, but now she wanted to engage. She wanted to be a part of their lives.

"I'm better than I have been in a long time. I—I just realized it, just now."

A second realization hit. The Doctor was right. Almost right. The reason the Metaverse made linking so taboo was because the Metaverse's stalled-out version of humanity was bent on entertainment and pleasure. Connection, adversity, and challenge were the keys to progression. To wanting to live.

Horn, oblivious as always, brought them back to reality. "It's on a four-second timer once Timmic throws it at your command. Junip, you listening? You've got to get a bullseye on the Doctor's node with this bullet." She slapped a cartridge into their hand.

Pik let go of her insight. Her mind raced, but she had to leave the philosophical reordering of her world to another time when her team wasn't going on a death march.

"Ah, yes. I've got it, Horn. I still am not sure I'm the best suited for this role in our plan," Junip spoke, distracted. They were staring at Pik. They'd picked up on the difference in their team captain. Pik felt her face heat as Junip's eyes bore into hers with curiosity.

Pik opted to redirect the attention, interrupting Horn's incoming assurance with her own, "You are our best marksperson. I wouldn't trust anyone else to it." Any concern she'd had at the team's least-experienced member taking on the most pivotal part of their plan had evaporated. Junip *would* succeed. The connection between them and Horn would guarantee it. Junip would hit the Doctor's primary node with their package.

"The packet ready?" Pik asked.

"Yes, we're good, as long as Junip is on target," Horn assured her captain.

"I will be."

Pik left the two as they walked through the plan for the fifth time. Junip's eyes trailed their team leader, only to be drawn back to Horn.

Pik had one last check-in before the assault.

"Timmic, you ready? The resurrection sickness worn off yet?"

"Eh, I've felt better, but I'm good to go."

"What's still causing you trouble?" Pik studied the man. His golden beard, normally his prized physical feature was patchy. It hadn't grown back in fully, even after a half dozen medkits. His self-image flickered a moment, showing a more scarred version of his face. One of the shrapnel bits had struck him across his eye, and the altered image had a long scar across his face bisecting an eyebrow.

"My head is still a little fuzzy. Like I've got an old-time concussion, a little reverb in the connection. Nothing I can't handle. My part in this operation is easy. I'm just the human meat shield again." His words were jovial, but his tone was depressed.

"Look, if we can get out of here alive with Trick, we'll find a new role for you. I'll be the meat shield." Pik shuddered silently, thinking of healing from the encounter with the mermaid. "We'll do what it takes."

Timmic's look was haunted. "I'm not sure I'll keep going as an Echo after this. Assuming we can get home." There was a tinge of hopelessness in his statement. Pik had finally identified the thread of dissonance in the team's link. She'd thought it was Brit. The thread of hopelessness. She just wasn't sure how to help Timmic.

"We'll get home. It may not be today, but we'll find Trick and figure out how to get home." Pik watched as his eyes went blank, numb. She knew a stupid platitude had been the wrong choice, but she didn't have an alternative. Connection, challenge, and adversity. She tried again, "You are such a critical part of the team. I would hate to see you leave us. As a historian, I think Brit alone has got to be a treasure. Imagine if the Doctor has records predating the Metaverse. That would be worthwhile. It's the single greatest find an Echo team could make." Pik had given it a shot. She watched as Timmic rifled through her words.

"Do you think Brit would work with me?" A purpose began to solidify for him.

"If we save her daughter? Absolutely. I think she'd sign on for anything." Well, that may have been a stretch, but she would definitely be willing to talk to Timmic about the time before.

"Pik, we talked about what those bodies in his lab mean. Like, mean for this place and the Metaverse. It just can't be real, can it? Like we're real, we're separate from this horror." Timmic's unraveling suddenly made sense. He was afraid that their home, the reality of the Metaverse, was some sort of experiment of the Doctor's. Brit's conspiracy theory had taken root—that this was some part of the creation of the Metaverse was a horror to haunt them all.

"I don't think the Metaverse is his experiment. He may have influenced the Architects, but those tubes, those people, they were here before the Metaverse existed." Pik put as much confidence into her words as she dared. "We are more than digital footprints in any world, Timmic, we have souls. We have our unique thoughts, likes, and dislikes. We have love. Not just the romantic love"—she glanced at Horn and Junip, who were still talking in the corner—"but family love, connection. Look what we're doing for Trick. This love for each other makes us human. It also sets the Doctor apart as a monster. I would do all of this to save you too."

His face softened. "Would you? I wonder about that sometimes. I'm not exactly easy."

"We wouldn't want it any other way, Timmic. You're part of the crew. The friction we have makes the team better. *You* make the team better."

"That sounds like a recruiter line."

Pik shrugged. It probably was. "That doesn't mean it's not true. Now stop being so morose. We're at the finish line. We didn't use both of our rezzes on you because you're not needed or valued. Timmic, you're as integral to this party as I am. You've helped unlock the Doctor for us."

"You better remember that when the lasers are flying." He gave her a slight grin.

"Damn right."

The team was together, connected. Insecurities aside, they were in pretty good shape. They had a solid plan, and they had explosives. What else did a party need? Trickshot was ready. They were locked and loaded. They could do it. Pik believed it. For a brief moment, she considered that she might have been trying to convince herself more than the team.

She stood in front of the cargo bay door, flanked by her team. Each was nervous for their own reasons. She took one last look at the party: Brit had determination etched in every line of her face, Horn had her HUD up ready to battle, Junip clenched her sniper rifle with white knuckles, and Timmic gave her a smile. He'd accepted what was to come. Pik turned toward their fate.

"Let's go!" Pik kept her voice loud as her shaking hand slapped the access button.

Chapter 26

Do you want to engage in the OBLIVION protocol? Warning: You will only get one chance.

Pik hesitated, realizing this was the moment Trick sealed his fate. She hit accept and received another pop-up.

OBLIVION protocol active. All deaths are final; you only get one chance in life, and you only get one chance here. Shield, health, and ammo are boosted by 100%. Good luck!

The door slid open in a whoosh.

Before them stood the scaly monstrosity that she and Trick had conquered together the first time: Iraxinus. The challenge had mounted with the party. Masses of humanoids with glowing, sunken eye sockets sensed the party and focused on the Echoes. So many Pik couldn't count them all. Red tendrils of influence ran along the lines of filament connecting the shamblers to Iraxinus.

"Defilers. Defilers." A unit, the web-wrapped mummies began to shuffle forward, chanting.

"Aim for the head! Junip, let us know when you've got a bead on the node," Pik said, taking command of the situation.

Brit was plastered to the wall, frozen in fear. Thankfully she wasn’t required for the first phase.

"Momma? Are you here to save me?"

Pik closed her eyes at the sound of their plan going to hell.

"Jada? Is that you?"

Pik shot a shambling horror in the face. Glancing at Brit, she saw fevered hope replace terror on the woman’s face. Through their link, she could feel the desparation to save her daughter.

"Brit, this isn't real," Pik warned, trying to salvage the situation.

"It was—it's real enough for me." Brit pulled out a knife and ran into the horde of monsters. For a brief moment, Pik thought about leaving Brit to her fate as everyone watched her crazy attack. Connection. Brit was one of the team now. They had to support her. And Brit was right: the Doctor's games were real for those trapped in them.

"Timmic, Horn, cover Brit. I've got Junip. Go, quick!"

Pik switched her load to dual-wield. She'd trained her ambidextrous skills a long time ago and picked up the skill. Standing in front of Junip, she trained her right hand on a shambler and squeezed the trigger. Another replaced it while she fired her left pistol on a second shambler. The staccato of her guns filled her ears as skull fragments went flying. Pik had engaged the enemy.

"How's it going?" Pik's voice was level as she called back to Junip. She kept her calm, trying to keep the shamblers off of them.

Junip's voice was tense, "I've spotted it, just trying to identify the pattern."

"Where is the node?"

"It's right between the eyes of the main boss."

"On Iraxinus?" Pik scanned the boss, a pop-up informing her that this was Iraxinus Prime. The beast's head ducked and dodged, presenting a moving, fluctuating target. "Can you hit it?" Pik fired off her left gun, knee-capping a shambler scurrying toward them. It'd still reach the two of them, but it'd be slow, and the aggro wouldn't designate another shambler for their small group until it was killed.

Between gritted teeth, Junip answered, "I don't have

a choice, do I? Now shut up so I can concentrate."

Pik did as commanded. She capped the crippled shambler in the head. Raising both hands, she started a rapid-fire sequence, thinning the herd focused on them.

Her eyes roamed, trying to spot if anything had happened to Brit, Horn, and Timmic. Nothing. Her job was to focus on Junip, so she would. The three still existed in their link. They weren't down.

Nothing got within two meters of the medic. Her pistols popped, her aim unerring. Fragments of slime and bone and viscera sprayed. Her field of focus narrowed. The only way she could help Brit was to draw the shamblers' attention. Pop, snap, auto-reload. Her ammo was lowering with every round, but it was okay. Everyone had dumped their pistol ammo on her, so she had more than enough.

"Defilers." The moan ran through the room repeatedly, chanting off-tempo.

"I've got the shot." Junip's hoarse whisper broke Pik's concentration.

"What do you need?"

"I need three meters and two minutes for the pattern to reset."

"Check, let me know when to push."

Pik continued clearing, upping her fire rate. Three meters was doable. She'd have to increase the spread. She started ramping up.

"Now!"

Pik used a speed skill to boost her reflexes. The line of shamblers crumbled in front of them. Junip squared up, held their breath, and fired. The gun popped once. Then again. A two-chamber rifle.

Pik watched the first bullet fly through the air when something horribly unexpected happened: the monster reacted out of its pattern. A clawed hand whipped up, taking the shot. The claw burst into fragments. It wasn't the node, meaning Horn's special bullet was wasted. Pik turned to look at Junip to share in the horror, but the sharpshooter still concentrated on the alien.

"Junip?"

An explosive concussion hit the room. "I did it!"

Pik blinked, looking back at the monster with her node overlay. Iraxinus had been hit by the second bullet right between the eyes. The node had shattered. The shamblers groaned simultaneously, tentacles of red influence pulling back from them.

Pik looked at Junip. "We're going to talk about that later."

Junip gave her the smuggest grin Pik had ever seen on the medic. "At least there's going to be a later. Let's do this."

They had to find out what happened to the rest of the team. Pik swapped her load to a Cosmic Sabre and a pistol, ready to go melee. Junip swapped out for a spray-and-pray machine gun. They wouldn't get many kills with it, but she'd do damage. The two of them rampaged toward the rest of the team when Iraxinus opened fire.

Pik had forgotten Iraxinus had a significant bite. It'd ignored them up until now. Blowing off a claw and hitting it between the eyes ignited its ire. The beast focused its laser attack right at the two Echoes. Pik dived to the right, but Junip suffered a direct hit. They flew, hitting some cargo netting hard. Pik watched and swore as Junip crumpled to the ground. She pivoted and ran straight to the prone medic. She skidded to a stop, dipping down to feel for a pulse. The shamblers moved slowly but spawned anew every minute.

Her cold fingers pressed into the medic's neck. Pik caught a thready pulse. She quickly dragged Junip behind a stack of crates. Each Echo had a stash of medkits since the hydrazine incident. Pik activated one immediately while pulling out a rifle. She opened fire, trying to keep the shamblers away from their position.

Splitting up as they had wasn't part of the plan. Pik didn't have enough firepower beyond a stalemate with the waves of shamblers. And without Junip, they weren't going to make any progress against Iraxinus. The boss seemed to have an unlimited number of minions it could throw at them. Pik saw the glow swelling. It was her only warning. She ducked just in time, hair singed.

Junip moaned.

"You there? Can you heal yourself for the rest? Trying to keep them off of us."

The crate they were behind had taken the brunt of the laser's damage. Their "safe" place wasn't going to stay that way.

Junip didn't respond. A glance down between shots confirmed the medic was still unconscious. Pik activated another medkit. The kit would work better if they weren't in combat, and she could take the time to apply medical knowledge. Junip could maybe do it on the fly. Pik was left with hitting its instant-use function as she fired. Where was her team? She tried to send her sense of panic into the link.

Pop. Aim. Pop. The rifle recoiled into her shoulder. It was reassuring, like the growing pile of collapsed shamblers. She could hold out as long as their cover and her ammo lasted. An energy beam shot across the room. She hadn't seen a warning glow, and it was five seconds faster than expected. The beam slammed into the crate, blowing it to bits.

Pik was lucky. The shot would have killed her. Instead it destroyed their cover. The timer on survival had started.

"Junip, I need you awake. We've only got fifty seconds or so." Pik couldn't leave them. Junip was the best of them. They pieced the Echoes back together over and over. Besides, she didn't want to explain to Horn she'd left her partner for dead.

"Junip. Come on. WAKE UP!"

Shooting again, she cursed. The rifle was out. For that gun, she'd given most of her ammo to Horn. She swapped back to dual-wielding pistols. Thankfully, Junip sat up, the healing finally taking effect.

Pik looked at her medic, making a decision. "I need you to sprint to the right when I tell you. You got this?" Junip was dazed but gave an affirmative.

Pik switched to her mini rocket launcher. It'd been effective the first time around. They had ten seconds before the laser attack refreshed.

"GO!"

Junip didn't hesitate. They ran toward the crate on the right side of the room. It wasn't a quick sprint, more a shambler-like limp, but they moved.

Pik gripped her rocket launcher, aimed, and fired directly at Iraxinus's head. The creature switched focus from Junip back to Pik. After firing, Pik stored the launcher and sprinted in the opposite direction of Junip. Iraxinus fired on her heels. She'd swapped to the Cosmic Sabre, beheading a shambler as she ran.

Pik had bought them another cycle. Nothing more. She wasn't sure she even bought Junip that much time. Could they hold off the shambler horde as dazed as they were? Pik leaked despair into the link. If the part hadn't split, if Brit's daughter hadn't been used as bait, maybe the plan would have worked. Pik wasn't even angry.

Impossible choices. Sometimes in a dive, it happened. They had to go after Brit's daughter. Junip had made the shot. They hadn't predicted it would draw the central weapon fire. Seconds ticked by as Pik cut down shambler after shambler. Each one she cut down was replaced by the next.

Sweat stung in her eyes. Pik was about to give in, give up, when she heard the sweetest voice.

"Pik, we're coming! Everything's set." Timmic was coming to save them.

They'd done it. They'd done it!

Pik could feel Junip, the team, all of their joy. It lasted a moment before the full force of Iraxinus's weapon struck her. Her vision went white as everything exploded in shrapnel and pain.

Chapter 27

"I've got to stop doing this," Pik murmured as her vision slowly returned, the world on fire.

The skill Death Below, Death Above triggered, and she'd been saved. She'd hoped to never use the skill she'd gained after her last near-death experience. The anti-assassination skill had canceled out death, but it'd still knocked her health down to 5%.

Disoriented and with her health bottomed out, Pik waited for a shambler to finish her off. It'd just take one good snap of a maw. Her vision blurred, and she wasn't sure her hands could hold a weapon.

One moment became two. The death blow she expected didn't come. The only thing she could hear in her ruptured eardrums was the beating of her own heart. Her ears began to itch, and her skin, too, as everything began to heal.

The muffled voices of her friends came through the fog. Even their link felt muted.

"We've got you, Pik. Give it a minute, and you'll be on your feet," Junip's mild voice reassured. Pik's mind eased. She began to feel the firm, professional hands of the medic touching her body.

"Timmic, you have your shield in place? Will it stop the laser?"

"We're set. Brace in ten seconds. We should be fine. Remember, I built this to withstand. Horn, where are we at with phase two?"

"We've got the charges set. I need a minute to get everything synced up. The worm is active. Great job, Junip."

The words flowed over Pik. They gave her hope, but it wasn't done. It was almost too good to not be a hallucination. An afterlife where she imagined success? What happened to a soul when it died for good in the game or Metaverse? Even the reincarnation protocol had some data loss. Where did those fragments of humanity go?

"You should be good." Suddenly Pik's eyesight returned. The world flashed brilliantly as, out of nowhere, another laser shot hit the team. Timmic's shield held as he'd promised. Pik was flat on the floor. A half-dead shambler pulled itself toward her position. Its mouth, no longer connected to vocal cords, still mouthed the word "defiler." Pik couldn't turn her head. The grotesque monster inched closer.

A voice she didn't recognize spoke, "I'm counting the recharge time."

Horn replied, "No need. I've got a timer set. It seems to vary between twenty and forty seconds, which is fairly quick for such a strong shot."

Junip's back was to the monster, who moved, jaws gnashing. Pik tried to form words. Her own mouth mimicked the shambler's, unable to vocalize the words. It moved closer to the unsuspecting medic. The leathery, desiccated arms pulled. The shambler had no lower half.

Junip!

Pik tried to leverage the link, but her brain was still scrambled. Suddenly a boot stepped between her and the shambler.

"Junip, hold still." Pik felt the impact of bullets hitting the deck, even though a leather boot blocked her vision. She strained her neck muscles, a healing infusion taking hold, and glanced up.

Above her stood a dark-skinned woman covered in tendrils of shambler filament. Dark curly hair framed a grinning face as she looked down at Pik.

"Who are you?" Finally Pik's question came out—though as a dry whisper. As soon as she said it she knew it had to be Brit's daughter, Jada. She was just nothing like

Pik would have guessed. Brit and Jada couldn't have been physically more different.

Jada's eyes twinkled with humor. "Not what you expected?"

With a blush of embarrassment, the team captain tried to save face. "Uh, I mean, we weren't expecting you here."

Brit joined the trio. "We think the Doctor put her here as a distraction. It did almost doom us." Her voice softened, offering an unspoken apology.

Junip moved in front of Pik's view of the mother and daughter. They added their two bits, a shimmer of resolve moving between their link. "We're still standing, relatively speaking, so no harm, no foul." Pik gave a slight nod. Brit had ignored the plan, and the team had almost wiped, but she let go of her anger. The knot she didn't realize she'd been holding dissolved. Leaving her daughter as a shambler was too much to expect a plan to endure.

Another chunk of Pik's health and function returned in a flash as Junip finished applying a medkit. Pik sat up, trying to assess the disposition of the team. Timmic clutched a shield in one hand, ready to spring into place, while his other hand held a gun that he was firing at the incoming shamblers. Horn was working through her interface, trying to set up the next phase of their plan. Junip had returned to firing, performing crowd control. The shambler masses were getting closer. Brit was taking shots at the monsters, her low stats having trouble making much of an impact on the crowd.

"Can you fire a weapon?" Pik asked Jada, wondering if the woman had the same constraints as Brit.

"I can, but I don't have any in my inventory." Pik lifted a hand and began dropping guns onto the floor. Jada seemed to be part of the game and, unlike Brit, able to make a difference.

"Jada, take this. You take the left side." Pik tugged

at Brit's pant leg. She wasn't having much of an effect on the crowd. "Brit, if you can help me sit up, I can take the right."

Jada got to work. "Taking the right" was a little harder for Pik than she anticipated. She still only had 45% of her health back. Pik's vision and hearing may have returned, but her ability to aim had been impacted. Her first five shots hit but maimed instead of killed, which didn't do them a whole lot of good. Brit held a Cosmic Sabre. She'd hack at anything that got too close, but with her nonexistent health, it would be a risk.

"How long, Horn?" Pik asked.

"Almost there. Brace for impact." Timmic's shield slapped up as they got hit by another laser attack. Everyone's vision whited out for a moment.

"Horn?" Pik wasn't sure how many more shots Timmic's shield could take.

"Almost there."

Pik went back to firing. The shamblers with vocal cords and enough lung power were still howling their chant. She couldn't imagine what it'd been like for Brit or Jada to be a minion of Iraxinus. The air was hot. The laser attack threw up dust as it superheated everything it went through. Several shamblers evaporated with each shot, but with an unlimited supply, there was no actual cost to Iraxinus. The beast could hammer them into submission.

A cough wracked Pik's body, throwing the last shot off. She glanced at Junip's side of the battle. They were holding up okay, Jada and Brit trying to help. The encroachment of shamblers kept shifting closer and closer. Pik fired a shot into their mass, trying to help with an assist.

"Horn, it's got to be soon." Pik didn't bother hiding the urgency in her voice. If Horn didn't trigger the trap, they weren't going to survive.

Two more pops and Pik's ears picked up something among the moaning.

"Help!"

Pik blinked. Was it another survivor? Had someone else been shelved as a minion of Iraxinus? She strained to hear the dissonance in the chaos. "Help! Pik? Anyone? Help!"

The voice sounded like Trick. He'd known her name. None of the other victims of the Doctor on this hellship would know.

"I've got it!" Horn's voice was tense. She wanted Pik to make the decision. "We ready?"

Pik fired both her guns, downing two shamblers who had gotten too close. She looked at Horn. They were about to get overrun.

"Pik! Help!"

At that moment, Pik hated the Doctor. She hated the fact that she was the one who had to make the call. She even hated Trick for getting caught in the first place and putting her in this situation. She wanted Trick here, deciding to sacrifice one for the rest. She realized it wasn't a choice. She knew what he would have picked—what she would pick. Knowing the right answer didn't make her hate it less.

"Execute. Horn, GO!"

The team collapsed into a ball. Timmic hit a special ability, and they were enveloped in an energy shield just as the remote detonators ignited the hydrazine barrels they'd placed around the bay. Every inch of the cargo bay, except for their small enclave, went stark white with fire. The team huddled as close as they could. Pik put every positive thought into their shield as she watched the power indicator drop. Their bubble of safety started to get hot.

"Is this going to hold?" Pik was glad Jada wasn't part of the link. The whole team was panicked. Except Timmic.

"It'll hold. Have faith." Timmic's face was strained, but Pik could feel his calm spread across the link.

Pik knew he was saying this to reassure them, but it made her feel better. Her skin itched. It was still sensitive from being rejuvenated the first time around. She shrank back from the heat. The outside was no longer simply white but a whirl of colors. This meant the initial blast was starting to cool. She wasn't the praying sort; she just grabbed Timmic's arm and squeezed it.

The energy countdown fell to 20%. They weren't going to make it. Pik's mind raced. She couldn't infuse the shield. She started prepping her self-healing skills.

"Get your defenses ready." Pik left the "we're not going to make it" out. When the shield collapsed, Brit and Jada would be dead. They didn't have any abilities or levels that would save them. Pik and Junip wouldn't be far behind. Junip's specialization didn't lend for high hit points, and Pik was still half dead from Iraxinus.

10%.

"We're going to make it," Timmic insisted. He was living in a fantasy. They had twenty seconds of shield left and at least a minute of the explosion. She didn't know where their estimations had gone wrong, but they didn't calculate the shield-strength-to-explosion-power ratio correctly. She scanned her teammates, then her eyes rested on Jada. She was the missing variable. Their bubble was larger because they'd included Jada.

"Shrink in. Everyone get closer." Pik pushed in toward the group's core. Nobody hesitated; everyone was practically sitting in each other's laps. Pik's arm wrapped around Timmic, her legs were in Jada's lap, and her torso mushed against Brit.

8%.

They'd gained themselves a couple more seconds. It still wasn't going to be enough. Pik couldn't think of another solution, so her mind began to spiral.

3%.

She wished she could see Trick again and have one

last conversation to say goodbye. To be honest about how she felt. To tell the whole team how much she loved them before they left this plane of existence. Pik put all her regret and love into the link. Each frightened, angry, determined thread flooded with her acceptance and love.

As the shield went down, the heat was unbearable. A wave of hot, ashy air ate at their exposed skin. Pik held tight.

"I WILL protect you!" Timmic yelled, and the shield was back. Miraculously the air cooled. Pik willed her strength into him as she squeezed his arm. He was doing it. She didn't know how, but she was so completely, utterly grateful.

The hydrazine explosion ended. Experience notifications popped into her vision. Pik waved them off. The shield finally popped. The cargo bay was nothing but dust. Pik untangled herself, standing up in awe. Ash fell from the ceiling. It was like they were silent witnesses to a volcanic explosion.

Timmic rocked back on his heels, toppling over in a boneless pile. Junip was there instantly. They had a medkit out and were examining his frame. Pik looked across the bay, hoping the ash would part and Trick would materialize.

"He's dead."

Pik knew Trick was dead. It'd been another trick of the Doctor's.

"Pik, Timmic's dead."

She looked down. *Timmic?* That couldn't be right. The man had just protected them from the inferno. She knelt, studying Timmic's face, which was frozen in determination. They didn't have a resurrection. They'd never found the third one. They'd been convinced that the hydrazine ploy would work.

"What does this mean? Is he with the Doctor? Are we compromised?" Pik turned to Horn, looking for answers. If Timmic was with the Doctor, their plans would get tortured out of Timmic. Pik reached for the link to their historian, but she found only a void.

"I think this means he's dead." Junip's voice was soft.

"He can't be dead. Trick didn't die. Why would Timmic . . . ? It's just a game."

Junip wrapped an arm around her waist. "Trick had the connection back to the Command Center. He was saved because he swapped with Brittany."

Horn cut in, "I'm reviewing the logs now. It looks like Timmic used an overcharge skill. He fed his stamina and health into the energy shield to make it last." Horn looked up, her face stricken. Pik knew the truth in the look. They'd all chosen the Oblivion Protocol. Final death had been the threat.

Pik was in shock. He couldn't have. If someone was going to sacrifice themselves, it was to be her. She remembered some of his last words: *I'm not sure I'll keep going as an Echo after this. Assuming we can get home.* They all had to believe they'd make it home, even without hope. Even if the hope was fake, they had to believe. If they didn't, it wasn't worth it. It was easier to die than to forge onward.

Pik had butted heads more often than not with the man, but there was a hole burrowing deep inside of her at the thought of him gone. Kneeling, she placed a hand over his eyes and gave a silent wish for a better tomorrow. Yet part of her still didn't believe it. They'd meet up with him down the road. Whether in the Doctor's lab or on the feed back to the Command Center. Echoes didn't die, not in games.

"May you find the peace you always wanted," Horn said solemnly. Her words convinced Pik more than anything else that it was true. Timmic was gone. She was numb.

Junip and Horn hugged, Brit and Jada clung to one another, and Pik stood alone. She let them each have a moment to mourn. Phase three wouldn't be harmed by taking the time. She needed to return to business and distract herself from the gnarled knot in her chest. They—the rest of them—still had to succeed.

She avoided thoughts of Timmic. His sacrifice. It may not have been kind or worthy, but she couldn't deal. Instead she began evaluating her level-up and the choices it presented.

She'd gained heat resistance. Self-healing also made a jump. She put some points into her agility and aiming skills. She examined the balance and read the description of her new ability, Redirect. It allowed her to shift damage from a teammate to her or vice versa. The game gave her the ability *after* Timmic died.

One last push. She thought of Trick. Of his reaction when they told him the team lost Timmic in an effort to recover him. Trick would be devastated. She forced her mind to let go of the present. They had a job to do. The decisions and consequences had already been made. Second-guessing anything wouldn't bring Timmic back, and an emotional retrospective wouldn't help her make a better decision. They were too committed to stop.

"Horn, are we ready to execute the next phase?"

She coughed. Pik looked up to find Horn's face tear-streaked. Horn had fought the most with Timmic; they had the least in common and the least empathy for each other. They'd frequently butted heads. It surprised Pik that Horn held such emotion for him. Junip's teary face made sense, but not Horn's. Pik reached up to her own eyes, swollen from the ash particulates, but she hadn't cried. Timmic deserved her tears, but she was too numb to cry.

She felt like a cold-hearted bitch.

"Phase three, Horn, we ready to go? We're going to need to move quickly before the Doctor recovers from the loss of his boss. The portal connection won't be live forever."

A light glow of the HUD illuminated Horn's watery face. "We're good if everyone can step into the blast circle." There'd been a patch of unwashed ground where Timmic's shield had been. The five surviving team members huddled together, guns drawn, waiting for the final push.

"I'm executing in three, two, one, execute." Horn's voice was even, and, as expected, the world streamed around them as the data transfer for their upload began.

Chapter 28

Transfers were discombobulating but rarely painful. Pik wasn't sure if the searing pain was from the transfer or the Timmic-sized void in her chest. Either way, she screamed as the protocol pushed her through the space between programs and loaded her into the Doctor's lab. She materialized none-too-soon in a dull, dimly lit lab that was a run-down cousin of the one they'd been trapped in earlier.

This lab was unaugmented, and the equipment was dated a few centuries prior. It was as if they'd loaded into a grungy garage lab. It was gross, unaesthetic, unclean.

"Horn, *go*."

Pik pulled from her inventory. Nothing materialized. They'd hoped the inventory protocol would load immediately, but it hadn't. Pik looked around, trying to locate something she could use as a weapon. She spotted an emergency axe hanging in a fire suppression case next to a coiled hose. Pik walked over to the box and broke it.

This was a mistake. Fire alarms started blaring. Pik cringed and snatched the axe. At least she had a weapon. She guiltily turned to her team.

"Was that worth it?" Horn said annoyed. Pik gave the axe a few swings and staked out a location close to the door, preparing to defend them against the inevitable show of the Doctor.

"Too late." She gave the programmer an apologetic head bob. "We need our inventories."

"I'm working on it."

Brit, Jada, and Junip scanned the room, looking for their own weapons.

"Brit, how's your inventory working?" Pik had to know.

"We're still good for plan H." The team had used

coded plans for their tactics in case the Doctor was listening.

Pik's shoulders relaxed. This would end one way or another. Junip grabbed a microscope to use as a club. Jada looked like she had found a couple of jars of chemicals. Brit found a small tube of compressed gas, though the label had been rubbed off. The canister was light enough to swing and would no doubt pack a wallop.

The glow of Horn's HUD was up and running. She was frantically typing, trying to outrun the footsteps they knew were coming. Pik stood, tense. There was no going back. They were committed.

She tried focusing on the door, but her thoughts inevitably drifted to Trick. Had she killed him when they blew up Iraxinus? Was Timmic's sacrifice in vain? What would Trick say when he knew Timmic was gone? That Pik hadn't been able to save them both? She'd contemplated sacrificing herself for the team, so it shouldn't have surprised her that they'd all probably considered it. It'd never occurred to her that it'd been a possibility. Timmic, of all of them, had been the most selfish of the lot. He'd stubbornly stick to his plan, stances, and opinions even if it hurt the rest of the team. Self-sacrifice hadn't been his style.

Pik knew that the trip had been risky. The team had left the Metaverse knowing they may be trading any of their five lives for one. They'd cut ties to their only home on the off-chance they could rescue Trick. His life was worth the possibility of each of them losing their lives, and one person had already paid the ultimate price.

They had all committed to self-sacrifice. Brit had done it for her daughter, not Trick, but it'd been the same decision. Pik was prepared to sacrifice her life, but not Timmic's. She'd reverse the decision to come if they weren't already committed to the next move. If given the chance, she'd rethink the whole gambit. Gambling with all of their lives on the remote possibility that Trick was still alive suddenly seemed like insanity.

Was Trick even alive, or had he been extinguished along with Timmic in the boss battle? Why would the Doctor want to keep him around? What purpose could he serve? The thoughts bounced around, none of them helpful. Pik gripped the axe, holding onto the decisions she couldn't take back.

Today's course of action had already been decided. Her past self had drawn a clear line from Iraxinus to victory and hadn't seen any doubts between those two outcomes. Timmic's death changed everything and nothing.

Horn was twitching her hands, running through her programs. "He's here," she whispered hoarsely. Horn's fingers danced as she worked her magic.

Pik let go of her doubts. It was time for action. She held her axe tight. The door creaked open. The Doctor stood in the entry wearing Trick's face. Pik's heart ached a moment, but the reptilian smile snapped her out of her trance.

"I'm so glad you're back." The voice was Trick's, but the inflection wasn't.

Pik threw the axe as hard as she could. It whipped the six feet between them and bounced off an invisible shield. For the moment, they were still in his domain.

"That was unwise." He raised a hand. Like an invincible villain, he waved his hand and Pik flew across the room. Her back smacked into a table. The equipment sitting upon it went flying, clattering across the room. Then Pik's head slammed against the floor. She sat up in slow motion, dazed.

Horn was still working. Junip had closed distance and swung her useless microscope at the Doctor. Jada waited, ready to throw her acid bath once Junip moved out of the way. Pik thought the Doctor could see Jada, unlike Brit, who stood motionlessly before him. He ignored Brit, bringing an arm up to block Junip. With superhuman strength, Junip sailed across the room like Pik.

Jada swung into action, throwing three jars in rapid succession. All three were in the air for a brief instant, then the Doctor looked up and snapped his fingers. The shield shimmered as the first, second, and third jars shattered. Hope blossomed. The shield flickered out as the third jar hit. Acid splashed on the Doctor's form.

"I'm melting!" the Doctor cried in muted anguish. Pik was finally on her feet. She ran forward to take advantage of the moment, grabbing a metal tray. The Doctor's cry turned into an evil, deep-throated laugh. "Do you think you can touch me? This is my domain. You're mine." With a flick of his hand, a force field slammed down around Jada. Pik's tray bounced off his shield and rebounded on her face. He looked at Junip, who'd found a few more jars to chuck in his direction, and they, too, were imprisoned in the blink of his eye.

"What's the point?" Pik muttered, throwing her tray to the ground. She faced the man, "You've got us. I'm not sure why you want us, but we're here. You're right. It's your domain, and you've got our friend's face. I've lost two of my team, and I'm not willing to risk anymore." She almost believed it as she felt herself let go in the moment. "I give up."

"You can't, Pik," Junip cried, heartbroken. Pik hadn't previewed this plan with the whole team, she wanted their reactions to be honest. The only person who knew all the details was Horn. Pik kept her eyes on the Doctor. She didn't dart her eyes to Horn to ensure she was still working. She just had to keep faith.

"I just want to know why. Why are you doing this to us? What's the point?" she whispered, trying to convey as much hopeless despair as possible. It wasn't hard to summon it.

The Doctor paused in his assault on the team and

watched Pik, studying her momentarily. "I don't owe you anything."

"But why not? You can wipe our memory. It doesn't cost you anything."

The Doctor shrugged. "This isn't a villain monologue moment." He snapped his fingers again, and Pik was surrounded. She made a dramatic attempt to slam her hands against the energy barrier, causing them to shimmer in response.

Horn and Brit were the only ones still free. Pik waited as the Doctor turned his attention to Horn.

"And what are you working on, my dear?"

Horn ignored the man, lost in her world. The Doctor stalked toward her, and Pik held her breath. His trajectory would take him right past Brit. She waited, surrounded by the energy field, a faint ozone smell assaulting her senses.

Horn finally glanced up. Her hands stopped twitching. After years of working with the woman, Pik knew she'd accomplished her goal. Horn's mouth was her tell. As neutral as she held her face, the right corner of her lips was slightly upturned in a smile. Without knowing her, it couldn't be deciphered.

"What did you do?"

Or maybe it could be.

"Me? What could I do?" Horn tried to look innocent, but her smirk was unavoidable.

The Doctor paused. He'd brought up a diagnostic tool. Brit picked that moment to swing into action. She shifted her body weight and twisted. The compressed air tube lifted and swung around through the Doctor's shield and hit him in the back. His body flew forward violently. For an instant, Pik saw the shock on his face. She could do nothing but watch, still trapped behind his barrier.

The swing threw Brit off balance, and she was out of position to do a follow-up. Horn moved, her inventory active. She brought up a low-impact pistol and immediately unloaded a round of bullets directly into the Doctor's prone form.

Pik let go of her breath. It was over. They'd won. Trick's corpse—*the Doctor*'s bloody corpse lay on the ground. Pik tapped at her force field, trying to draw Horn's attention. She conveyed *Let us out* through their link.

Horn, however, was still focused on the Doctor. Pik couldn't make out the details until Trick's fractured body raised back to a sitting position. Blood dribbled between his teeth as he smiled.

"You shouldn't have done that."

Pik felt Horn's confidence falter as she brought up her interface to enter a new command. The Doctor's eyes began glowing a brilliant red.

"Duck!" Pik shouted. The sound reverberated within her prison. She couldn't reach Horn.

They all looked on in horror as lasers shot from the Doctor's eyes, slicing Horn in two. Pik avoided looking at Junip, knowing what she'd find. Brit regained her balance and dodged the laser as it swept across the room. The Doctor still couldn't sense her, although he knew someone else was in the room.

The energy weapon hit Pik's force field. It glowed red hot but held. Her heart dropped. Horn was critical to any plan that they enacted. She was the only one who could hack the Doctor's system. Without her, they had no hope of their inventories or memories returning. Pik had sacrificed another in their hopeless cause. The hole in her chest grew, as she was overwhelmed by grief.

Brit walked in front of the bloody doctor and knelt beside Horn. The Doctor, unaware, walked over to Junip's prison. "I've observed you two. I know you had feelings for her. Don't worry. I'll erase those in the next iteration. You won't miss her. It's a shame, though. Such a waste of a good personality profile."

And then Junip vanished.

The Doctor walked over to Jada's trapped form and said, "And you. I still haven't found your mother. I thought that using you as bait would tempt her into the open. She's a cockroach, that one. Good thing smarts don't run in the family."

Jada opened her mouth to protest, but the Doctor gave a command, and she vanished too. Pik watched as her doom approached. The corners of Trick's mouth were bloody, and his eyes were bloodshot. Holes in his torso oozed blood. He walked as though in pain, confirming to Pik that they did do some damage. He wasn't invincible.

"And you, Pik. I must say, Trick had a lot of hope that you'd rescue him. I'll admit your team has been more challenging to capture than expected. Nonetheless, here we are."

He sounded bored. Disappointed. Her mind raced.

"Is he still alive?"

Not-Trick's eyes scrutinized her. "Can't you tell? He's right here." The Doctor moved a hand and gestured to his face. "That's the irony of your crusade. Kill me, kill him. You can't win."

Brit moved across the room carefully so as to not draw his attention. Pik watched his face, concentrating on breathing normally. She would not, could not, give Brit away.

The Doctor tapped Pik's prison, and once again, everything went black.

Chapter 29

Pik was surprised to wake up. After seeing her whole team wipe, a large, nauseated part of her wished she hadn't. She could give up if she were dead. She wouldn't have to carry the uncertainty and the heartache. She wouldn't have to look Junip in the eyes.

On the other hand, Pik woke up exactly where she expected. She was in the Doctor's original lab with all of the unconscious personalities in their tubes. She stood up immediately, face plastered against the glass, searching for everyone else. She was in the same containment tube she'd been in before. A recognizable, unconscious black woman stood right across. Orienting herself, Pik looked to her right, squinting, hoping she could make out Junip. Pik smiled. The medic appeared to be in their tube, still unconscious. Further on should be Horn.

Her heart fell. Horn's tube was empty.

A sound interrupted her investigation: a light tapping in one of the team's recognition codes. She twisted and stifled a squeal. Brit's face was hovering directly behind her, fogging up the tube. Brit was tapping out Horn's identity confirmation code. Pik tapped out her own in response, watching the tension in Brit's face evaporate. The woman brought up a HUD, something she hadn't seen Brit do since they entered, meaning somehow Horn was controlling Brit's features.

Before she could say anything, the tube holding her slid down. Pik took a breath of fresh air and instantly regretted it. The place smelled putrid, like body odor and decay. The real Doctor seemed not to care about personal hygiene. He was also nowhere to be seen.

"Horn?" Pik coughed out, trying to recover from the deep breath of fetid air.

Pik looked Brit in the eyes and was astonished to see them shift from brown to Horn's green hue and back again.

"We're sharing this body for the moment. I can't reconstitute anything for myself, so Brit's graciously agreed to be my host." The face shifted a second, bringing back a quirk of the mouth and Brit's looser vocals. "It's crowded in here. We need to free everyone."

Pik nodded, and they began to work. Of the fifty tubes present in the lab, only twenty-two contained bodies. Timmic and Trick were nowhere to be found, but Jada and Junip were present. The rest were nineteen strangers. No one was conscious. Two of the people were in an active experiment, and they left those two unconscious ones in their tubes for the time being. Horn started wake-up protocols on Jada and Junip. All of the strangers were dragged to the back of the lab. They'd have to analyze the consciousnesses to see if they'd actually survived the Doctor's torture over the years.

"I need you to barricade the door. The Doctor appears to be in one of the simulations with those two." Brit waved at the two unfortunate souls being tortured. One was a heavyset man in a suit sporting thick eyebrows and a prominent chin. The other was a small Asian woman the age of a grandmother. Pik stifled a moment of rage at their lost lives. All of them. Brit, Jada, the two dozen souls that had been sacrificed to the Doctor's insanity.

Not much in the lab was movable. Most of the space was taken up by the retention tubes. Jada found an old, heavy desk in the corner. It was covered in yellow paper. Pik couldn't make sense of any of the markings on a quick inspection. The two only managed to lift the desk a hair off the ground. On their tiptoes, they shuffled it over to block the main door into the lab.

This left the side door unblocked, however, and there wasn't an obvious solution. Junip regained consciousness as though a marionette had taken up their strings. They'd been unconscious one moment and fully aware the next. Dark circles curved around their eyes, and tear streaks raced down their face.

"She's alive!" Jada's voice rang with humor.

"Junip goes by 'they,'" Brit corrected in Horn's voice.

"Oh, right! They're alive!" Jada fixed her mistake with a smile. A spark of hope hit Junip's eyes.

"Horn? How?" Their voice rose hopefully.

"She's cohabitating with Brit."

Horn gave Junip a genuine smile. "It's the only way I could get past the Doctor's filter. Thanks to the link, it wasn't too hard. It's a little crowded in here, though."

Brit returned to manipulating settings in her HUD, which was a very Horn thing to do. But physically the woman was Brit. Pik found it odd as well. Unlike the manipulations of Trick's identity, Brit/Horn were both active and moving.

"I'm glad you're . . . both here." Junip's voice was unsettled. They were struggling, like Pik, with the meld of the two individuals. Even her mental link to the group seemed to blend the two together in Pik's head.

Jada had started moving anything not nailed down in front of the side door to the lab. Microscopes, computer monitors, and even the paper scraps from the desk were piled ineffectually in front of the door. Pik hit the internal locking mechanism. A locked door wouldn't stop the man with all the keys, but every second counted.

Horn had walked Brit's body over to the main controls of the room, the wall of monitors where the Doctor watched his experiments run. They poked at ancient keyboards and zoomed in on the currently active experiment.

"I've found something," Brit voiced this time. One of the screens was full of text, a log of some sort. "It looks like the Doctor actually was a part of it all. Horn, look at this."

Pik came over, studying her friend. "What does this mean?"

"It looks like the Doctor helped create the Metaverse. Look here." Horn splashed a matrix onto Pik's HUD. "The Doctor's research was on uploading consciousness, which we knew, and the effects of emotional strain on the stability of those matrixes. Over the years he mapped out not only how to upload a complete consciousness but also the mechanisms to keep them viable."

Brit/Horn's voice contained a bit of awe. Pik didn't like it. No part of her wanted to admire any bit of the Doctor's work.

"I've got a filter we can add to our HUDs here. Give me a moment," Horn's confident words again came out of Brit's mouth. "Here. You should be able to activate it in your HUDs. Except for you, Jada, since you're not linked yet. Unfortunately I don't think any of these other folks in the lab will be able to come with us."

Pik loaded the filter in seconds. She looked at the prisoners they'd liberated, the bodies propped in the corner. All of them glowed in a sickly burnt red color, compared to Junip, who was a brilliant green. Pik swung her vision to examine Jada and Horn/Brit. Jada was orange-sick looking, but not as bad as the others.

Studying the monitors, Horn expressed what Pik was thinking, "Even the ones he's experimenting on are effectively brain dead. I don't expect his current active experiment to take much more time."

Brit and Horn didn't show up in the filter. The duo completely vanished. Pik lifted an arm, showing a healthy green glow. Even the dark blotches of scar tissue on her arms from the mermaid encounter radiated a deep green.

"No wonder he was so obsessed with us. If he's

been living virtually, we looked like juicy treats. He's a psychic vampire."

Brit's voice cut in, "Yes, exactly. I realized it when you and Trick came into the game. He'd offloaded me to Iraxinus because I'd hit the same lethargy as everyone else. He didn't grow bored with me; I'd just become too unstable to play with. Look at the screen. Somehow Jada and I stayed viable longer than anyone else, but even we were hitting the limits."

Pik moved to the Doctor's terminal station. She subconsciously cracked her knuckles as she examined the displays. Even the Doctor showed up with a sickly brown glow around his body. She squinted. He was a swirl of two different colors. And the realization hit: he was a combination of Trick and the Doctor. A green swirl mixed with a red that resulted in a brownish hue. The Doctor should have been red, dormant, or dead like everyone else. The two folks he was lording over were deep red. Pik investigated their tubes, connected to the Doctor's internal network. They were never going to wake up from the nightmare.

Brit was looking at one of the bodies. "I think this is Tammy from season one. That monster collected all of us, everyone who lost the game."

"Horn, can you split you and Brittany? Can you build an external matrix and split your consciousness?" Junip had shuffled up next to Pik, leaning in to hear their response.

"I think so. It's my code, so it should be possible," Horn said, pausing. The two were having an internal conversation. Finally they looked up. "We'll have to deal with it later. The attempt will take some time."

"How about the Doctor and Trick?" Pik couldn't stop herself from asking, even though she was afraid of the answer.

Horn's lips compressed. "Yes and no. One of the

reasons I'm relatively confident about Brit and I is because I know my physical matrix well. The problem we have with Trick is he has no container here. We'd need to eradicate the Doctor or put Trick into something else. I could perhaps build him something new, but it would take time. And that's a problem. We don't have time; without a physical matrix, he'll degrade rapidly if we split him."

Brit's inflections took over. "What this research is saying, assuming I'm interpreting it correctly, is two things: To stay viable in virtual reality, you must have a purpose, which kept Jada and me relatively intact. You've also got to have a strong sense of self."

Junip snaked an arm around Pik's. They had hope, but it was marginal. Their physical closeness was heartening.

"What do we do now?"

"First, we split us," Horn/Brit said.

"You don't want to be Brorn for the rest of your lives?" Junip's combo name for the two made them all smile. Humor was needed.

"No, it's hard for me to think." Their voice glitched as if both tried to respond at the same time. "Ouch, let's not do that again. Every time we try to override the other, it causes our matrix to mesh and for someone to be shunted into a submissive role in our head."

"How long do you need?" Pik walked over to the Doctor's central console, examining the possibilities. They could try to delay the man in his study. Somehow keep him engaged and entertained with his current investigation.

Brit and Horn conversed for a moment internally. Horn seemed to answer, "I could use a lifetime to study this better. I could do an okay job splitting us up in an hour, but we have more pressing needs."

"I've got the Doctor. You work on you, Horn." Junip gave her a side hug in thanks. Pik couldn't take losing another party member, and Junip didn't like Horn meshed up with Brit any longer than she had to be.

Pik pondered the console. The man had monitors from every angle. Physically he was in place, giving the villain monologue he'd never given to them. Pik typed on the manual keyboard, hunted and pecked, and brought up a command window. It allowed her to pull up the protocol for the experiment. She and Junip stood motionless as they examined the Doctor's madness.

"This guy is sick. He's a fucking monster."

Pik raised her eyebrows, looking to her friend. She'd never heard the mild-mannered Junip use that sort of language.

"It's not great, but this protocol could be worse. What do you object to so strongly?"

"You see here? The BF Skinner reference? He's conditioning them all. Theoretically building resistance to defragmentation, but I think he left that goal a long time ago. Everyone here is past the point of no return on fragmentation." The medic slid into place in front of the console. They started clicking around the system. Pik, more the action hero than an analysis nerd, just watched as they went to work.

"Here's a flowchart of his research goals in the last two centuries. He found the solution to defragmentation here." They pointed at a box. "It looks like the main problem with prolonged consciousness is the need to reboot. Immortality doesn't serve. And if you look here, he had a lot more subjects. Hundreds even. But once he solved the immortality problem, he dropped to the numbers he has here. These folks were too fragmented to break up."

They clicked on a profile that represented Brittany Jasmine Montgomery. Jada had finished wedging the secondary entrance closed and joined them at the console.

"See here? If someone loses cohesiveness, they need his long-term lab matrix to keep them stable and can't be released into what he designated as the Ether." Horn explained

"What's the Ether?" Jada asked.

"No idea. There's not much on here. The Doctor might have been part of a network of labs working on what was called "Project Afterlife." There's old communications stuff from Brit's age. Everything went silent two hundred years ago."

Pik's mind raced. The Metaverse was in an accelerated time state. Two hundred years was about fifteen thousand in the Metaverse—close to the creation of the system they lived in. Pik looked at Brit, not having put it all together until that moment. The Doctor was one of the intellects that helped create the Metaverse. It was true. But why not join the Metaverse? Why stay in this lab?

All of the problems his research addressed were problems that needed to be solved in order for the Metaverse to exist successfully. Her mind raced. Was it possible that the Doctor was one of the Architects? They had lost all of the original Architects that were uploaded into the Metaverse. Each had succumbed over time to the need to reboot their consciousness. The last, Ubesrtia, had rebooted a thousand years before Pik had been born.

They'd lost many of the Metaverse admin privileges when Ubesrtia passed into her next life. "Horn, the Architects, there were twelve of them, right? You have those in Timmic's archives?"

"Yeah, all of us have access to the file."

"Okay, Junip, look for the Doctor's real name. I'm going to do some Timmic research." A pain of sadness clawed at her throat as Pik brought up Timmic's historical database. The man would have loved this revelation.

Each Echo had been responsible for specific areas of knowledge to be downloaded in their HUDs before loading. Timmic had pulled historical data; Horn favored her modern algorithms and binary shortcuts; Junip kept pages on modern game design, psychology, and digital first-aid; and, as the leader, Pik pulled the team's backup logs and personal files.

Horn had set up a transfer across each Echo's instance so the data could be shared. It allowed for quicker research and insulated them against data corruption and loss, in the event that one of the Echoes got ejected from the game. Or died . . . in Timmic's case.

Pik brought up the correct file and began leafing through the Architects. Theoretically her parents made her take a history class, but it wasn't something she'd ever been passionate about. She'd opted for a human load instead of cybernetic in this reincarnation, which meant she didn't have an enhanced memory. She brought up the minor AI-assisted search.

Immediately, she was rewarded with the names and bios of the twelve Architects:

Jason Jones
Rraaxus Two
Mary Lyn Frye
Andrienne Anzaldua
Joe Ursa
Ubesrtia Swrai
Taven Kli
Grace Wu
Dixit Ramakrishnan
Gloria Rich
Jain Patil
Frey Williams

Twelve was a suspicious number. A historical number. She wasn't surprised when Junip returned with a name that wasn't on the list.

"Richard Langley."

"Of course he'd be a Dick." In the tense moment, no one laughed at Pik's joke, so she continued, "There's no match here. Let me try to find something. Junip, go ahead and work on the Doctor's distraction. We're going to need some time one way or the other. He should feel confident so he won't be suspicious."

"Aye, captain." Junip gave her a small grin. Pik felt herself sliding back into the role of team captain. Timmic's death had shaken her, but old habits died hard.

Pik picked at the problem. Searching for thirteen Architects brought up nothing. The number thirteen stood out, but her vague recollection of history class wasn't helping. Thirteen disciples—or was it twelve? She searched and found the Bible. The thirteenth disciple was the betrayer. She searched for Richard Langley, but nothing came up. She searched for dissenters and still came up blank. She searched for controversy.

Finally a thread to pull.

Early research into uploading consciousness had multiple issues that held humanity back. With the world facing increasing physical limitations, a subsection of humanity resorted to unsavory, inhumane practices to secure the scientific advancement needed. These researchers, once renowned, have been redacted from the historical record. This historian believes, however, that the nature of the atrocities committed by this group of people needs to be recorded, even if their names are forgotten. The only sure way to prevent a replication of this historical event is to know of it.

The scientific group, Isa'N, compelled humans to volunteer or be coerced into giving up their humanity in early experiments. The known limit for humans to exist in a virtual environment without suffering permanent damage at that time was roughly 150 hours. This group knowingly kidnapped individuals and performed experiments on them to prolong their time as an uploaded consciousness. This researcher believes that not only were individuals—as recorded—returned to society damaged, but some practitioners ended up dying during these experiments. One of the most notable individuals who participated in this sort of inhumane, coercive experimentation was [name redacted]. This Doctor was one of the primary Architects of the modern solution of the Metaverse, and his insights were used to help the Twelve Architects achieve their accomplishment. This scientist was left behind on purpose during humanity's migration. He was denied entry into Eden and remains lost in humanity's physical destruction.

That was it. No more data was available, but the text had capitalized Doctor, which was a tidy link. This Richard Langley was a brilliant mad scientist. He was perhaps the last Architect of the Final Solution for Humanity, the creation of an Afterlife when they recognized that the Earth's habitability quotient was doomed. He'd built the keys to Eden and been barred from entering.

Which meant they couldn't kill him. Not really. They'd be killing one of the only souls that could help fix the Metaverse. Since the last Architect had moved on, humanity had survived—and thrived even, but over the years, the stability of the Metaverse had been called into question.

Echo teams were commanded to pay specific attention to any external programming that may lead to solutions or knowledge of the Grand Architecture. Pik had ignored the directive through the years. The team had never encountered anything nearly as sophisticated.

"How's it going, Junip?" Pik asked, having gotten what she could from the historical notation.

Junip gave a raptor's predatory grin. "He's dancing for me. I've hacked into the psyche of the two he's testing. Right now he's obsessed with the non-standard results."

Pik studied the monitors. The Doctor had an old-school electric pad out and was taking notes. They could see what he was recording on one of the monitors to himself. The man was convinced that absorbing Trick's patterns and interacting with the team's independence had given him some new subconscious insights into interacting with what he termed his 'zombie' consciousnesses.

"You think you can keep him distracted for hours?"

Junip nodded. "Easy. This guy's got an ego a mile wide."

Pik patted them on the shoulder. "Good. I'm going to read the Doctor's early journal entries. I want you focused here. Horn and Brit will work on the split. We'll get Horn out. And then figure out what we're going to do with the Doctor." Pik tried to convey confidence.

Junip nodded, their attention plastered to the monitors. Junip knew their best chance of seeing Horn in one piece was giving her the most time possible to extract. They all had immediate missions.

Chapter 30

Pik tried to channel Timmic, tried to be as interested as he would be in real, unedited historical documentation. She read. It didn't take long for her to move beyond faking fascination to being sucked into the drama. Some of the entries were mundane, but gold nuggets of the Metaverse's history were scattered across the expansive journaling.

Pik downloaded the entire file but highlighted the entries she found particularly compelling:

Journal Entry 302

I can't believe that blowhard Rraaxus doesn't see the logic in my argument. They were the one I thought would be most open to my technique. They're cold and logical. They have trouble connecting to the rest of humanity. And yet they denied me on moral grounds as though there's morality when humanity is dying. The doomsday clock has passed; we have hit the point of no return, and anything and everything we can do to preserve the human race is a necessity.

Journal Entry 303

I've begun efforts to identify a base with the Dark Net. It's a chance I'd rather not care to take. If I'm being investigated or watched, they will immediately pick up on my illicit activity. Thankfully, no one's knocked down my door yet. Everyone's trying to "save humanity" even if they're unwilling to take the necessary steps to break the immortality barrier. My nephew is the only family I have left, and he is on terminal life support. I can keep him alive as long as it takes, as long as it doesn't take too long.

Journal Entry 308

It's been a week of digging around, and I've finally found them. The rich bastards will pay for whatever I need to lock down their future. The SpaceLaunch program is not a viable solution, and it's out of reach for these men anyway. Might as well drill into the caverns with the Umbrella emporium. They have a better chance of survival underground than in space.

Journal Entry 320

We've figured out the architecture. Rraaxus and the self-styled Architects of Humanity will work through the legitimate corporation funding of the Afterlife project. They were already working together across academic institutions and companies. Now, it'll just be official. Meanwhile, I'll be doing black ops research through a front. The group I'm working with has deep ties to Hollywood. They've got a new idea for a colosseum-like lottery. With enough money and the end of humanity on the horizon, what can get green-lit is amazing. I will begin to build my virtual laboratory for my research purposes. The goal is to strip people's consciousness from the game. They're gambling with their very life. If they win, and we'll make sure some will, they get a ticket to the next life. They get survival, money, whatever it is that they dream of. If they lose, however, they're mine. I get to experiment with them as I please.

Journal Entry 375

The games have begun, and I have now received my first participant. The process of swiping his consciousness did not go entirely as planned. The participant's name was

Randi Sase. May he rest in peace. He landed in my lab in the psychic equivalent of a splat. I must devise some containment field to keep the consciousness intact when it lands. I hypothesize that the trauma induced by way of transfer needs to be countered by a containment device that allows the consciousness to self-conceptualize long enough to provide a self-imposed containment.

This may be trained out of people, which we'll see, but this needs to be done more delicately for the initial transfer. I've let Randi's psyche pass on to the next life, assuming there is one. He was so fragmented that there wasn't enough cohesiveness to perform even the basic psychological testing that I needed to.

Journal Entry 395

The second capture was done with more finesse and success than the first. I have my first captive in the lab. I'm not sure how much Abigail understands her situation. She's just mad at this point. I've got her in a very old idea of a force-field-based container. Thankfully, I don't have to follow the rules of physics here. If I can program something and make it so, then it is. There is almost unlimited power available at my fingertips. It's too bad my genius isn't in design, or I'd simulate something better.

It doesn't matter. My tests don't need to be pretty, just effective.

Journal Entry 396

I've done some baseline tests. Abigail seems to fall within the normal expected psychological parameters of humanity. She participated in the game to save her child. This is a standard expectation of a mother. There is some inherent trauma with failing and associated guilt. This is causing some degradation of the stability of her matrix.

It is curious. The initial hypothesis was that mental health was physical, and even if things like guilt and shame were ported to virtual reality, they wouldn't have much impact besides motivating a virtual individual into doing tasks. Some of the early directions the Architects were pursuing was to use shame and guilt as motivators. In a world where immortality is the expectation, how better to get humanity to still function within normal parameters? This will not work if it causes instability in the matrix. Curious indeed.

Journal Entry 405

Grace Wu is an idiot. I was probably the closest to her professionally as any of the other Architects. I approached her with my knowledge of shame and guilt and how they affected matrixes. She wouldn't listen to me. Flat-out refused to hear what I had to say once I started saying it. She instead insisted on me telling her how I'd come to know what I knew.

I walked away. I'm not going to compromise myself further. We need a mole in the organization to whom we can leak information. The Architects have the global funding to make the Metaverse a reality, but they won't know how to get it to work quickly enough. I've discussed this with my compatriots, and they agree. They will work on the thirteen Architects and find one we can leverage. They all have egos. I'm sure one of them will bend so they can get the accolades. They are only human, with human foibles.

Journal Entry 424

Abigail imploded today. Her consciousness gave in.

Without the knowledge of her daughter surviving, she gave up the will to live. It's funny, as she didn't have a physical body. Her refusing to eat or drink virtually shouldn't have had any effect on her mental capacity. But it did. Her subconsciousness translated her lack of care for the physical, virtual body into a lack of cohesion in the mental landscape. This is a fascinating development that I will have to work out. Unfortunately, this will make my research harder, as all of my test subjects have been uploaded from a game in which they're gambling their lives for something they will ultimately lose.

Journal Entry 430

I've got it. What if I give them what they think they've lost? Maybe not the loved one that was dying, although that's a possibility. But they need some reason to live. I have control over their environment, so I just need to research their lives before we upload them into my lab and provide the appropriate motivator to live. The next competition in Infestation is four days away. I've got to move rapidly on this idea, or I will lose the chance of my next participant. I will also talk to the board about upgrading my space to contain more than two consciousnesses. I need to rapidly experiment once I prove I can keep someone in here and viable long enough to experiment on them. Also, if I'm going to research the participants and keep up with the latest that the Architects are doing, I will need some time dilation protocols. This technology is old. It was proven to touch on a person's physical body, but with humanity ending, who cares? My consciousness will be uploaded with everyone else's anyway, so there's no need to care much about the state of my body.

Journal Entry 335

Marcus has been successfully uploaded, contained, and is now in one of my simulations. His health in the system seems relatively stable. I've provided a combat simulation similar to the game he was gambling his life in. He thinks he's still fighting for the life of his niece. She's got terminal brain cancer and only a month to live. It could be treated, but the treatment costs more than Marcus could make in his entire life. I don't know how long I can keep the game going. I'm not much of a game programmer. One more skill I need to work on. But it should do for the next week. I've played with his perception of time, too, so he won't have the thought that this is taking too long to beat the real game.

Journal Entry 350

I've pulled Marcus out of the game. He started getting suspicious when he hit the same level for the fifth time. I tried to vary it up, but I can do only so much with my skill. He's unconscious in my containment zone. I'm going to set up a new challenge, give myself the skin of his sister, and have her break the news of his dead niece. Then try to simulate real life for him or just the general ambiance of real life. The board agreed to give me a research assistant, Evelyn. She's programming the simulated life game off of his original profile. She seems on board with what we're doing but refuses to participate in a virtual environment. She's a smart woman.

Journal Entry 434

Marcus has passed on. With the time dilation effect, he effectively made it a year before his matrix lost cohesion. Looking at the logs, it looked like the new environment Evelyn and I gave him was too dull. He didn't have the motivation to get up in the morning. This boredom factor is going to be a problem. No matter how interesting the environment is, they will eventually experience severe boredom, given a timescale of forever. The immortality problem has been recorded for thousands of years in the form of gods and goddesses who simply live to torment humanity.

There isn't a long-term solution for needing to entertain a group of people for eternity. At some point, the limit of humanity runs out of options to experience and create. I will have them grab me a creative on the next game. Give me someone who can create new experiences to get them out of the hole Marcus found himself in. God knows Evelyn and I are not creative enough to keep them busy.

Journal Entry 476

We lost the last upload, our artist today. Evelyn thinks it was a freak accident, but I know better. There are no freak accidents in a contained virtual environment. The man was a genius. He finally figured out what was going on and ended it. I admire his tenacity and his lack of ego. He was brilliant, but he understood that living in a realm where people's only interaction is with their creative intellect is ultimately not very satisfying. Rather than create on his own forever, he lost cohesion.

I suspect there's an analogy to being deserted on an island, a go-crazy-by-yourself element. There's been a long history of torturing humanity by enforcing solitude on those who are deemed "deserving." This "rightful" consequence frequently causes the bearer to go insane. Humanity is meant to be social.

So, with this argument, I've convinced the board to allocate more space for me. It's not a small amount of space to upload a consciousness. Human brains are complex—2.5 petabytes on average for a modern scientist, more to allow the self-actualization, with significant processing power to keep up with the expected bodily reactions and environments humans thrive in.

My lab alone was one of the most significant expenditures in my dark web network's history, and I'm effectively asking the board to quadruple the investment. Although they are getting increasingly desperate as the Architect's efforts stall out, I personally haven't produced the results that would justify this kind of investment yet. Thankfully, the gameshow has been wildly popular. Evelyn made a logical analysis that they are making plenty of money to justify the investment. The entertainment business is hot right now, even more so than in humanity's past. Everyone wants a distraction from today. That gives me leverage.

Journal Entry 501

So, with my entertainment module, we've managed to increase the stability of a participant. Evelyn subcontracted out an entertainment AI to provide some different takes on the type of entertainment she—Kai—enjoys. She participates in virtual entertainment regularly, which helps with boredom. I will add my second consciousness into the environment tomorrow once the game concludes. Between the entertainment factor and boredom, we should have a good mix. Hopefully, this will prove my theories, and we can apply these to the Architect's plan. They already have a sophisticated Metaverse planned out, but it's too static. They need a universe that challenges its inhabitants.

Journal Entry 555

We've got a teeming colony of five participants at an accelerated timescale. They are flying through time and interacting with one another. We've pushed the time speed as much as possible with the entertainment AI still able to generate quality games for them to consume. Evelyn has noted some drops in Kai's readings now that we've hit their five-year mark. It's not anything to worry about. Normal humans have fluctuations in their self-conceptualization.

Journal Entry 565

I was wrong. Evelyn was right. I hate to admit this. I hate being wrong. Kai fragmented this morning. We tried pulling her back from the simulation, but she was too far gone. It was like a house of cards. Once that first card slips, nothing can be done to save the whole. The other participants have dipped, noting Kai's disappearance. I'm afraid we're going to have a mass extinction event. Kai was the longest-lived, and she impacted the whole community.

Journal Entry 567

The whole group died off as of this morning. The last one lost cohesion in his containment cell. I've been thinking about what happened. I've had to—the board wants an explanation and wants some conclusions to share with the Architects. They've got their conduit in place. We need a refresh cycle built into the system. Something that creates a new environment or experience for the participants as they degrade. A reconstitution or reincarnation event that prevents them from getting bored.

Evelyn is working on a way to measure the degradation of human consciousness with more detail than what we have today. I hope this gives us more insight into what's happening. These participants lasted ten years within the environment, but it was almost an instantaneous collapse once Kai was gone. I'm passing a formal report of what we know and what techniques have worked—creation, engagement, entertainment, and community are all key. I'll save the refresh for when we've got it played out.

Journal Entry 650

Our first successful cycle is working. It's taken a few failures, but the reboot protocol is in place. This Oblivion Protocol, as I've named it, evaluates an upload's cohesion and makes a determination on its health. If deemed healthy, the individual is allowed to pass through with all memories intact. If the fragmentation factor is too high, it reboots the individual into a new instance. That rebooted memory will depend on their personal preferences, if they're conscious of this act like me, or be a determination of the protocol.

At first, we had complete wipes of knowledge for the humans we uploaded. However, that proved exceptionally frustrating as Evelyn would pick moment by moment to load back into the consciousness, which was a terrible waste of time.

I was able to discover, by looking through her memory tags, a pattern in memory creation. Based on the brain's perception of time and memory storage, we can extrapolate out a time tag for events using the new algorithms. This gets translated into their matrix. We've upgraded the processing component of our brain software to include two additional metadata fields to associate with this data. One will designate the iteration the person is working from. Is this a base memory? Is it a third reboot memory? And one will suppress the memory from the current iteration of the intellect. This allows us to control what the entity remembers at any given time.

This allows us to iterate a lot quicker on causes of

defragmentation. As Evelyn's monitoring program picks up on any fragmentation, we stop, rewind, and hit play to determine the exact cause. This has allowed us to send significant data to precisely refine what causes fragmentation and a lack of cohesion.

I've sent innumerable reports to the Command group—that's what they're calling themselves these days. But I'll summarize things here: The closer the virtual experience is to humanity in the worst ways, the longer people survive. The environment must provide challenge, meaning, and struggle. Love must be offset with heartbreak. It turns out humanity is the act of survival. We don't do well in a utopia. There needs to be darkness tempered by hope. We're starting to see that play out in physical society. Humanity has started to self-destruct as they realize the doom our collective recognized five years ago.

Journal Entry 750

The fucking idiot of a mole. I should have known better than to trust some weed smoking flower child. We've been working with him for two years, and the Architects were making great progress on their grand design, the Metaverse. The idiot let slip some knowledge he has no reason to possess. Gloria was too clever. She'd been suspicious of him for a long time. When he introduced the reboot protocol, as much of a leap as that was for the group, she monitored his communications. It didn't take long for her to trace back some of the information he had to our conglomerate. I don't think she knows about me, but the damage is already done. He's out, and now every revelation he provided the team is under suspicion. He's played his last trick.

Thankfully he didn't know my name and couldn't give it

even to save himself. I'm sure he would have. They are trying to keep his betrayal secret so as to not affect the project. The Metaverse can't afford a loss of belief that it will work.

This means that Evelyn and I will have to institute Plan B. We cannot ensure it'll function correctly in the long term without a way to influence the Metaverse's design. We've introduced more equipment needs to our conglomerate, the Central Command. At this point, they are willing to give us whatever we need to make a difference. Never waste a crisis.

We're going to infiltrate the Metaverse by hooking up directly to it and influencing its code to get some of the improvements needed into the environment. This shouldn't be too difficult. They're allowing thousands of third parties to hook up to fund the Metaverse. This is how they're providing some of the vehicles of entertainment and other new content into the verse. I'm not sure how they got these companies to agree to it. It's not like virtual individuals can output gold for them to leverage.

Journal Entry 785

Living on Earth has become more dire. New York had to be officially evacuated today as the last levy threatens to break. The food shortages continue. Even though people are starving, there's no rebellion because the next episode of DeathGate is airing tomorrow. People will focus on anything but their doom. Another lesson.

We've officially sunk our claws into the Metaverse. They're constantly monitoring the connections to the gate, so Evelyn's replicated her content creation AI into the interface. Once everything is started, they will likely have less strict controls over who uploads what. No one will be monitoring these ports in the long term. In reality, even if the Architects upload into the environment themselves, they're the only ones who have enough knowledge to fix anything. They will eventually have to reboot their own consciousness or risk defragmentation. We'll ultimately win, assuming we can stay whole longer.

We've also officially hit some personal records on being interactive only in the virtual sense. I'm still running off my physical biology, but I can now spend two weeks (or about nine months in VR) within the environment. Evelyn is even better; she hasn't left the virtual environment in two months. The logic and discipline she operates at is incredible. It feeds her cohesion.

Journal Entry 825

I don't know why we didn't think of this sooner. If a participant thinks someone they love's life is on the line, they become intensely focused. This act of focus helps increase their short-term cohesion by a factor of four. Nothing works better. It's the most effective way to prolong someone's virtual existence.

Evelyn and I are talking about taking the final step to slow down time and move wholly into the game. Our physical bodies are starting to degrade, the ambient radiation levels where we're at have increased significantly in the last year, and we're both worried about getting some sort of brain tumor that would ultimately impact our ability to upload. We've harvested twenty last souls from DeathGate. They're even talking about shutting down production because, at this point, there isn't much that can be done to save anyone anymore. What's the point in risking your life if there's no actual meaningful benefit to winning?

The Metaverse has made significant progress. It is expected to be fully up and running within the next two years. The Architects and the initial participants—wealthy people who have been funding the effort from around the world—have been moved to the underground complex where the hardware of their future will be stored and preserved. They've invested in an architecture network to keep the contraption working robotically. Hard lines are still set up in the general network, so we can still reach it through our link. They've covered up our mole nicely. I hear he's even going to be uploaded into the Metaverse himself. That man has more lives than a cat. Evelyn heard rumors that he wasn't "caught" at all, that instead he betrayed us. Either way, there'll be a reckoning for negligence or betrayal.

Journal Entry 865

Today is the day. We're loading in together. I must admit that there is no one else I'd rather be uploaded into a virtual environment with than Evelyn. She and I have grown professionally close over the years, and I think we may be able to explore a relationship beyond work once we're officially non-corporeal. With humanity on the brink and our experimentation the sole thing standing between the Metaverse and disaster, we just haven't felt right about it. Now though . . . Now, we'll have eternity.

Journal Entry 890 Virtual

I decided to restart my journal. The work must continue. I will only speak of this once, as I don't want to remind myself what happened. Simply put, Evelyn's upload failed. She defragmented and lost cohesion when she hit the lab's loading zone. Considering how long she could exist on the network without returning to the physical environment, I should have seen this coming. She had lost her sense of physical self, so when she tried to actualize without biology backing her up, it failed utterly.

I should have performed the clean-up protocols but couldn't bring myself to do it. It makes me feel better that the environment may have a bit of Evelyn looking after me.

I may not have her companionship, but I have twenty-two uploads to experiment on and a mission. My life is the mission. How can I keep humanity afloat by whatever means necessary?

Journal Entry 950 Virtual

They have discovered me, my connection. The remaining Architects. I am locked out, no longer able to influence the success of humanity. They will not survive without me. Evelyn's sacrifice will be meaningless. I still have most of my uploads. I will continue to experiment. One day I will break back into the Metaverse and set things right.

Chapter 31

Pik kept reading beyond the Doctor's upload: Pages and pages of him bashing the Architects, the Metaverse's most sacred heroes, for idiocy. How he infiltrated the Metaverse like a virus, instituting changes without anyone knowing. His quick descent into insanity as his existence becomes his mission. The Doctor's punishment of his twenty-two uploads in the name of experimentation and science. The bucket of cold water at the realization that the original mole, the plant on the Architects, the flowerchild who liked to play tricks. He was *her* Trick.

Pik consumed all the information rapidly, but comprehension took time. What did it really mean? What changes was the Doctor responsible for in the Metaverse? What were the Echoes doing in the structure built by their ancestors and the Doctor?

Her first thought was to reject it all. She didn't want him to be part of her history or existence. Didn't want his reality to influence who Trick was. Didn't want to accept that *her* Trick was the Trick in his journal. The Doctor's methods were brutal and cruel. They couldn't credit any of the beauty of the Metaverse and humanity's virtual existence to a monster like him. Trick *couldn't* be a part of any of it. And the last bit—that Trick may have given up the Doctor on purpose. The only thing Pik knew for certain was that she needed to talk to Trick.

However, her feelings on the subject didn't do much to erase the facts. Pik looked up from the data pad she'd been reading, looking at the team. The Doctor's last few entries had started to become more erratic. He was always insane, but he was now losing cohesion himself. And then it clicked.

He needed to be rebooted. *He* needed the Oblivion

Protocol.

"That's it! Horn, I've got it!"

Horn was not herself yet. They'd been working for hours, and she still hadn't figured out how to draw her physical entity. Junip was still happily playing mind games with the Doctor. They reveled in the fair turnabout of it.

The Doctor had been eating it up. Pik began to understand why he was so much like the vampires of lore. He'd been missing true human companionship for a long time. His mission had kept him on his feet, that and Brit and Jada's tenacity. Torturing them with each other's existence and the need to be rescued kept the whole group alive longer than any of the other twenty-two uploads. Their system had reached the breaking point, his torture eroding their need to survive.

Pik was pretty sure the Doctor had forgotten who Trick might be. If he was the Conduit—the link between the Doctor and the Architects—he'd survived the millennia intact. Relatively speaking.

When Brit and Trick swapped fates, it had been a miracle to the Doctor. The Metaverse had finally reached out. His long solitude was broken.

"Horn, Ubesrtia was the last Architect, right? I remember her name, but I don't know why she was important other than being the last one."

Horn nodded with Brit's head. "She was the last one and ultimately the founder of the Echoes. She instituted our transfer protocols and our quarantine rituals. She's the reason why we exist."

The last puzzle piece fit into place. Ubestia must have suspected some outside influence on the Metaverse and locked down the connections to the entertainment world. Knowing that they needed entertainment to keep everyone going, she created a profession for the rest of them.

"Horn, I'm not sure we've got enough time to get

you out of Brit if you haven't figured it out yet. After reading these files, we need to put the Doctor in stasis. Both he and Trick need to be quarantined and examined. Jada and Brit will likely lose cohesion if not reinitialized themselves."

Jada looked pale, leaning against one of the workbenches, struggling to keep her eyes open. Mentioning Brit's fate flipped Horn out of control of their shared body. Brit went to Jada's side and pinched her arm. The two murmured for a minute.

"Brit, I know you care about your daughter. But if I'm right, the only way either one of you will survive is if we send you both back to the Metaverse with the Doctor and Trick," Pik tried to convince the two. As far as she could see, this was the only viable option for them.

Junip gasped from their console. "You can't send this monster"—they waved at the Doctor on the screen—"back into the Metaverse. He'll destroy our world."

"He's an Architect. The Metaverse is sick. We all know it. He could be the key. Look, we're not going to let him live as this vampiric monster in the Metaverse. We're going to send him through the reincarnation protocols. That's the problem. He never perfected them here. He made a gross version where he could reboot people based on their old memories, but he didn't allow a true reincarnation—a true rebirth. We're having trouble with the Metaverse as it exists today because he was the one creating many of the techniques that the other Architects used. Like it or not, some of the base code that our existence relies on is the by-product of his experiments on real humans like Jada and Brit."

Pik's pronouncement was met with silence. She felt everyone but Jada in her link, and they were all tired. Tired of the struggle, the truth, tired of the Doctor. Neither Horn nor Junip objected. The remaining Echoes could feel Pik's determination and truth.

"What exactly is your plan?" Brit's voice came out listlessly.

"I know Horn put a trace back to the Metaverse so we could find our way back home. I want you to use that trace as a zip cord for the five of you and boomerang everyone back there. If we tag everyone as part of the Grand Architecture, they won't automatically trigger the destruction protocol. Five left and five returned. Central Command will find this acceptable. Jada and Brit and Horn will march the Doctor to the Reincarnation Center. Horn will be able to pull from her files in the Metaverse to successfully split consciousness. Even if Jada and Brit choose not to undergo reincarnation, he must. You'll have Horn to make sure it's done right."

Brit and Horn nodded slowly. "Yes, I can ensure we follow the pathway. A Grand Architecture tag should get us through the initial kill protocol. But this plan of yours has a flaw. It leaves you and Junip stranded in this hellscape. And Trick, if I can't split him from the Doctor, he'll be reincarnated as well."

Pik knew. She knew before proposing the plan. She could be dooming Trick. Furthermore, and she suspected Horn kept this quiet to save Junip, it would be harder to split Horn once she went through the transfer back to the Metaverse. Her consciousness would be mixed even further with Brit's. Both Trick and possibly Horn would effectively die while saving humanity. "We knew it might be a one-way ticket to save Trick."

Junip had gone back to the console to tweak another response out of one of the participants. Their voice floated toward them. "This feels like one of the Doctor's sick, sadistic tricks. Save ourselves or save humanity. The choice is yours."

"Except with this group, that isn't a choice. Timmic taught us that. The whole is more important than the individual." Pik said this, but she wondered if the cost was worth it. The reincarnation pamphlets talked about an individual's experience being uploaded into the meta-subconsciousness of the Metaverse. Assuring those who stepped into oblivion that they were not truly lost. But she wasn't sure she believed it. She'd watched her parents leave reality and hadn't seen a wink of their existence since.

"How do we get the Doctor to agree to the trip?"

"Horn, I can handle that. You prepare the tags. Jada, you're with me. I must explain some things about the world you're about to venture into. Give you a download of our logs. Timmic's logs, in particular. You'll need to make sure they get back into that Reincarnation Meta-consciousness—if it exists." She felt like an atheist who couldn't entirely give up the thought that there was some universal power in the world. Maybe not God, but a connection to something bigger.

Junip played the Doctor like a fiddle. They kept adjusting the reactions of the two zombie participants in such minute ways that he couldn't help but be fascinated. They showed more low-level life signs than they'd had in fifty years. He was obsessed with the results and focused on repeating them but kept failing to repeat the same micro-reactions.

When the Echoes were ready, recalling him to the lab was simple. Junip just stepped away from the console. The zombies stopped reacting. Junip and Horn in Brit's body held each other, spending a few last moments together. Pik's heart ached as she watched them. The love that had sprung up was still new and fresh, and this sundering would be raw.

Horn had given Pik the mechanism to trigger the recall. Jada, Brit, and Horn were tagged as Grand Architecture Protocol finds. She just had to tag the Doctor and anything left of Trick. There was a chance the quarantine protocols would read Horn as a rider. A virus to be destroyed. But Pik didn't want to think about that.

Fists slammed against the back door of the lab. "What is going on? Why won't this door open?" The Doctor was in a rage. This didn't bode well for Pik's negotiation.

"Richard, we're in here, and we have a proposition for you."

Silence met her call. She waited patiently.

"Richard, I read your logs. I know you're responsible for most of the Metaverse. You're a genius." She nodded to Jada, who cleared some of the debris she'd wedged into the door. "You should be able to enter the lab now. No weapons. This is a truce. I want to talk to you."

The Doctor thrust open the door. Expecting more resistance, he stumbled into the room awkwardly. His face was calm until he saw the empty containment tubes.

"You killed them *all*? How could you?" Richard, the last Architect of humanity, fell to his knees. His hope snuffed.

"We both know they were already dead. Zombies kept alive by a will not of their own."

"But I just had evidence . . ." the man's voice trailed off, realizing the success of his experiment had been manipulated by the group. "It is done then. It is over."

"Not yet. There's one more thing that needs to be done." Pik watched him carefully, ready to tag him.

"Judgment. I deserve it." The same eyes that had haunted them in this prison looked at her. This insane intellect had fueled Pik's nightmares for the last month as they navigated the hell was now asking for a judgment that she was unqualified to give. "They launched the space expedition, and they sealed up the caverns, and we were left with two billion humans walking the Earth. Twenty percent of humanity left. Doomed to die horrific deaths. The Metaverse had to work, and it did." The madman lifted his eyes then, feeling resolve at the decisions he'd made.

The end justified the means. This fuel had sustained

him for hundreds of years.

"I refuse to judge you, but the Metaverse will. We're going to send you back."

"Why?" His righteous fury faded from his face in confusion.

"There are problems. That's our second directive: find evidence of Grand Architecture and send it back to the Metaverse to help. You're an Architect."

The Doctor searched her face. She watched him. She was telling the truth; he wouldn't find a tell.

"So there is hope," his voice choked with emotion. She almost felt sorry for the man. To be frog-marched unconscious into the rebirth protocol would be the worst fate the genius could probably imagine. Unconscious oblivion. She thought of Trick and hardened her resolve.

"I can see how you'd look at it that way. I'm going to be stuck here. The gate will only allow so much data, a matching number of consciousnesses." They'd left with five. And between him, Jada, Brit, Trick, and Horn, they couldn't return with more than five.

"Okay." The Doctor nodded. "Do what you have to but move slowly and talk me through it." An unsaid threat of "or else" simmered in the air.

Pik did not doubt that he could still destroy the whole group. They were on his turf in every sense of the word.

"I need to do two things. I need to attach the metadata of the Grand Architecture to your and Trick's profile. This comes with a package that may have to reconstitute a superficial level of your code to make it through the quarantine protocols. They must recognize you as a friend and not a foe. Then the hook must be attached for Horn to trigger the retraction program. This will pull you back through the Network to the Metaverse."

"This makes sense to me. The meta tag and superficial skin you're putting on me shouldn't go deeper than my identification programming, correct?"

Horn had briefed Pik on what to say. “Correct. It's just superficial," Pik lied with a straight face. It helped that she didn’t understand the truth. Horn was also planning on knocking the Doctor out.

They were going to add a tertiary tag that indicated that the Doctor may be infected, which when the quarantine protocols activated would ensure he was unconscious when he hit the Metaverse.

When the Doctor didn’t object, Pik stepped forward and began to pretend to fiddle with his settings. Horn invisibly manipulated things through Brit’s hands on another console.

The Doctor examined her work. She watched as he glanced over the tertiary tag. It was commented out, which means it wasn't executable. Horn was counting on his deep programming knowledge to shunt any commenting of code out as harmless. The filter on the Metaverse didn't care. It was used to working with those Echoes that were less technologically advanced. The text anywhere on a load out would cause the correct reaction.

After a few minutes of review, the Doctor said, "I'm ready."

"That's it? No goodbye to your home?"

"I've been wanting to walk the Metaverse since it went live."

Suddenly a bubble of doubt hit Pik. The Doctor was way too excited and confident.

Pik stepped forward and attached the retraction code to him. The countdown began ten seconds later.

"It's going to self-destruct when I leave." He gave her a wicked grin as though his last bit of revenge was served. She stamped out the urge to stop their transfer.

"You'll never see the Metaverse with your own eyes."

Fear streaked across his face as he saw the truth in

her eyes. The villain of their story retracted. Brit, Jada, Horn, and Trick went with him. The world changed.

Chapter 32

Pik watched the Doctor rip away. Surprisingly, Trick's body stayed. For the first time in a long time, she stood with Trick. The *real* Trick. He was washed out. A memory of the man she'd been chasing.

"Hey, is that you?" The lab began to shake. A filament trailed from Trick's body, attached to a very solid Horn.

"It is. It's all me. I can breathe again." Trick gave her the grin he would when he'd pulled off a ridiculous feat.

"*Can* you breathe?" The question wasn't the one she wanted to ask.

"I meant metaphorically."

Pik gave him a waned smile. He always joked at the stupidest moments. "I don't think this trick worked out."

Trick looked serious for a moment. "Not for me, anyway, which I think is fitting. I have struggled with the nature of the Doctor and his influence on the Metaverse for a long time. With my role in allowing it to exist."

"So you are the Conduit? *His* mole? Was his journal right? Did you betray him at the end?" Pik's hope was fragile.

"I've been looking for the Doctor for a long time. I knew he had to persist. Back when the world was ending, I was willing to do anything to make the Metaverse a reality. I still am."

Pik got her confirmation. Her heart dropped. Trick had allowed the Doctor's research to form the core of the Metaverse. The torture of souls. She couldn't look him in the eye. Instead she pivoted to Horn and Junip hugging in the background.

"Horn—why didn't you transfer? Why didn't

Trick?"

Trick spoke before Horn opened her mouth, "I kept us back, removed the retraction. We would have been classified as riders or viruses. Horn was too optimistic about how the quarantine architecture works."

Pik nodded. The lab shook, and ceiling tiles fell around the group. It was shaking apart. Digital pixels were absent, blacked out of existence. The Echo team would soon follow.

"Do you think anyone will know what we've done?"

"It's a story worth telling." Trick's ghost smiled. "I think you'll tell your children one day."

"What do you mean?"

Trick ignored her question. "I'm proud of you. You're the captain. Truly. And . . . I have one last trick. I found someone willing to help. An old friend of mine."

A ghostly figure materialized next to Trick. To her disappointment, it wasn't Timmic. Instead it was a woman she didn't recognize. The woman was plain, dressed in a lab coat with her hair pulled up in a tight bun. She looked rather severe. She peered at Pik through glasses, low on her nose.

"I can't say I approve of what you did to Richard, but it was time. He couldn't see it, but he was losing cohesion. He ignored the rules we'd put in place on how we were going to pursue the mysteries of human consciousness long ago. Anyway, I have given Trick the access codes. Go forth and see what you can learn. I'm ready to move on." The woman vanished without waiting for a reply.

"Evelyn." Pik realized. "She was here the whole time?"

Trick nodded. "In a way. When she lost cohesion, parts of her were integrated into the architecture of the lab." Trick's form spasmed. "It's time."

He waved his hand up and smiled as though he just

performed a magic trick. Then, the man bowed and faded, a hatch appearing behind him.

"Horn, Junip, over here. We've got a place to go." The hatch swung open, giving them access to the craft. Pik stepped inside in wonder—the place smelled of Trick. Horn rushed past, sitting at the command console at the front.

"We've got to disembark, or we're going to be pulled into the lab's destruction."

Pik nodded, turning around and hitting the close hatch controls as Junip stepped past her. Everything shuttered. They fell off from the lab's existence and, for a moment, freefell. Horn got the "engines" up and running and held them in place. Pik moved to one of the windows to see what was going on. They were surrounded by space, and above them was what she'd imagined the old alien-infested dungeon ship looked like. Blasts of fire let loose from different compartments. The ship was self-destructing.

"Good riddance," muttered Junip. Pik agreed. It'd be too soon if she never saw another game like that ship again.

The whole thing blew apart a moment later. They floated in nothing more than space.

"Hey, Trick, where should we go?" Pik asked. Ready for their next adventure.

When he failed to respond, she faltered, "Wait . . . where'd he go?"

Junip looked at her, confused. "Wasn't he right behind you?"

It hit Pik then. He'd been saying goodbye—she just hadn't heard it. His last gift to them had been the hatch.

"I think he's gone, Junip." There was heartbreak in her voice, but also acceptance. He left, but he'd given Pik the torch. The hollow part of her—the place she'd been trying to fill since her parents left—didn't feel so empty anymore. Junip put their arms around Pik.

"We've got each other." For the first time, Pik truly

believed Junip. They'd survived.

"This still leaves the question of where to? And what are we going to name this ship?"

Junip pondered and said, "I want to return to the Metaverse or the real world."

"You think that's possible?"

"I think anything's possible."

Pik made a curious face. "How about Trickshot?"

"The Last Trick?"

"Magic Trick?"

"How about Hat Trick?" Horn grinned with the reference to hockey. The three of them were still alive, a true hat trick. She'd won naming the ship. The three floated in Hat Trick and began plotting a course to their future.

Epilogue

Journal Entry 14,349

I have exhausted all my avenues of trying out new strategies with the specimens I have. Only two have a remote chance of viability. The mother-daughter duo I was able to land. I've verified fifty times that their bond and willingness to go to extreme lengths for each other have helped them survive. I believe this is also what is keeping me alive. It's so frustrating to be able to observe the Metaverse and yet be isolated from it.

We're floating in literal cyberspace, a living nebula full of stars, solar systems, and beauty. I can watch the superficial comings and goings and the leak. They're leaking data and lives. I've managed to pull my lab into the vicinity of the leak and have studied its contents. It's random data bits and bytes. I knew those idiots would build a failed design, and that's why Ubesrtia reached out before she passed. I still am not sure why she wasn't forced to pass. She'd discovered the leak, too, and reached out beyond the Metaverse to see if anyone was listening. The poor woman thought that perhaps someone left on Earth was still monitoring the whole project. Instead she got me.

Admittedly, I may be better than someone on Earth, but it'll take another five months for the message to get close to the endpoint at the edge of cyberspace. I've floated there too. She didn't like my response, but she gave me hope. She sent me a data packet that I'm still working on unsealing. It has several layers of security. I'm unsure why she sent me something I can't read.

The other form of hope came in the new activity I saw on the Metaverse Nebula. It has opened up. It's a hair, to be sure, but they're sending foraging parties out into the universe. Opening the door, even a crack, may allow me in. It's a risk. It could allow anyone in. Who knows what's been floating out here all these years—fragments of a long-forgotten world? Memories of Earth. Evolution in cyberspace happens much more rapidly than it does biologically, and there are fewer rules. Monsters lurk in the abyss between stars.

The possibilities are endless.

Journal Entry 14, 785

I observed a ripple, and I don't know what to make of it. Ubesrtia's last communication was answered by something other than me. I don't think she's around to hear it, but I heard it. It didn't sound human. There were no words or images associated with the ripple through the infrastructure of our universe. It was more of a feeling. A malevolence.

I wonder how much longer the salvation of humanity has left. Between the leak, which is growing bigger, and this other force. I must get into the Metaverse and warn them before it's too late.

I still haven't decrypted Ubesrtia's message. The only thing I can gather from this is that the message wasn't meant for me. I wonder who the intended recipient was.

Journal Entry 15,200

I've finally made contact with one of these exploration teams. They are called self-styled Echoes. Some sort of group that explores the more extensive universe outside of the Metaverse. I'd noticed that they kept hooking up to old game ports or holodramas. I resurrected the old DeathGate that my test subjects were stolen from. The game hasn't aged that well, in my opinion, but it's served a purpose. I've captured one of the investigators, my old friend Trick. Revenge will be sweet. I've implanted Brittany into the Metaverse in his place. If the upload process worked with her, it should work with me.

This new entity is full of life. I could begin my experimentations again and learn much about the Metaverse and how its people have adapted to near-mortality. If nothing else, though, I've got the answer: humanity has survived.

Journal Entry 15,203

I've learned so much from Trick. He has become very willing to connect and share information with me. I'm not completely sure he remembers me. The reboot protocol he's suffered over the years seems to have erased his knowledge of me. He was surprised to find a non-artificial sentient digital entity. I'm finding his complexity and energy addictive. I've had to force myself to put him in containment a few times, as he overwhelmed me personally.

His team has loaded into my reality. This is going to be a great source of wealth for me. I should be able to experiment for another three centuries. Hopefully I don't need that long to fix the Metaverse. I miss Brittany. She's been my subject for so long that we're connected. I don't think that I'll be seeing her again.
She didn't load with this new team. To think that she's walking around the Metaverse—it's inspiring. It's as though my plan was going to work this entire time. It will

take time, but she should be able to infect the Metaverse for me. This is the best outcome I could have dreamed of. To think that I'd just put her on a shelf this whole time, not knowing if anything I've done in the last four centuries could be viable.

Journal Entry 15,204

I finally got Trick to talk to me about the other Architects. I can't believe they've all passed on to be reincarnated in some form. I outlasted them all. I am the last one left of the original efforts to upload humanity. It's incredible to me how infantile this Trick seems. His team too. I watch them fight and am disappointed. If they are the best of humanity—and Trick sure seems to think they are—then humanity is in a sorry state. I'll be winning this war in no time as soon as I can bore through the Metaverse defenses. I've never been this close.

Journal Entry 15,508

[Monitoring Alert] The Owner Entity has been terminated. Backup protocols engaged.

[Activity Stamp] Journal Entries have been declassified.

[Activity Stamp] Journal is flagged for external use.

[Activity Stamp] Journal has been auto-sent to all nearby entities. Metaverse. Hat Trick. Darkstar.

Thank you for reading Echo. If you enjoyed this read – please think about leaving a review, every review helps push the book in the algorithms and gets it in the hands of more people.

Follow MJ Douglas on social media!

@mjdouglaswrites

@dtp.mjdouglas

@mjdouglaswrites

@mjdouglas

Thank You

No feat is accomplished without the help of others. I want to start off by thanking my own digital archivist and lovely spouse, Jen. I'd never have pursued this dream without their support and grace. Kat Hamrell was a partner in crime in getting this book from an idea to a physical reality. I'm ever in debt for your deadlines, creativity, and snacks.

Hope Houtwed has been a tireless and diligent editor. She's been a source of inspiration and given me key insights to make the text more approachable and clearer. Thanks for nixing that tsunami line, we both know it was terrible. Also – thanks Chase for backing me up on slagged.

Much gratitude to Luna Spark who was ever willing to lend an ear as I worked out plot details and Mark Whelan for an early, nightmare-fueling read. Nancy, ever willing to keep me company on a late-night writing session.

Finally, wanted to acknowledge that the cover art for Echo sets it apart. Thank you, Sienna Arts for a kickass cover, bringing my characters to life.

About the Author
MJ Douglas

MJ Douglas' groundbreaking work, characterized by its thought-provoking blend of science fiction and LGBTQ+ themes, has earned them a place among the new influential voices in contemporary literature. With a talent for storytelling and a deep commitment to representing diverse voices, Douglas crafts narratives that transcend traditional boundaries. Their unique perspective, often exploring the intersections of life and technology, continues to push the boundaries of literary conventions, offering readers a glimpse into worlds where inclusivity and diversity reign supreme. Their visionary work challenges societal norms, encouraging readers to question the status quo and envision a future where science fiction and technology blur.

Check out the debut novel from MJ Douglas, Augmented!

It's Kansas in the not-too-distant future where digital oppression holds humanity in its grip when two strangers unite to overthrow the digital tyranny of The Network. Envision a world where reality is pliable and augmented reality reigns over the masses. The populace can alter their reality at will and ignore the dull, damaged, and broken.

When Chris decides to try her luck in the world of augmentation, she never expects the fate of humanity to rest in her hands. That is until she meets Anita, a tech-savvy Latina seeking the truth about her grandmother's hacktivist past. The crucial key to salvation lies in Omega- her grandmother's vision and the only hope of stopping The Network. The future lies with these women and leaves Chris wondering why she didn't just stay home with her cat.

"Vonnegut meets Orwell! A fantastic story with interesting characters and a good twist. Highly recommended 5 stars. I cannot wait for the next MJ Douglas book."- Instagram Review

"If you're in the mood for a wild ride into a future of augmented reality, filled with moments that will make you burst into laughter, this book is a must-read."- Reedsy Review

"An entertaining cyberpunkish dystopian story."- GoodReads Review

Follow Dragon Tomes Publishing on social media!

@dragontomespublishing

@dragontomespublishing

@dragontomespub

@dragontomespub

Made in the USA
Monee, IL
30 March 2024